Undocumented Visitors in a Pirate Sea

An Investigation of Certain Caribbean
Phenomena by Dr. Thayer Harris

Jeffrey Roswell McCord

Jeffrey Roswell McCord

Jeffrey R. McCord
Box 37
Cruz Bay, VI 00831
St. John,
United States Virgin Islands

Book cover design by Alice Gebura

ISBN: 0989950816
ISBN-13: 978-0989950817 (Jeffrey Roswell McCord)

"I brooded by the hour over the map...I climbed a thousand times to that tall hill they call the Spy-glass, and from the top enjoyed the most wonderful and changing prospects. Sometimes the isle was thick with savages, with whom we fought, sometimes full of dangerous animals that hunted us, but in all my fancies nothing occurred to me so strange and tragic as our actual adventures."

— Jim Hawkins contemplating the pirate treasure map in Robert Louis Stevenson's *Treasure Island*, 1883, Chapter 7.

"I thought along some beach on some planet, there would be a small creature walking with its dad and they would see our sun in their sky, and they might wonder whether anyone was there...We are made out of stardust. The iron in the...blood in your right hand came from a star that blew up 8 billion years ago. The iron in your left hand came from another star... and we are now learning that planets are as common as stars."

— Dr. Jill Tartar, physicist and astronomer with the University of California at Berkeley and Director of Research at the SETI (Search for Extraterrestrial Intelligence) Institute. Ms. Tartar inspired the character portrayed by actress Jodie Foster in the movie adaptation of Dr. Carl Sagan's book *Contact* [See: http://www.npr.org/2012/07/23/156366055/jill-tarter-a-scientist-searching-for-alien-life]

CONTENTS

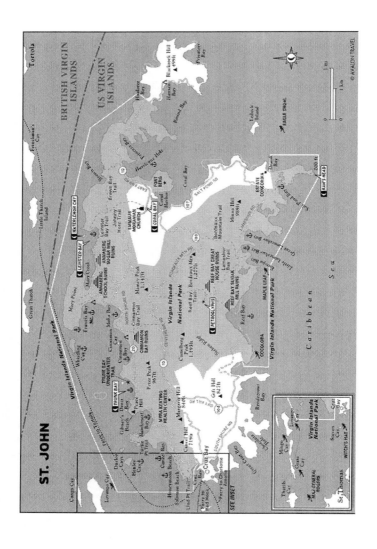

1 THE DEAD MAN'S CHEST

"The New Frontier is here, whether we seek it or not. Beyond that frontier are the uncharted areas of science and space, unsolved problems of peace and war, unconquered pockets of ignorance and prejudice."

— Senator John F. Kennedy, Democratic Party Presidential Nomination Acceptance Speech, July 15, 1960

Feet propped up on the gray, steel government-issue desk, sweat dripped from hands as I tapped on the keyboard. A whirling, humming ceiling fan did little to cool the room. Lethargically, I was fine-tuning lecture notes for the next term. But the view of the palm-fringed beach down the hill from my office was more enticing than struggling for new anecdotes and humor to engage students in Caribbean Maritime History 101. Sailboats swinging in unison to their moorings, as a breeze propelled white clouds across an azure sky and turquoise bay, were hypnotic.

Finally, drowsiness and a sinus headache caused, no doubt, by various molds growing in the former Navy barracks housing faculty offices drove me outside. There a fresh wind and strong midday sun startled the neurons and synaptic clickings in the old memory banks and I was fully awake again – despite the heat and humidity.

Suddenly, remembering the day of the week and items on my calendar – a challenge at times in these slow, warm latitudes – I looked down the brick paths for my scheduled noon day visitor. It isn't every day the maritime history professor of the Territorial College of the Virgin Islands gets a visit from a U.S. Naval Intelligence officer. A glance at my watch revealed he was late and that was a good thing.

I had no idea why he was coming to visit me – Thayer Harris, a historian whose last significant research had been completed years earlier. That work, done back in Washington, D.C. when I was an American University post-doc adjunct professor, had concerned Cold War naval activity in the Caribbean. It had also covered the phenomena of unidentified submersible objects – still unexplained, still unidentified.

Now securely tenured, I was more interested in family, sailing and exploring sugar plantation ruins in Virgin Islands National Park than career development. My six foot, lanky (albeit, filling-out) frame and salt and pepper hair were easily recognizable to Park rangers.

While waiting, I surveyed the college grounds. Above the campus the mostly green mountain sides were speckled with brown and yellowing trees and bushes. With April already upon us, leaves were dying and dropping. Funny how "Fall" occurs in the Spring down here. Spent Bougainvillea flowers were falling, floating around lawns like crinkled pink, yellow, red and orange tissue paper. And, the first of the "mists" formed by Saharan dust carried across the Atlantic on the Trades had appeared just a week earlier. Today, though, was clear.

No question. Summer was approaching. Tourists and snow birds were flying home. Red, orange and yellow flamboyant trees were blooming as humidity levels rose.

The loud, cackling Ada birds – big and black as crows, but with longer tail feathers – had arrived. Soon the laughing gulls and terns would pass through on their way back north from wherever they spent winters even further south of here.

As I watched pelicans circling above the bay, a white Ford SUV (the government vehicle of choice in these islands) drove through the college gates and ascended the hill leading to the scattered wooden barrack rectangles. Above these former enlisted men's quarters, stood the old officers' row of two story white brick houses that made up the rest of our campus. The structures, built before World War II, and the land under them were a post-Cold War gift to the United States Virgin Islands from the United States Navy.

On a hill overlooking the grounds, an old stone wind mill testified to the 18th and 19th century years when the principal islands of St Thomas, St John and St. Croix had been colonized by Danish sugar planters, merchants and traders (mostly Danish, Dutch and English) and administered as the "Danish West Indies." In 1917, the United States bought the islands for $25 million because of their strategic location vis' a vis' the newly built Panama Canal and north to south shipping lanes. St Thomas' outstanding deep water harbor was a big plus and the Navy built a formidable base and airport there.

The SUV arrived, parked in an oval of shade, and a suitably clean-cut, 30-something man emerged. He quickly climbed the steps to the History Department's lofty offices where I awaited him on the stoop. A gold-plated belt buckle and various badges glistened on his summer white, short-sleeved uniform. He stopped and saluted.

"Dr. Harris, Sir?"

"Lieutenant Taft, I presume?"

With introductions over, I invited him into my pale green plywood office and looked over his ribbons.

"Are those from Iraq or Afghanistan, Lieutenant?"

"Both, actually. I did two tours based in Bahrain as an intelligence analyst and managed a couple of fact-finding and other missions in both Iraq and Afghanistan. Now I work at the Office of Naval Intelligence in Washington, D.C."

I had read about the rigors and perquisites of headquarters life in Bahrain – the Fifth Fleet's base and one of the wealthiest and most luxurious principalities in the world.

"Well Lt. Taft, what brings you from Washington to our humble tropical outpost? Not too many Pashtuns or muhjardins here. And, no sightings of Taliban naval craft that I know of. Still, plenty of sand."

He wasn't amused and we hadn't yet established eye contact. Without responding, he abruptly pulled a typed manuscript out of his brief case and plopped it on my desk.

Bloody hell! It was my paper on Unidentified Submersible Objects – USOs. No good would come from it, my wife Mary had warned years ago. Was she to be proven correct?

"Your former History Department chairman at American University had the sense to pass this on to the Office of Naval Intelligence. Thirty years ago, it was considered one of the more credible, objective analyses of these mysterious objects or craft. You mostly relied upon mainstream media reports and the few military officers and defense contractors who spoke about them. And, of course, the UFO buffs were sources. I gather that people spoke more openly about such things in those days."

Yes, I recalled vividly. People were more forthcoming back then, less worried about non-disclosure pacts and secrecy laws; and, of course, the abuse and ridicule associated with open discussions of USOs or UFOs had not yet been institutionalized in the media.

An image of Dr. Mecklenburg, American University's history department chairman, mailing my paper to Naval

Intelligence came to mind. Or, perhaps, the wizened old academic merely ambled with his cane across campus on a nice day, traversing Ward Circle and Nebraska and Massachusetts Avenues to personally drop it off at Naval Intelligence offices. They were only a block from our campus, after all. Now the property has been subsumed by the Department of Homeland Security and the old Naval Observatory, a few blocks away, is the official home of U.S. vice presidents.

Like so many well educated white men of military age, good breeding, and above average intelligence in his era, Dr. Mecklenburg served as a naval officer during World War II – probably in intelligence, given his academic achievements. No doubt he kept-up his contacts in the "club" after the war.

But, Dr. Mecklenburg – God rest his soul – couldn't be faulted. And, Lieutenant Taft sitting here before me was both insightful and disarmingly forthright – a young innocent, perhaps. I thought of something to say about Dr. Mecklenburg's generation.

"People were more open and honest in the post-World War II years. Today, do we have anyone like Admiral Roscoe Hillenkoetter – an early CIA chief, for goodness sake – who publicly said UFOs are real and called for Congressional hearings? Or, would a British Admiral of the Fleet such as Lord Hill-Norton, the former head of the Ministry of Defence, today publicly say as he did that UFOs are real and then badger the House of Lords into holding a hearing on them, as they did? But, Admirals Hillenkoetter and Lord Hill-Norton were World War II vets and heroes. Not ones to be intimidated by bureaucratic functionaries or secret operatives."

"I agree, Professor. And, I learned about them in your paper."

"You're probably too young to have heard about the UFO sightings by Presidents Jimmy Carter and Ronald Reagan. I bet those incidents never made it into your history books at Annapolis."

Having noticed his Naval Academy ring, I felt free to opine self-righteously.

"On the other hand, I'm sure you were taught that Jimmy Carter served in Admiral Rickover's nascent nuclear submarine service. The President was very proud of being a submariner."

"I knew President Carter was an Annapolis man and submariner, but must admit I had no idea he and President Reagan had witnessed UFOs," he said a little skeptically. "But, we did learn the protocols on how to deal with reports of unidentified flying or submersible objects, as I believe you know."

I did know the military once had instructions on how to handle sightings and reports, but was out-of-date on the details.

"I knew the Air Force and Navy had protocols, but heard they had been rescinded when researchers made them public. Are they, or revised versions, still 'operative', as you people say?"

"That's a question I am not at liberty to answer," he said off-handedly. "How did you learn of the Carter and Reagan sightings?"

"Well, Jimmy Carter told his story to several newsmen, freely admitting he had no idea what it was that he saw; but said he did see a maneuvering object in the sky. And, Ronald Reagan described his tale to no higher authority than the Washington bureau chief of The Wall Street Journal. Carter and Reagan were both governors when the incidents occurred, and, of course, they, too, were of a generation of leaders who spoke their minds. Right or wrong, you knew where they stood."

I made a note to myself to check on the details of the Carter and Reagan sightings. More information might now be available.

As I thought about the Presidents, I realized I had been rambling on, but still didn't know why the Lieutenant was sitting in my office.

"So, I assume you're here because of my paper."

"Yes, sir, I am. It's complicated. I'm investigating the death of a retired Marine Corps gunnery sergeant. His name is Roger Baskins, age 65, place of birth: Gulfport, Mississippi. His last base was Pensacola. His body washed up on St. John's East End on April 5th."

Since my family and I live on St. John, we knew about the body. In fact, we had actually seen the rescue squad and EMS Boston Whaler respond to its discovery out at the East End, where we happened to be snorkeling that day in Hansen Bay. Later, an ambulance boat brought the remains over to Charlotte Amalie, the capital of the US Virgin Islands on St. Thomas. That's where I work. I get a kick out of telling visitors from New York or Washington about my hellish commute. It's a ten minute jeep drive across National Park mountain ridges with majestic views on either side; then a 20 minute ferry ride to St. Thomas watching smaller mostly uninhabited islands slide by while sunning on the top deck.

I replied, "Yes, I heard a little about that, but no details. What does a deceased Marine have to do with me? Or, for that matter, a Naval Intelligence officer?"

"Sergeant Baskins was last seen alive on April 2nd on board the 'Willy T' – that floating bar in the harbor on Norman Island. Three days later his corpse was discovered in the rocks near St. John's Privateer Bay."

Ah, the Willy T! Formally known as the William Thornton, she's a 100-foot steel schooner anchored in The Bight, the sheltered harbor of Norman Island. She's served boaters' liquidity needs for decades. Willy was named for a Tortola planter, amateur architect and British citizen who improbably submitted the winning design for the United States Capitol building in 1792. George Washington himself praised the plan for its "grandeur, simplicity and convenience." For his effort, Thornton was awarded $500.

Today, we can only guess what Squire Thornton or President Washington would think of "Willy." When planning our first sailing trip from St. John to Norman Island, my wife looked up the floating bar on a travel advisory site and found a few indecorous reports. Allegedly, any woman who takes off her shirt and dives into the water from its pilot house is given a round of applause and a free T-shirt. Free drinks probably follow.

We deleted Willy from our itinerary on our first sail to Norman. In any event, rather than half-naked girls, Norman Island brings to my mind Long John Silver and his mates searching for treasure. Most consider the uninhabited British Virgin Island the model for Robert Louis Stevenson's "Treasure Island." Pirate loot was actually found there around 1800. We have snorkeled in the very sea caves where treasure was found hidden behind a false rock wall.

"OK," I said to the good Lieutenant. "I fully understand why a retired Marine would hang out at Willy's. But, surely this is a matter for BVI officials and the U.S. Virgin Islands Police Department."

"They have investigated it," Lt. Taft replied with a slight grimace contorting an otherwise well sculpted face. Had Taft been British, I'd have pegged him as an aristocrat.

"The problem is," he continued, "the Brits have no record of him entering the British Virgin Islands. We do know he flew to the US Virgin Islands. He caught a direct flight from Dulles airport in Washington, D.C. to St. Thomas on March 26th. That's ten days before he was found washed up on St. John. He has no family ties in D.C. or anywhere else that we could find. He received his pension and social security checks in a Northern Virginia post office box."

"It's not unusual for someone to 'forget' to clear B.V.I. customs before visiting Norman," I observed. Since Norman is only a two hour sail from St John's Coral Bay, some people neglect to first make the longer trip to Tortola, the main BVI island, to clear customs and immigration. After all, the USVI and BVI are part of the same archipelago, separated only by the relatively narrow Sir Francis Drake Channel. My family, however, makes a point of clearing British customs first before venturing further in BVI waters. Penalties for customs violations can be stiff and include confiscation of your boat, if the Brits wish to make a point.

"So, some intrepid person must have sailed or motored directly to Norman Island with Sergeant Baskins aboard – they probably departed from Coral Bay," I continued.

"That's what the police believe, but no one has admitted taking him over and Virgin Islands Police Department has no budget or incentive to investigate further. The coroner ruled death by drowning with no evidence of foul play. We got involved because the Sergeant's only identification was his Vietnam War era dog tags and a fascinating tattoo on his chest: a disc-like image that looks like a flying saucer with "JFK 1971" beneath it. On his bicep was another tattoo - an anchor astride the world and 'Semper Fi'."

To say I was surprised would be an understatement. The Lieutenant handed me photos of the tattoos.

"JFK and a flying saucer? Could this guy have been a conspiracy nut and a UFO nut?"

As a conspiracy buff myself, I was enthralled by the possibilities. Fortunately, the sight of the tidy, earnest young man sitting opposite me arrested my wild speculations. There must be a plausible explanation for the Marine's pictogram.

"It *is* a very distinctive tattoo," I agreed. "And the dog tags. I assume some vets proudly wear their old tags as sort of souvenirs or good luck charms. And, we all know they like tattoos related to their service. JFK? My guess is he once served on the old aircraft carrier, the *U.S.S. John F. Kennedy*. Correct?"

"All true," confirmed Lieutenant Taft.

A wave of self-satisfaction washed over me. My Sherlock Holmesian deductions were on target and my interest in this matter was soaring.

The lieutenant continued, "Sergeant Baskins survived unscathed during two tours in Vietnam that included long range reconnaissance patrols into the highlands. They were the most dangerous missions of the war. He was then assigned to the *U.S.S. John F. Kennedy's* Marine detachment responsible for vessel security."

I had read of the horrors of long range recon patrols – vermin, poisonous snakes and centipedes, spiders, constant threat of ambush, heat exhaustion. Service on an aircraft carrier must have seemed like resort living by comparison.

"One question, lieutenant. If the dog tags were his only ID and he hadn't cleared BVI customs, how do you know Baskins was on Norman Island?"

"Elementary, my dear doctor!" He said it with good humor. "He paid his bill on the Willy T with a credit card that we easily traced. But, the card and a wallet he probably carried it in were missing when the body was found."

I was surprised Willy took credit cards.

"One other noteworthy point about the body – its pants zipper was closed. The Coast Guard tells us that many men fall off boats while in the act of relieving themselves over the side – particularly when intoxicated. But, the zipper was closed and an autopsy revealed he'd likely had only two or three beers, hardly enough to incapacitate an old Marine gunnery sergeant."

Fascinating about the zipper, I thought.

"So, what about the flying saucer, Lieutenant?" I asked

Taft actually squirmed in the straight backed, wooden chair as he looked over my desk, establishing direct eye contact for the first time.

"We're not sure. We believe it's possible that the

saucer and even Sergeant Baskins' death are related in some way to his service on the *U.S.S. John F. Kennedy*, which was tattooed under the saucer as I said. During 1971, Baskins' tattooed year, the *Kennedy* was in the Caribbean and had even docked here in Charlotte Amalie at the old Navy yard. The crew enjoyed a 48 hour liberty during their week here."

"Why not just check the ship's logs and records?"

The lieutenant crossed and uncrossed his legs, seeming to be in pain as he explained.

"Part of the log for certain dates and hours during that cruise are highly classified. Worse, the only other related records I can find have been heavily redacted. Unfortunately, I am the only one assigned to this case and I don't have the clearance or rank to locate the original classified sections and unredacted docs, even if they could be found. Sadly, the Captain during that period who likely ordered the classifications – possibly after secure radiophone conversations with superiors – is deceased. Yet, reading between the lines, I conclude that something phenomenal happened to the ship in the Caribbean that year, but can't prove it."

Taft's problem was not as shocking as it might seem. In today's federal government, hundreds of millions of pages of documents have been classified. Millions more are added each year. With the deaths and retirements of senior military officers or government executives who may have witnessed "secret" events or collaborated in classifying incidents, orders or policy decisions, it's inevitable that some records evaporate from history – particularly when they date from pre-desktop computer and e-mail days.

"Let me make sure I understand this," I said. "You can't adequately investigate a retired Marine sergeant's death and resolve your suspicions about it because you, a commissioned intelligence officer in the U.S. Navy, are denied access to or can't find the Navy's own records?"

"That is correct."

"So, that brings us back to the flying saucer tattoo. You must think that is indelible evidence – so to speak – of a possible phenomenal event."

"That is correct and that's why I came to see you, Dr. Harris. Although it does appear to be a flying saucer, it could also be an unidentified submersible object. It is possible Sergeant Baskins may have witnessed or been involved in some way with a USO or UFO incident during the *U.S.S. John F. Kennedy's* 1971 Caribbean cruise."

"And, now you are interested in trying to recover that lost knowledge about the hypothetical incident. Is that it?"

"Yes. Several of us mid-level naval intelligence officers think its time we – I mean the Navy – seriously study and evaluate whatever evidence we *already* have in-house about UFOs and USOs. We might then build a case for more open reporting of these phenomena in the future. Some day we hope to bring in the broader scientific community to assist. The material could be provided to the President, as a possible prelude to public release."

A remarkable statement. And, if true, a very promising development.

"Quite laudable. But, where do I come in?"

"We liked your paper. Liked it enough for me to come down here with a proposal. It's now April 15. Your spring semester will soon be over. We'd like to give you a *sub rosa* grant to investigate Sergeant Baskins' last days, any links he and the *Kennedy* may have had to unidentified flying or submersible objects, and uncover any new or previously unreported evidence related to the phenomena."

"Interesting assignment," I replied, suppressing my excitement. "But, how do I get compensated?"

Also, would Mary give her blessing to such research?

"We believe the Annapolis Institute Press might be persuaded to generously fund research into the role of the U.S. Navy during the Cuban Missile Crisis. Such funding would be more than sufficient for you to also investigate the more important subject at-hand."

"So, let me get this straight. I write an article on the Navy and the Missile Crisis and, at the same time, clandestinely investigate Sergeant Baskins, the *U.S.S. John F. Kennedy* and any UFO/USO connection?"

"Precisely, Dr. Harris."

My family had no definite plans for the summer break other than sailing, working on the house and avoiding hurricanes. Assuming the money was good, this sounded enticing.

"How 'generous' is the grant we are discussing?"

The grant, paid in monthly installments, was most generous – exceeding my salary – and one month would be advanced immediately.

"We would require regular progress reports sent directly to my attention and, at the end of four months, we will want a paper with your findings and conclusions. Of course, discretion is paramount."

As interesting as it sounded, I had to discuss it with Mary before accepting. And, it might be a hard sell.

"I must discuss this with my wife since it will affect our plans for the summer," I explained.

"By all means," the lieutenant replied, giving his cell phone number and the name of his hotel. I agreed to get back to him the next day.

That night, during cocktails on our deck while watching the sunset, I eased into the subject. Mary, a petite blonde with a big heart and strong mind, did voice misgivings about such research.

"What if the Dean heard you were studying UFOs? What would he or, for that matter, other faculty think?"

"This would be very confidential research for a reliably closed-mouth client," I assured her. "And, as far as anybody knows, I'm simply researching and writing an article for the Institute Press."

"Nothing is confidential on this island for long," she

said. "You know what they say, 'if you don't know what you're doing, someone else does.' And, if it got out that you believe in these things, it could harm your reputation."

She had a point. Her justifiable concerns brought to mind the mixed feelings of one of the few journalists in recent years to study UFOs. In her well-regarded 2010 book, *UFO's: Generals, Pilots and Government Officials on Record*, Leslie Kean recalled that she was increasingly concerned about keeping her expanding interest in UFOs quiet:

"I began to feel as if I were covering-up something shameful and forbidden, like the use of an illegal drug . . . The subject carried a terrible stigma."[1]

I replied to Mary that my client had no interest what-so-ever in making this research public. She asked for a bourbon refill, took a sip and replied: "Well, everyone here knows you're a professor and somewhat eccentric."

"That's right, honey, and who on this island isn't eccentric?"

Finally, Mary agreed to my taking on the project, as long as I didn't talk about it outside our home and I kept her informed.

I phoned the lieutenant immediately.

"When do I start?"

"Not so fast," he intoned. "We need you to sign a non-disclosure agreement and   contract with the Institute to produce the Cuban Missile Crisis article. Fortunately, I happen to have both documents with me."

"Sounds like a done deal to me," I answered.

We met the next day over lunch at Tickles, a waterside bar and grill overlooking Crown Bay Marina and the new cruise ship docks and shopping complex. It was a highly appropriate venue. The Marina and cruise ship center had been carved out of the Navy's old docks, yards and even a submarine base.

That oversized concrete cruise ship dock, just a few hundred yards across the water from where we sat, was likely the very spot where the *U.S.S. John F. Kennedy* had once tied-up for liberty and re-supply.

The *U.S.S. John F. Kennedy* was a beautiful ship born in a poignant, family ceremony. Nine-year-old Caroline Kennedy had to swing the champagne bottle twice to break it across the bow and christen the *U.S.S. John F. Kennedy* on May 27, 1967 – two days before what should have been President Kennedy's 50th birthday.

Caroline's younger brother, John Junior; their mother, Jackie; uncles Ted and Bobby; and Aunts Joan and Ethel were all there. Even grandmother Rose attended.

As though it were the christening of an infant, the ceremony was overseen by clergy. In this case, Cardinal Richard James Cushing, Archbishop of Boston, who was no stranger to the Kennedy clan.

Aside from immediate family, John Glenn, the World War II Marine flying ace and pioneering astronaut attended the ceremony as did President Lyndon Johnson and Secretary of Defense McNamara.[2]

The largest and last U.S. aircraft carrier propelled by conventional power, the *U.S.S. John F. Kennedy* was built in Virginia by the Newport News Shipbuilding Company and officially entered service a year later in 1968 – the year Bobby Kennedy would be assassinated as his big brother had been.

The *Kennedy*, though, was just springing to life. Her eight petroleum-fueled boilers drove four propellers that pushed the ship at cruising speeds up to 34 knots. She measured 1,052 feet overall.

By comparison, with an overall length of about 652 feet, on her first and last voyage in 1912 – just 56 years before the *U.S.S. John F. Kennedy's* launch – the *R.M.S. Titanic* was driven by three propellers powered by 29 coal-fired boilers. She could only reach and maintain speeds of 21 knots.

When the *Kennedy* called at the port of Charlotte Amalie in 1971, she was virtually brand new. No doubt, Gunny

Baskins and his buddies walked around joking and looking for bars and other diversions in the very waterfront neighborhood in which Lieutenant Taft and I sat talking and downing beers.

Back then, President Kennedy's roots as life-long sailor and combat Navy skipper were fresh in every seaman's mind. His comments on why the sea is so special to humans, delivered in Rhode Island in 1962 on the occasion of an America's Cup race, are hard to argue with or improve upon:

"I really don't know why it is that all of us are so committed to the sea . . . I think it is the fact that the sea changes and the light changes, and ships change; it is because we all came from the sea. And it is an interesting biological fact that all of us have in our veins the exact same percentage of salt in our blood that exists in the ocean, and, therefore, we have salt in our blood, in our sweat, in our tears. We are tied to the ocean. And when we go back to the sea, whether it is to sail or to watch it we are going back from whence we came."[3]

After long and eventful service, the *U.S.S. John F. Kennedy* was decommissioned in 2007 and now rests mothballed with the reserve fleet at the old Philadelphia Navy Yard. Many hope she will become a floating museum.

"So, Dr. Harris, just one final item," Lieutenant Taft said, interrupting my reverie. He opened his brief case and pulled out a USB device.

"Before you send me an email or open one of mine or send emails to third parties related to this case, please plug this encryption card into one of your USB ports," he explained, handing me the whirligig.

"A bit dramatic, don't you think?"

"It's standard practice in Naval Intelligence research. In fact, when you phone me, please use this number. It's a secure line. If I don't answer, feel free to leave a short message simply asking me to phone you."

I took his business card with the number written on the back and assured him I'd follow the procedure. Pure bureaucratic nonsense, I thought.

After Lieutenant Taft and I had shaken hands, I caught the ferry back to St. John. It struck me as ironic that I had to sign a non-disclosure agreement and conduct secret research to (hopefully) serve the cause of greater government transparency about UFOs in the future.

And, of course, even if I didn't honor the non-disclosure agreement, my work could still be very plausibly denied by the Navy as the product of a whacko academic. On paper, I was simply researching and writing a story on the history of the Cuban Missile Crisis. While exploring anything further, I was on my own.

Still, why not keep a log of this investigation? It might come in handy, serve as a useful record and help me sort out my thoughts as I proceeded. So, I started this narrative.

I had no idea then, just how dramatic and potentially dangerous this investigation would become.

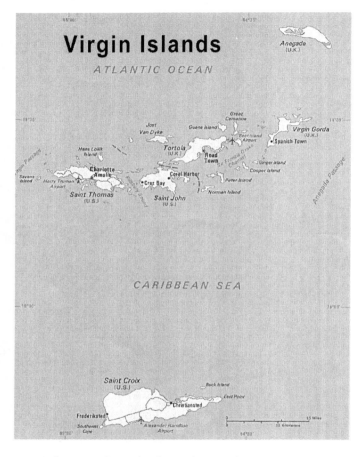

"Sailors are the only class of men who nowadays see anything like stirring adventure; and many things which to fireside people appear strange and romantic, to them seem as common-place as a jacket out at elbows."

— Herman Melville, preface to *Typee, A Peep at Polynesian Life*, 1846

While completing the spring semester's work, I made little progress on the Navy project. Whenever we sailed in and out of Coral Bay, where our own sailboat is moored, I made quiet inquiries among sailors about Sergeant Baskins and recent trips to Norman Island. Nobody knew anything.

As the semester ended in May, Mary and our teenage son, John, went about routine chores of maintaining home and garden. I worked out of my home office. John, who has many medical challenges including a seizure disorder, is tutored at home. At 5 foot 10 inches with chestnut brown hair, he was growing rapidly. His handsome features were catching the eyes of young ladies. We needed to keep our eyes on that.

We make a point to get away weekends, sailing to one or more of the scores of nearby U.S. and British islands.

On Memorial Day weekend, while moored overnight in a deserted National Park bay, the waters around our boat came to life with bluish-green light. Bioluminescent plankton on the surface blinked on and off like fireflies in summer grass on the mainland. Mary described them as watery Christmas lights. A foot or so beneath those twinkling specs, glowing oblong creatures – perhaps six to ten inches long – slowly moved around our boat. They are small squid who use light to attract prey. In daylight, these remarkable organisms change colors to blend with the coral or sand bottoms beneath them.

It was a very clear night. With the Milky Way above and bioluminescent waters below, we seemed adrift in space.

"Our boat is a starship," I told Mary.

"You watch too much Star Trek for your own good," she replied.

Meanwhile, we could feel summer coming on as heat and humidity rose a few noticeable degrees and the Trade Winds calmed considerably. Our thoughts turned toward the rains and inevitable storms that would arrive sometime in August and accelerate into September and October before ending in early November. Possible hurricanes and the safety of homes and boats were nagging, but suppressed, concerns in the back of every islander's mind. Everyone simply ignored the occasional minor earthquakes that can occur any time of the year.

As needed, we sought local palliatives. A painkiller is a frothy, coconut milky iced rum drink said to have been invented at the Soggy Dollar bar on the Brit island of Jost Van Dyke. It's an elixir that eases such worries and also helps salve the normal climatic aches and pains of the Continentals who emigrate here.

Once Europeans used daily quinine and tonic water spiked with gin to ward off tropical fevers. Today, malaria is gone and gin is in decline. But, rum remains the number one beverage, as it was for the post-Columbus seamen who sailed these waters. As Robert Louis Stevenson's character Captain Billy Bones put it when speaking of these buccaneer isles in *Treasure Island*:

"I been in places hot as pitch, and with mates dropping round me with Yellow Jack [yellow fever], and the blessed land a'heaving like the sea with earthquakes, and I live on rum, I tell ye! Rum!"

Rather than Jost Van Dyke's Soggy Dollar, however, the first break in my investigation occurred at Coral Bay's favorite watering hole – Skinny Legs. A plywood and mostly open-sided, tin roofed establishment nestled along the Bay under a canopy of mangrove and sea grape trees, Skinny's is headquarters of the Coral Bay Yacht Club. Neither the elegant New York Yacht Club nor Marblehead's Corinthian Club can match the Coral Bay YC when it comes to authentic waterfront color.

At days-end Coral Bay sailors – many of whom live aboard their boats – tie up their dinghies at the old stone Danish pier located a few yards from Skinny's and inevitably drop in for some cold ones and company. It was one of the most experienced seamen I spotted there one late afternoon who provided the breakthrough.

Sir Keithley sat astride a stool. A graying black pony tail emerged from his oil and salt stained white Royal Naval captain's hat. Its gold crown atop anchor was thread bare, though still visible above the visor. A closely cropped salt and pepper beard and moustache clothed his thin, red face. Skinny, sun mottled legs emerged from weathered, baggy Gurkha shorts. The sleeves had been cut-off of his grimy khaki tropical officer's shirt. It was opened half-way down to his navel, revealing a thin silver chain from which hung three Spanish pieces of eight. In short, he could have leapt from the pages of a Joseph Conrad novel.

Keith claimed to be the bastard son of the long deceased Lord Claymore. He maintained he was the only surviving direct descendent. But no one in Coral Bay had a copy of Burke's Peerage to look further into the matter. Although someone else got the title and what was left of the estate, in West Indian sailing circles he was nevertheless known as "Sir Keithley." Some even addressed him more formally as Lord Claymore.

Regardless of ancestry, Keith had come to the islands 30 years earlier with his common law wife from their home town of Croydon, a London ex-urb not known for landed gentry. Keith and his fair lady had first touched shore in the port of St. George's, the capital of the British island of Grenada. Unfortunately, "Lady Claymore" promptly sailed off with a rich Yank yachtsman, leaving his Lordship to fend for himself.

In the years since he had slowly migrated northward up the island chain, taking a wide-range of sea port jobs from which he learned to be a skilled shipwright, diver and treasure hunter. He had built a classic wooden boat and gained fame as a champion racer in sailing regattas.

I had certainly seen him around – he is hard to miss – but had never spoken with him. My curiosity and interest in old boats and all things English made him *one* islander I wanted to meet. Then one afternoon, there he was in Skinny's.

"Is this seat taken?"

"She's all yours."

Sitting down, I introduced myself and asked if what I'd heard was true: was he heir to Lord Claymore's title?

"Aye. If blood and kinship meant anything in this world, today I'd be sitting in the House of Lords instead of 'ere on Skinny's barstool."

Never good at small talk, I wracked my brain for some other comment or question to keep him engaged.

"I'm something of a novitiate sailor in these waters. I wonder how long a sail it is from Coral Bay to The Bight and do they have a customs house there?" (The Bight is the main bay on Norman Island.)

I already knew the answers, of course, but have found seeking advice to be a great ice-breaker. Most people enjoy giving it.

Sir Keithley looked at me, blue-eyes reddened and glassy.

"You've come to the right place. Surely, I ken tell you everything you want to know about sailing these islands."

As he spoke, he lifted his empty glass and looked into it philosophically. Taking the cue, I bought him a drink. He preferred Pusser's rum, of Royal Navy fame, straight up – no ice, no nonsense.

From its earliest days, the Royal Navy issued seamen a daily ration – or "tot"– of rum. The officer who administered this medicine, kept the ship's books and managed all rations was the "Purser" (corrupted by sailors to "pusser"). A tot was a pint and seamen were given one per day and two tots before battle. How many tots were Sir Keithley's daily rations? I hoped not to discover on my tab.

"From Coral Bay to the Bight t'is an easy sail," he said. "And when you go, you don't want to pass the Willy T."

"What's that like?" I asked to keep the conversation going.

"Well now, t'is only the best place to drink in these Leeward Isles," he asserted, as he drained his glass. "Last time I was there, though, something mighty peculiar 'appened," he added, looking into his glass and glancing at me.

"Another Pusser for his Lordship," I called to the bartender. When it arrived, Sir Keith continued.

"Yes indeed, last time I was in The Bight at my table on Willy, something very queer 'appened. It was either the last week in March or first week in April; a fine clear night, seas calm, wind light. Suddenly, Willy's deck lights went out and the background hum of her generator stopped. All was dark and silent. Even more strange, out in the 'arbor, all the mast and stern lights of every moored boat went black. An outboard engine on an inflatable dinghy comin' toward Willy stopped. Dead in the water, she was. All was silent, 'cept the slap of water on Willy's side and waves washin' on the beach. Never seen the like."

Keith paused to drain half his glass. Thus fortified, he continued.

"Next thing any of us knows, a bright orange light – so bright it 'urt eyes to look at it came a' skimming at a fearsome pace out of the open sea racing a few feet above the water. It flew past Treasure Point and into The Bight in a blur.

"Faster than any jet plane, it wove through the anchored boats without 'itting a mast, splicing a line, or nipping a stay, and then flashed past Willy, heading to the beach. It seemed certain to knock down palms and slam into Spy Glass Hill. It didn't, though. Instead, at the last minute it made a ninety degree turn straight upward and shot into the sky until only an orange speck could be seen. That, too, quickly disappeared. At that, the boat lights came back on across the harbor, the dinghy engine sputtered back to life and those of us on Willy could only look at each other. Stunned, we was.

"Finally, some bloke said: 'Bloody 'ell!' what *was* that?' A Scotsman at my table yelled: 'A fooken' rocket ship, is it now? What next?' Every one 'ad an opinion, of course. But, me, I sat silent-like lookin' up at the stars.

"Praise be to *him*, the Willy's bartender took charge and gave us all a couple free rounds to settle our nerves. And, things got back to normal a'gin."

Amazing. After years of reading reports of very similar incidents, this was the first live witness I had ever spoken with.

"What night of the week was that, Sir Keith?"

"I'll never forget that one. T'was Saturday. Later, the Cap of a boat heading south out of Coral Bay told me the orange a'flamin' ball came right out of the water somewhere a few miles south of Norman and headed straight at 'im. Thought he'd be dismasted, 'e did. But, it veered away and shot toward Treasure Point on Norman."

"Who was that captain?"

"None other than Hap Collins. He has that old yawl *Slow Hand*; takes people out on sunset cruises." Sir Keith chuckled. "Folks got their money's worth that night, they did."

I was on friendly terms with Hap. Always gave him a "Hello, how are you today?" as I rowed past his mooring out to our own boat. He was always pleasant. I'd need to speak with him next.

As his Lordship sipped his rum, I thought over the information he'd provided. Saturday, April 2 was the night Sergeant Baskins disappeared – last seen on the Willy. And, Keith said the sighting had been on a Saturday; might have been the first week in April, he said. Baskins could well have been on-board that night *with* that flying saucer tattoo of his.

"How close did this object come to the Willy? And, did you or anyone you know of have any skin burns or rashes – like a bad sun burn – or nausea, or any other effects?"

Keith thought about that. I knew there are cases in which witnesses do have such problems, depending upon how close they are to the object and how intensely they are exposed to the lights.

"It seemed we could reach out over Willy's gunnel and touch the thing. It passed that close. But, not one problem a' t'all, 'ave I 'ad. I often think about it, though. H'aven't been back to Willy since."

"How big was this orange ball?"

Sir Keith grunted, licking his dried lips, as though considering his answer. Another glass drained.

I ordered yet another Pusser for him and a Virgin Islands Pale Ale for me.

"Reckon t'was in the range of about thirty to fifty feet across. I'm guessen' *that* based on what it blotted out on shore as it whizzed by. Came by about main deck level. Close-up, it looked to 'ave a smooth metal-like surface; but the shimmering orange, red and shades betwixt made it 'ard to look at it. Went past us in the blink of an eye before we could get a good look-see."

I gave him a description of Sergeant Baskins and asked if he'd seen him. But, beyond the orange fireball, all he could remember were his own drinking companions and, of course, the two women who, before sunset, had made their topless leaps from Willy's pilot house to win T-shirts and the crowd's sincere gratitude.

"Praise the Lord, the jumps were made in full light and before all the commotion."

Judging that was all Sir Keithley had to say and being speechless myself, I thought about an exit strategy. Mary was expecting me back home soon, since I had only come out to Coral Bay to check on the boat. As I thought about how to politely depart, his Lordship motioned for another drink. I ordered one more for him.

"Thank ye, brother! I thank you."

In a fine display of etiquette, Sir Keithley stood up, saluted and exclaimed for all at the bar to hear:

"Here's to a better 'quaintance lad and to the 'ealth of Prince William *and* the Queen herself!"

With that, he winked and drained the glass of Pusser in one gulp.

"Well, must be gettin' back to my boat before sun down."

He then spun around and ambled down the steps out of the open sided bar, crossed the sand yard and horse shoe pits down the path between mangroves to the harbor. He had the rolling gait of a man who'd spent years living off-shore.

I knew Sir Keith would be taking a wooden rowboat out to his 48 foot boat, the *Bonne Chance*. Built many years ago in the somewhat ram shackle boat yard next to Skinny's, the *Bonne Chance* – "Good Luck" – was often called "a small tall ship." All wood, she boasted a foremast and mizzen mast. She was rigged as a brigantine, meaning her fore- mast had a real yard arm for dropping a square main sail. The mizzen carried a big lateen sail and off her bowsprit she'd run a head sail. In-board of that she could also carry a stay sail, run up her forestay. Under her bowsprit, a carved mahogany Indian maiden kept watch.

When carrying all her canvas, the *Bonne Chance* looked just like a 19th century trading vessel. Lord Claymore and his pals certainly looked as though they, too, could have been manning her back then.

After Keith left Skinny's, I looked around the crowd for Hap Collins. No luck.

The next morning while in Cruz Bay to get the mail, I stopped by St. John Hardware to pick-up a couple things. And, there he was.

As in many small towns on the mainland, the hardware store is something of a hang out for folks early in the morning. Nursing coffees, they'd lean against pick-up trucks or jeeps, swapping news before starting work.

Though Hap lived in Coral Bay, he'd come to town to do some shopping.

"Hap, how are you today? What brings you to the big city?"

"I'm doing fine; had to come all the way over to get some stainless steel screws, a new hack saw, and groceries. But, I can't get back fast enough. Too many people around."

Though Coral Bay is only eight miles away, it is eight tough, mountainous miles and people who live out there do so because they like the remoteness, spectacular views and close-knit, sea-based community. Hap was from Marblehead, Massachusetts and always wore his sun faded Red Sox hat with pink chino pants and a sports shirt. He says he came down to the islands because he got tired of boating in waters too cold to swim in.

We were standing in the shade of the store's stone arched porch by the water cooler. "You know," I said, "I heard of a strange story about an odd occurrence last month out near Norman one evening just after sunset."

"Strange, isn't a strong enough word for it," he quickly replied. "I saw it. We all saw it, whatever it was. Scared the hell out of us."

"What happened?" I asked.

"Well, I was taking a nice young couple – thirty-something tourists from Philadelphia, an accountant and his wife – out for an evening cruise. Figured I'd sail far enough east out to sea for them to get a good view back westward of the sun setting over St. John with the mountains in silhouette. Then we'd sail around star gazing and be back in harbor by about 9:30.

"We were out beyond Flanagan Passage sailing southeast and the sun had just set. Our guests were downing rum punches at a good clip and enjoying the distant lights of St. Thomas and Tortola. Suddenly we saw this reddish-orange ball burst out of the water a few hundred yards or so off our starboard bow. It came out like those submarine launched missiles you see in movies. Went straight up fast, then stopped dead, made a sharp 90 degree turn, and started coming right at us – thought it would hit our foremast and carry off our rigging.

"Came so close it nearly burned our eyes out looking at it.

"At the same time, all our navigation lights and electronics went out. I barely noticed as the thing kept coming. I had just ordered Billy, my mate, to open the lazarette, grab and pass out the life jackets, when, at the last second before it hit our head stay, the thing made another sharp turn and headed straight northeast toward Treasure Point on Norman.

"Meanwhile, the couple was screaming and I saw the white froth of a wave coming from where the thing had emerged. We had been on a windward tack in light air, so I fell off the wind a bit to pick-up speed to better ship the wave. It was coming fast, but was a queer 6 to 8 foot short wave – not like the wake made by a boat; more like the wrinkle in the water made when you skip a rock across a pond. We went up over it with a big splash and that was that."

I could visualize the whole episode – pink twilight on Navy-blue water, distant island lights and suddenly hell fire coming at them.

"What did your guests do?"

"The couple calmed down surprisingly quick once the fireball veered away. Then, we all took deep breaths and watched it speed toward Norman like a low flying comet. It made another sharp turn and disappeared behind the hills of Treasure Point for what seemed like a minute or so. Then, it shot straight up right beside Spy Glass Hill; kept going up straight as a rocket and disappeared into the stars.

"By then, our nav lights had come back on and I had Billy bring up some more rum punches. We all had a couple glasses.

"Of course, the guests asked me what it was. How the hell should I know?"

He chuckled and continued.

"I just said something like 'the Caribbean is known for strange lights at sea.' Then I told them about the Green Light you sometimes see after sunset in these latitudes. They accepted it.

"But, you know, the green light is a natural thing – something like the aurora borealis we occasionally see off New England coasts. Nothing like this."

"So, what did you do?"

"What could I do? We sailed on a couple comfortable broad reaches, back and forth enjoying the stars and lights of the islands and then returned to Coral Bay. By then, we had our guests very comfortably lit up with rum and they paid full freight; gave nice tips to Billy and me. No question, they got a great story to tell the folks back home in Philly."

"Did you report this to the Coast Guard?"

"No. There was no emergency, per se, and I wouldn't have known what to say. Plus, who needs them coming around asking questions?"

No one, until or unless you're in trouble, I thought.

"I can see why you didn't report it. So, as far as I can tell, no one on any other boat or on Norman that night notified anybody, even though as many as a hundred or more people must have seen it. Makes you wonder how many such events occur and nobody says a word to any authority."

"Can you blame them? They'd be called nuts," Hap said plaintively.

"Right you are."

On that note, we went our separate ways, each running morning errands.

Later, I thought over his story and got out a chart.

About twelve miles south of both St John and well beyond Norman Island is the deep water where the "shelf" of shallows, reefs and undersea mountain tops that form the Virgins falls off into what is called the "South Drop" by locals. Like a cliff on land, the depth drops steeply from about 30 meters to nearly 700 and keeps dropping to 1200 meters and more. Hap most likely had seen the USO emerge from the Drop.

His story confirmed Lord Claymore's. It was now clear I would need to visit the Willy T the next Saturday I could manage it. Hopefully, the Willy's Saturday crew would be the same as on April 2nd.

And, the very next Saturday, Mary, John and I departed Coral Bay early in the morning, sailing up-wind to Tortola to clear British customs and then across Sir Francis Drake channel to Norman Island.

3 TREASURE ISLAND

"After an uneventful Atlantic crossing we were crawling slowly along, in thick haze and heavy rain . . . in a gray shore-less world of waters, looking out for [our first sight of land, the island of] Virgin Gorda; the first of those numberless isles which Columbus . . . discovered on St. Ursula's day and named them after the Saint and her eleven thousand mythical virgins. Unfortunately, English Buccaneers have since given to most of [these islands] less poetic names. The Dutchman's Cap, Broken Jerusalem, The Dead Man's Chest, Rum Island, and so forth [to]

mark a time and [their brutal] race . . . [but] not one whit more wicked and brutal than the Spanish Conquistadores, whose descendants, in the Seventeenth Century [the English privateers and buccaneers defeated] with great destruction."

— Reverend Charles Kingsley, Ph.D., *At Last, Christmas in the West Indies*, 1871(Project Gutenberg e-book version, pages nine and ten)

"What happened to Flint's gold, says you? Ben Gunn's cave, says I."

— Long John Silver, *Treasure Island*

White caps driven by a fresh trade wind met us outside Coral Bay as we cut through sea swells toward the line-up of the British Virgins. Their respective green mountains overlapped each other in a seemingly continuous range, sharp and distinct in the clear, dry air that morning. The strong sun, multi-hued blue-green sea and exotic isles brought to mind the buccaneers who sailed these same passages, using the same prevailing winds and enjoying the same inviting bays and harbors since at least the 1600s.

Like Sir Francis Drake, the first English privateer to fight the Spanish along the coasts of Central and South America in the late 1500s, buccaneers, privateers and outright pirates used these islands as a refuge – a place to hide, reprovision, repair and "haul over" their ships onto their sides on gradually sloped beaches to scrape barnacles and sea worms from wooden hulls and apply fresh coats of tar. They would await the time of year when they knew the great Spanish treasure fleets would depart Cartagena and Panama on their way to Cuba, the last stop before Spain.

By the early 1700s, 200 years after Drake, the Spanish

treasure ships were fewer, but other merchant men more numerous. And the Virgin Isles were still open for business. One of the greatest pirates, Samuel "Black Sam" Bellamy, led a fleet of captured ships manned by 170 young men that might have included the talented seaman named Edward Teach or Thatch (he used both surnames) who would later become famous as Blackbeard.

In 1717, following an unsuccessful sea battle with a French Naval frigate off Puerto Rico, Bellamy and his flotilla fled to the Virgins. Hiding and licking their wounds, the pirates spent October and November on and around the main islands of St. Thomas and Tortola.

"The islands were then a sparsely-populated archipelago contested by four nations. Five hundred Danish colonists lived on St Thomas, overseeing the labor of more than 3,000 African slaves and several hundred Englishmen lived on Tortola... The Danes and English both claimed thinly settled St. John and the French and Danes argued over St Croix."[1]

Confusion and rivalries over nationality and authority on the mostly uninhabited Virgins, with their secluded bays and forested mountains, made them perfect hide-outs for pirate bands. While there, Black Sam visited Spanish Town on Virgin Gorda to sell some booty to a renegade Dutchman who would then fence the goods on St. Thomas. The island also boasted a valuable copper mine, the ruins of which can still be seen.

With about 300 mostly British inhabitants, Virgin Gorda, with its distinctive mountain, was usually the first island in the archipelago transatlantic sailors would see as they followed the trade winds from the Canary Islands. After a day or so in its port, Spanish Town, many would sail on to the next and larger island of Tortola, anchoring in Road Harbor. Over the years, the town that grew there – Road Town – became the main port and capital of the British Virgin Islands colony.

After sailing from St. John, it was at Her Majesty's

customs house in Road Town that Mary, John and I cleared immigration and started our sail back across Drake Channel toward Norman Island. Our course took us between The Indians – red rock pinnacles rising from the sea like giant crocodile teeth – and the small wild Flanagan Island. Flanagan is labeled "Witch Island" on old Danish charts. No one remembers why.

As we steered closer to Norman Island, to the right of The Bight, we could see caves carved from the bases of cliffs by eons of water and seismic turbulence. The story of how pirate treasure came to be hidden in the caves reminds us of historical links, illicit and otherwise, binding these isles to North America.

Many years after Black Sam Bellamy visited Virgin Gorda, another English pirate captured quite a prize along the mid-Atlantic coast. According to St. John historian David Knight, in the late 1700s, the pirate William Blackstock and his pals managed to take a Spanish merchant ship – the *Nuestra Señora de Guadeloupe* – off the Carolinas.

They transferred the *Nuestra's* cargo onto their own sloop and sailed down to the West Indies, looking for a safe, secret place to rest and take account of looted coinage, captured tobacco and other goods. They sailed past Virgin Gorda and looked northwest up Drake's Channel at the parallel string of mostly uninhabited islands lining either side. Sailing past the crumbling cliffs and rocks of the island called Fallen Jerusalem, they looked for the best bay.

"Leaning hard into the bulwark to steady himself, [the pirate skipper Blackstock] stared, studying the maze of hills and hummocks that slowly began to come into view. 'And there' he bellowed, an arm outstretched as if in introduction, 'Norman's Island - as proper a place to share up a booty as any in the West Indies!' "[2]

They did their business at anchor in The Bight, Norman's well-protected harbor surrounded on three sides by mountain ridges. There, they divided some of the specie, but hid most of it in the sea caves just outside the harbor, around what is now Treasure Point. When they eventually entered port it wouldn't do for the crew to have too much gold and silver coinage in their pockets, a dead giveaway of their occupation. They could always come back and get more over time as needed.

The lads then sailed across Drake's Channel to Road Harbor in Tortola to sell the plundered tobacco and dry goods. Little did they know that their work on Norman had been observed by fishermen in small boats obscured from the pirates' view by the Indians and Flanagan Island.

As the pirates celebrated on the The Bight's empty beach, believing their anchorage was well hidden, the fishermen were already alerting British authorities. Blackwell and his men were seized soon after they dropped anchor in Road Harbor and rowed ashore to town to try to sell their plundered dry goods.

Brits from Tortola then thoroughly searched Norman and uncovered 93,000 Spanish silver pieces-of-eight coins behind a false stone wall in a sea cave. However, 57,000 coins remain missing to this day, rumored to still lay hidden on Norman.

No doubt the story of Blackwell's pirate treasure found its way into London gazettes. But it was the colorful name of a small, nearby island (Dead Man's Chest) mentioned in a travel book that caught Robert Louis Stevenson's eye and inspired him to write Treasure Island.[3]

Near sunset, Mary, John and I sailed into the legendary Bight and found a good mooring. I rowed them in our dinghy to the Pirate's Bight Bar and Grill on the beach – the only structure on the island. There, they could eat a civilized meal. After promising to be back to pick them up as soon as possible, I rowed out the 100 yards or so to the Willy T, where I tied the dinghy to its floating wooden dock and ascended the steps up her steel hull.

A mix of 60s and 70s rock music and reggae came from

speakers and colored electric lanterns were strung from Willy's rigging. Wooden tables were packed mostly with middle aged sailors clad in weathered top-siders, cargo shorts and open necked knit shirts – the dress code for those who owned or chartered boats. A sprinkling of teenaged and twenty-something tourists rounded out the crowd, now drinking to the sun as it set behind the distant mountains of St John. The blasts of boat horns around the harbor heralded the sun's drop.

The restaurant-bar manager was easy to spot. He was the thirtyish red-faced Brit wearing chino pants and a blue pin striped, long-sleeve shirt. I went over and asked about that most unusual Saturday of a couple weeks past. He hadn't been working that night. By good luck, Lizzie, one of the waitresses then on duty had been.

I sat down at one of her tables. Lizzie took my order for a beer and mutton roti. Small talk revealed she was a British emigrant who had been in the islands about two years. On both the U.S. and Brit isles, young adults come for two or three years and then either leave, looking for fortune elsewhere, or stay for the rest of their lives, evolving into Caribbean characters.

Assuring Lizzie that I was neither a policeman nor a military person, but merely a UFO enthusiast, I asked her about that amazing night.

"The thing scared us speechless. When the lights went out, I stumbled and almost dropped my tray of drinks. Then, my night vision came on and I saw everyone lookin' out at the 'arbour where an orange or reddish ball was flying straight at us. I screamed and then did drop my tray as that fiery ball flashed past us so fast I couldn't even focus on it."

So far, she was spot on with Lord Claymore's story. Then, I gave her a description of Sergeant Baskins and asked if she remembered anyone like him. Again, fortune was with me. She remembered him sitting at one of her tables. Like so many other old timers, he had closely watched the topless women jump off the pilot house while downing his pints. He had sat alone.

"He 'ad a bit to drink, but was 'olding his own. I remember him well, cause 'e left me a hundred as a tip. I watched 'im get up and head for the companion way and ladder. Moments later the lights went out and all 'ell broke loose."

She said he wasn't drunk. He was an old hand at drinking, Lizzie was sure. I asked about the cash tip because I had heard he used a credit card. That, too, was par for the course. Many pay for their meal with a card, but leave tips in cash. As for what happened to him, she could offer little.

"I assume he got in 'is dinghy and then off to 'is boat. But, that was a very strange night, and t'is 'ard to say what 'appened to him, or what 'appened to any of us, really."

I wondered why Lieutenant Taft hadn't told me about the UFO sighting on the Willy T. He must have learned of it from the police.

"Did the BVI police interview you and your friends working that night about what you saw?"

"Yes, indeed, they asked about it! And we told 'em."

"I didn't read anything about a UFO in the papers, though they did report the Sergeant's body washing-up."

"Sir, you must understand something. Such strange 'appenings, or ugly crimes for that matter, can upset the tourists. We can't 'ave that, now can we? So, police keep certain things quiet down 'ere. Couldn't ignore a body, though, could they?"

Made sense. No one made that big a deal about the outbreak of dengue fever during the previous year's rainy season, even though it struck some well-known locals. The nasty, mosquito-borne disease also hit Florida and Puerto Rico much more severely. But, the news media gave it little coverage. I guessed the local police had told Lt. Taft nothing but the facts about Sergeant Baskins' drowning, discreetly leaving out the phenomenal.

I finished my beer and dabbed some mango chutney on what was left of my roti, thanked Lizzie profusely, and left a good tip – not a hundred, but generous enough.

By the time I rowed to the beach to pick-up Mary and John and then rowed back to our boat, twilight was ending, the moon was out and it was time to settle in. The wind and sea had picked up and we learned a small craft advisory had been issued, as full dark came on. The rising wind slapped our halyards against the mast, playing a high pitch chord as it whipped through the rigging, in harmony with the music being played on masts and rigging on other boats moored nearby.

Mary and John went below to their bunks. I remained on deck. I added an extra line to our mooring, and looked for our phosphorescent friends. The agitated water seemed to reveal and light-up more than usual. They, of course, reminded me of the orange fire ball Lizzie, Lord Claymore and Hap Collins had described. Three witnesses.

Since I had my laptop on-board and a signal across the Channel from the tower atop Tortola's Sage Mountain, I quickly did a search for reports of similar objects from reputable sources. I went to the website of the National Investigations Committee on Aerial Phenomena (NICAP).

In the 1950s, Admiral Roscoe Hillenkoetter (an ex-CIA chief) had served on NICAP's board in its early days and it remains one of the most respectable UFO organizations. There I found the Congressional testimony of Dr. J. Allen Hynek, then head of the astronomy department of Northwestern University, associate director of the Smithsonian Astrophysical Observatory and a scientific UFO consultant to the U.S. Air Force. He was testifying at a 1969 U.S. House of Representatives hearing:

"One of these [major] patterns [of sightings] might be called 'Nocturnal Meandering Lights.' Reports falling into this category are characterized by the sighting of a bright star-like light, perhaps of -2 or -3 stellar magnitude which floats along without sound, frequently hovers, reverses its field without appearing to turn, and often abruptly speeds up. The light is most frequently described as a yellow, amber or orange."[4]

Bingo. Many such lights (or objects emanating light) have been seen coming out of, or going into, water – oceans, lakes and rivers. Several have been seen hovering above water dangling what appears to be a hose apparently taking in water.

Unlike our bioluminescent sea buddies, these strange lights simply cannot be explained in conventional terms.

That led me to think about old Gunny Baskins. What did he make of that highly strange orange sphere? Had he seen something like it before? And, how odd for a battle tested Vietnam Vet to have experienced such a thing (possibly, twice) and then end up dying in these idyllic waters.

In the moonlight, the palms swinging in the wind on the beach and the agitated tropical forest on the mountain side could have been a jungle anywhere in the world. Then, it hit me.

Like Vietnam, without the war.

That was how a Navy Seabee in 1969 described the mangrove swamp and jungle-like woods around Great Lamshur Bay on St John. He had been there constructing a dock and buildings on that remote bay in support of Project Tektite. Tektites are small molten glass rocks formed when meteorites strike the earth. Project Tektite *was* space-related. It was an astronaut training project in which a team lived deeply submerged for several days in an air- tight, space ship-like habitat. The purpose was to record the psychological stresses and physical strains on humans isolated in a restricted, alien environment.

Mary, John and I had attended a lecture on Project Tektite in an aging Quonset hut built under the mangrove canopy that now covers the old base (used today as a research center by marine biologists). To this day, to reach the base by land, one must go over steep rock strewn dirt roads and then down into the mangroves where drivers frequently face car-wide water pools a couple of feet deep.

Like Vietnam, without the War.

That understandable quip brought to mind a comment made by a friend who, like Sergeant Baskins, had also served on long range reconnaissance patrols into deadly Vietnamese jungles. Even to this day, he cannot watch classic Vietnam War movies like *Apocalypse Now* or *Platoon*. They're too realistic. They make him nervous, panicky.

So, that fateful night, our Sergeant Baskins, a Vietnam jungle combat vet, found himself in an environment that likely brought back panicky memories. Then, suddenly, the lights went out as he was either descending the Willy's ladder or shoving off from her dock in a dinghy. Next came a blinding UFO, racing toward him like a bat out of hell. Possibly, it was the second time he had experienced the shock and alarm such inexplicable visages summon in even the bravest hearts.

Traumatic, to say the least. Traumatic enough for a sixty-five year-old with potentially unresolved post-combat stress to fall into the water in a hyperventilating panic and drown? Quite possibly. Indeed, a Veterans Administration psychiatrist says such trauma can strike vets years after combat:

"Medically speaking, there is some evidence to support what psychiatrists call reactivated post-traumatic stress disorder. The literature is dotted with cases of veterans of World War I, World War II and the Korean War who, after briefly showing signs of stress disorders in the immediate aftermath of their ordeals, led productive lives for decades before breaking down in their 60's and 70's."[5]

Satisfied I was getting somewhere, I closed the lap top and went below for the night. Mary and I didn't get too much sleep on the rocking, noisy boat. Grating sounds marked the mooring lines scraping along the bow stays, halyards slapped the mast and wind rumbled like the proverbial train commonly described in storms. John, though, slept soundly.

Next morning we had an adventuresome sail back to St. John in 25 to 30 knot winds and five to seven foot swells. Hardly heavy weather by old salt standards, but wild enough for us middle-agers sailing a 32-foot sloop. We sailed down wind halfway back, passing The Indians and rounding Flanagan.

With a following sea and wind, our *Perseverance* rocked and flopped, starboard to port until we couldn't stand it. So, we veered off-course closer to the wind on a broad reach, gained stability as the bowsprit rose and fell six feet up, six feet down each swell with sparkling sheets of water flying fore to aft upon the three of us huddling together in the cockpit.

My wife was a fair weather sailor and was scared. Given the circumstances, I kept quiet about what I had learned about the orange ball.

Eventually, we jibed onto another reach and raced into Coral Bay between Rams Head point and the small Le Duc Island, a bird sanctuary. We were happy to see the overgrown old Danish fort on its hill top and the bell tower of the 18th Century Moravian Mission (still, the largest building on the Bay) welcoming us to our mooring.

On the drive back home through the mountains toward Cruz Bay on St. John's west end, I was satisfied we now had a plausible explanation of how Sergeant Baskins ended up in the water and drowned. I was then unaware that there were direct witnesses – indeed, perpetrators, but not the kind that can be arrested.

I had more questions to answer: how did the Sergeant get to the Willy T and how did he expect to return to St. John, assuming that was his intention?

We learned the next weekend.

At the end of a great day of sailing, we often stop to buy beer and wine at a discount store and raucous West Indian bar, Cases by the Sea, built out of old shipping containers. On the way we saw a couple of Rastafarian men selling fish out of the back of their pick-up truck parked between two banyan trees along the bay. This was a common enough sight on St. John and a great way to find fresh tuna, mahi mahi or Caribbean lobster.

Local fishing boats can easily make it to Norman Island. Fishermen or their friends are well aware of all vessels coming and going in Coral Bay at all hours day and night. Smuggling is not unheard of.

We stopped the car next to their pick-up and Mary and I got out to check-out the fish. While she took a close look, negotiated and then watched them gut, skin, slice and weigh her order of tuna steaks, I had noted an older, thin man on a wooden bench. The bench was nailed between some of the banyan branches that had sent trunk-like roots into the ground, forming a sort of cave. The man had graying dreadlocks and wore a faded Bob Marley T-shirt. I walked over to him.

"Good afternoon."

"Afternoon. What's up? What can I do for you, Mon?"

I asked about the fishing business and also the best power boat for cash- only charters. He knew we lived on-island, were regular customers and not police.

"Ah, the Silver Bullet! She's the one. Goes anywhere – day or night."

I told him about the strange flying lights on Norman.

"You sure someone not mashin' your corn?"

"I have it from reliable witnesses."

"Why you interested?"

I told him I was a professor at the college and doing a study of these mysteries. Also, I brought up Sergeant Baskins, saying I needed to know how he got to Norman Island that night and what he may have told the skipper who took him.

Most importantly, I didn't need to know the name of the captain or even the boat, but just wanted the information for my studies. West Indian islanders have a lot of respect for the territory's college.

"Come back t'morrow."

With that, we took our tuna steaks and bid him farewell.

"Have a blessed night."

The next afternoon we returned and Rasta man was right where we left him. He had news.

He nodded his head toward the Silver Bullet, a sleek steel speed boat moored a few yards off-shore from the mangroves. A friend *had* taken Sergeant Baskins (although he didn't know his name) to Norman Island that Saturday. At about noon, the Cap left Baskins and an old kayak – a yellow one seater – on the beach of The Bight. Baskins had paid in cash and asked the skipper to come back and pick-him up same time the next day.

Since people can rent a tent from the beach bar and spend the night in the bush above the waterline, I figured that's what the Sergeant planned to do. And, a kayak was adequate for Baskins to go between the beach and Willy T and explore the bay, if he chose. All sounded reasonable.

Rasta man continued. As planned, his friend did go back to Norman the next day to pick-up Baskins, but couldn't find him or the kayak. So, after circling around The Bight a few times, he came back to Coral Bay and that was that.

Later, when the body was found, the skipper realized it was the same man and was scared.

"He kept 'is mouth shut tightly. An, now he don't want no trouble, Mon."

"No worry. No one will get in trouble."

"Have a blessed day," he said, none too subtly indicating our conversation had ended.

Meanwhile, Mary had purchased mahi mahi from the younger Rasta men.

"Thank you, Mommy, and be blessed," he sincerely said to Mary, handing her the fish wrapped in a newspaper. Calling an older woman "Mommy" was one of many charming West Indian endearments. I am "Papa."

Back home I phoned Lieutenant Taft on his secure number, explaining I had three witnesses to a UFO sighting the night of April 2 and gave him the coordinates for Norman Island. I asked him to contact air controllers at Beef Island airport on Tortola and Cyril King airport on St. Thomas to see if their radars had recorded any unidentified craft that evening.

Two days later, he got back with a "yes" from both airports. An unidentified solid craft had been on radar, but only for about five minutes. It had seemingly appeared from nowhere south of St. John and west of Norman, then moved over the Bight, hovered for a few moments, and disappeared in a straight trajectory up into space.

I found it interesting that radar showed the object hovering over The Bight. No witness mentioned that. Indeed, they all described it as racing past them.

Thinking back, though, Captain Hap did say that from his boat off St. John, they had lost sight of the object for a minute or so when it sped behind the hills above The Bight.

A new mystery.

Fortunately, because of the inexplicable nature of their instrument readings, the airports had made and kept copies of the radar reports. The Navy had obtained copies, but would not share them with me because they were immediately classified.

We now had witnesses and electronic evidence. Like so many other UFO sightings, an actual flying object had been irrefutably documented.

.

4 ST. URSULA'S BONES

"They that go down to the sea that do business in great waters; these see the works of the Lord and His wonders in the deep."

> — Book of Psalms 107:23-24, attributed to King David of Ancient Israel

"A few times we anchored for the night; and when we did not anchor we kept the ship hove-to, and this in order not to make any headway and for fear of running afoul of these islands, to which, because they were close one to the other, the Lord Admiral gave them the name of Eleven Thousand Virgins [after St Ursula and the 11,000 virgin martyrs of Cologne]."

> — Count Michele de Cuneo, an officer on Columbus' second voyage in a letter home [1]

It was on a Sunday afternoon that I discovered the first concrete evidence of the investigation, beyond the radar readings.

That morning we attended the service at St. Ursula's Episcopal Church in Cruz Bay where our son John was an acolyte. He was never more content than when carrying the Bible in the procession that opens every Episcopal service world-wide.

Few people know anything about Ursula, the church's patron saint. But she has special meaning for the Virgin Islands. It was St. Ursula's feast day (October 21, 1493) when, during his second voyage of discovery, Columbus first spotted these islands. In one version of the story, the islands were so unspoiled and numerous he thought of Saint Ursula and the eleven thousand beautiful maidens she led. Sadly, they were beheaded by Attila and his invading Huns during the late Roman Empire in what is now Cologne, Germany. Ursula is said to have led the maidens in prayer as they met their fate.

Today, some believe the Ursula martyrdom story is mythical. Still, the Catholic Basilica of St. Ursula in Cologne contains her alleged bones along with those of thousands of her companions. Their remains are piled in the Basilica's crypt. From Wikipedia, we learn more:

"The crypt contains what has been described as a 'veritable tsunami of ribs, shoulder blades, and femurs...arranged in zigzags and swirls and even in the shapes of Latin words.' The Goldene Kammer (Golden Chamber), a 17th century chapel attached to the Basilica of St. Ursula, displays sculptures of their heads and torsos; some of the heads encased in silver, others covered with stuffs of gold and caps of cloth of gold and velvet; loose bones thickly texture the upper walls."

Despite her tragic patron, the church of St. Ursula in Cruz Bay has happy, easy-going services mixing Caribbean and Anglo-Saxon cultures. We sing the weekly psalms and many hymns West Indian style – backed by steel drums. The lilt and inflection of West Indian voices mix with the accents of mainland transplants to make even the songs sung from the traditional Hymnal particularly melodious and joyous.

After church that Sunday in early June we had planned

a special treat. Rather than sail our own boat, we would be passengers aboard one of the most famous charter boats in the Caribbean – the *Pulse*, a 42 foot gaff rigged ketch whose lines, sails and wooden decks bespeak 19th century adventure.

Pulse was one of the largest boats built on St. John in modern times. When *Pulse*'s owner/builder first arrived in Coral Bay in 1969, the only other vessels there were open rowboats and small island sloops.

The boat has sailed to the Azores, Portugal, Spain, Greece and Africa; even sailed up the Gambia River. In those days, the owners' family lived on-board. The boat's saloon still has a set of *Encyclopedia Britannica* snuggly stowed in carved mahogany racks, evidence of two children raised on the water.

That Sunday, we departed Coral Bay and entered Drake Channel in 15 to 20 knot winds and sailed along St. John's undeveloped coast to Newfound Bay. We anchored just outside the coral reef, about 200 yards from the sandy, mangrove encroached beach. While Mary and other guests snorkeled along the reef, John – with life preserver on – and I swam to shore to explore the flotsam and jetsam that had washed in from the nearby British islands.

In the branches of a mangrove, we found a dirty, yellow ocean kayak. Although its deck was punctured in a couple of places, its hull was sound. We pulled it down out of the tree and emptied rain water from it, trying to decide if it was worth taking and fixing.

That's when John had a seizure. It was a routine episode and I knew he'd come out of it. Still, I wanted to get him quickly back to the boat. We were too far from the *Pulse* for a cry for help to be heard.

Looking over all the other junk washed up on shore, I quickly plugged the kayak's holes with fabric torn from a broken beach chair. I laid John across the deck of the kayak and secured him with some torn fish netting I pulled out of the sand. From old green buoy line dangling from low branches, I made a tow line.

I started swimming, pulling John back toward *Pulse*. It was tough going, but adrenaline kicked in. About half-way there, the boat's dinghy was launched and a crew man met us, towed us back, and helped us board. We also pulled the kayak up on to the deck where I gallantly presented it to Mary as a gift. She'd been asking for one for years.

John quickly recovered, but rested as we returned to Coral Bay. His neurological events happened too frequently, but we knew they would pass and wouldn't let them dictate how we lived. He deserves a life just like every other teenager.

Once ashore, we tied the kayak on our car roof rack and drove home as the sun set.

A few days later, I looked over the battered little vessel to see if she could be repaired. On the kayak's deck was a rectangular manufactured hole about the size of a paper back book, which I planned to plug with resin and fiberglass. Threads lining the hole indicated it had originally been stoppered with something removable. As I poked around, I saw a bit of plastic below the hole. Covered by mud and sea detritus was a zip-lock plastic bag duct taped under the top deck, just beside the cavity. The edge of the bag would have been visible when the original plug was pried off.

After brushing away the caked mud and pulling the seaweed and other trash, I recovered the whole bag, still zipped shut, but torn. That it had survived at all was testimony to the powers of duct tape, plastics and zip locks. Inside, was a waterlogged black wallet and a soggy, pocket-sized spiral notebook.

Excitedly, I opened the wallet and saw a middle-aged, jowly face with crew-cut hair looking at me from a Virginia driver's license. Roger Baskins. An Arlington post office box was the address. One credit card and 300 soaked dollars in a mix of denominations were the only other contents.

Shifting my focus to the notebook, I found most of the pages stuck together. A few in the beginning could be gingerly pulled apart and fragments of writing deciphered despite the ink runs:

". . . night after night living dreams calling me back . . . Melissa's camp . . .

". . . Melissa calming jitters and cold sweats, pushing away nightmares . . .

" . . . Putain's Bier Garten . . . still there? Iggie's Beach . . ."

That was all that could be made out on the first few pages. An apparent lost love named Melissa, a beer garden and a beach.

The inside pages were stuck together as though glued. But, with care, I opened the last page containing blurry, runny writing:

". . . couldn't find her. Having black feelings. They swallow me whole. . . . black thoughts hit buddies in Nam before a patrol they never came back . . . Something will happen."

A few empty pages followed.

Chills crept up my spine. This was the voice of a dead man who only a few weeks earlier had been alive and writing that premonition.

I recalled what Rasta man had said. On the way to Norman, Baskins had told the power boat skipper that he was going to meet someone. Melissa?

Had powerful dreams of a lost love who had calmed his inner storms led him back to the islands? Life-like dreams that pushed away darkness? Relief from post-traumatic stress? The writing seemed to confirm my earlier surmise about his possible state of mind when the UFO bore down upon him in The Bight.

Vivid and strange dreams often precede contact experiences.

Had the UFO somehow drawn him to Norman Island for a meeting?

Some researchers believe that's possible; that UFOs and the apparent intelligences behind them can establish communication with the human mind at the subconscious level through telepathy or some similar means. The humans are then manipulated to travel to remote areas where a contact experience can occur unseen.

Consider that Harvard medical professor and psychiatrist John Mack, MD interviewed more than 200 people who believe they have been similarly drawn into contact and even abducted against their conscious will. Dr. Mack, without doubt the most qualified and eminent researcher of this phenomenon, could not explain what happens to these otherwise normal people. In a 2005 BBC news story, however, he said:

"I would never say, yes, there are aliens taking people. [But] I would say there is a compelling powerful phenomenon here that I can't account for in any other way, that's mysterious. Yet I can't know what it is; but, it seems to me that it invites a deeper, further inquiry. . . . I have come to realize this abduction phenomenon forces us, if we permit ourselves to take it seriously, to re-examine our perception of human identity - to look at who we are from a cosmic perspective."[2]

The U.S. Navy might well be skeptical of the doctor's findings. Nevertheless, the notes from Sergeant Baskins and their implications could not be ignored.

Like it or not, I was entering a cosmic realm. I sat cross-legged in our yard under a coconut palm lost in thought staring at the filthy kayak. Where does one seek information about Dr. Mack's "cosmic perspective"? Science first; religion second.

Like millions of other Americans of a certain age, I first learned of the cosmic realm watching Carl Sagan's PBS television series *Cosmos: A Personal Journey*. Eleven years before his influential television series, Dr. Sagan, then a Cornell University astrophysicist, testified before Congress in 1969:

"It now seems probable that the earth is not the only inhabited planet in the universe. There is evidence that many of the stars in the sky have planetary systems. Furthermore, research concerning the origin of life on earth suggests that the physical and chemical processes leading to the origin of life occur rapidly in the early history of the majority of planets. From the point of view of natural selection, the advantages of intelligence and technical civilization are obvious, and some scientists believe that a large number of planets within our Milky Way galaxy - perhaps as many as a million - are inhabited by technical civilizations in advance of our own."[3]

Dr. Sagan, a Pulitzer Prize winner, supported using radio-astronomy to search for signals from extraterrestrial civilizations. And, for decades the SETI (Search for Extraterrestrial Intelligence) project has utilized time on some of our most advanced radio telescopes, including Green Bank in the mountains of West Virginia, Arecibo in the rain forest of Puerto Rico, and our own Virgin Islands telescope on St. Croix, the eastern terminus of the Very Long Baseline Array. Individually and collectively these installations monitor and analyze the electromagnetic waves pouring from space like silent, invisible, dry rain showers.

Although some anomalous signals have been received, no true contact has yet been reported from SETI.

So much for conventional cosmic science. I next turned to theology.

I left the kayak in the yard and retreated to my home office to sail the electromagnetic waves of the World Wide Web. At the helm of my desk top, it didn't take long to discover a seldom visited harbor of theory within the mighty Roman Catholic Church, arguably the most conservative of mainstream Christian denominations. Turns out, Catholic clergy are already doctrinally on top of alien intelligences. Who knew the old men running the Vatican have an alien party line?

In 2000, mainstream UFO researcher Steven M. Greer M.D. interviewed Monsignor Corrado Balducci, who was a Roman Catholic theologian on the Vatican Curia (the Pope's governing council). Balducci said he accepted that UFOs are real and quite probably flown by extraterrestrials who could certainly be more advanced than us; somewhere in the hierarchy of life between humans and angels. Monsignor Balducci explained:

"The conclusion today of people of common sense is that there is something real happening here [with respect to UFOs]. There is not only witness testimony of general people of the populous, but also of people who are highly credible, cultured people, educated people, and scientists who were skeptical in the beginning. . . . When we are talking about extraterrestrial beings, we have to take as a supposition that a being is a body or material and a soul. God in his wisdom would not have created only us humans." (4)

What if extraterrestrials *are* more advanced than us sinning and all-too-destructive humans? No problem, Father Balducci says:

"It is desirable because if they are better than we are, they are going to intervene; then, they are going to help us. And it is desirable. It says in the Bible, everything that exists in the universe is in the creation divine. There are no extraterrestrials who are not part of the divine creation. If God created all of them, then He gives His love and He extends Himself to all. St. Paul says this."

In addition to open-minded theologians, the Vatican actually has an in-house astronomer and observatory.

In a BBC interview, Guy Consolmagno, a Jesuit Brother, astronomer and planetary scientist at the Vatican Observatory, said discovery of new forms of life does not mean "everything we believe in is wrong." Rather, "we're going to find out that everything is truer in ways we couldn't even yet have imagined."

Brother Consolmagno, who earned both undergraduate

and masters' degrees from the Massachusetts Institute of Technology (M.I.T.) and a Ph.D in Planetary Science from the University of Arizona, taught physics at Lafayette College, Pennsylvania, before entering the Society of Jesus in 1989. Here is his answer to the question "can aliens be made in God's image?"

"The traditional belief is that the Bible is referring to the aspects of the soul –intellect and free will. The ability to know that we exist, that God exists and the freedom to choose to love or not love. Anything, whether it is an intelligent computer or an alien with five arms – if they have those aspects, seems to me they'd be in the image and likeness of God."[5]

Sitting at my desk, surrounded by prints of 19th century sailing ships, I couldn't help think about the space farers who must be flying these extraordinary air and undersea vessels that changed course, altered speeds and otherwise navigated as though under intelligent control.

Shaking myself from these flights of fancy, I realized the kayak and the notebook it carried changed my initial conclusion about what happened to Sergeant Baskins that Saturday night in April. He must have made it down Willy's ladder, boarded the kayak, secured his wallet and notebook and then cast-off from the floating dock; and, then, fell in the water from the kayak's tiny cockpit.

Sergeant Baskins' notebook was of such importance, I decided a phone call to Lt. Taft was in order. Following procedures, I left a short message on his secure line and waited.

As I wondered how to explain the note and its possible implications, the phone rang.

"Harris, here."

"Taft, here, Doctor. What have you got?"

"Sergeant Baskins' wallet and a diary-like notebook found in the very kayak he had used during his visit to Norman Island," I began and then explained everything up to the work done by Harvard's Dr. Mack, leaving out the

Vatican.

"The notebook pages are soaked and stuck together," I told him. "Not much is visible or legible. Your technical people may be able to piece it together without destroying it. But, I could read enough to put together some of the pieces. They also provide some leads about his last days for me to follow."

After a long pause, Taft replied, "The note book and kayak are incredible finds – almost providential," he said. "Solid evidence. I need you to place the wallet and notebook in a very safe place. I'll send a team from the Naval Air Station at Roosevelt Field in Puerto Rico to bring them and the kayak in for forensic examinations."

So much for Mary's free kayak. Lt. Taft paused again, and resumed in a somewhat strained voice.

"As for this 'contactee' and 'abductee' research you cited, I find it very difficult to accept. But, I am willing to consider it. We have no choice, really. The facts and Baskins' own words would seem to speak for themselves. What my superiors might think, I can't say. I do urge you to be as skeptical and conservative as possible in your own thinking and analysis of all this."

"I'm trying, believe me. I'm attempting to use only eyewitnesses, physical evidence and reputable scholars and researchers to get a handle on all this," I replied. "We now have irrefutable evidence, in my view, that an unidentified flying object did come out of the sea and buzz Norman Island the very night Sergeant Baskins was there. I also believe his tattoo suggests this was not the first UFO he had seen. That's as far as the facts can take us at the moment.

"It is possible, though, that the kayak might have some trace chemicals, radioactivity or other residues if, as I suspect, the UFO passed close to the Sergeant while he was paddling away from the Willy T. It may have caused him to fall overboard and drown."

"That's all logical. We'll see what we find."

We then discussed my next steps.

The very next day, a white panel van with U.S. government plates drove up to the house. Two young men in Navy fatigues knocked on the door and took away the kayak and Sergeant Baskins' effects.

"Have a happy Fourth of July, sir," one wished me as he closed the van door.

I had forgotten another Fourth was upon us, although there had been a lot of visitors in Cruz Bay and the carnival had already been going for several days.

5 ZULUS AND THE END OF THE WORLD

"Another characteristic of the UFOs is electrical interference with various machines. UFOs have been notorious for stopping cars at short range. The driver will hear his engine sputter and it stops running. Besides cars, many other machines have been affected, including aircraft, motor cycles, buses, lorries and tractors."

— William Francis Brinsley LePoer Trench, 8th Earl of Clancarty, addressing the House of Lords during its Parliamentary Debate on Unidentified Flying Objects on January 18, 1979 (page 1248 of debate transcript.)

For islanders pondering the coming rainy (and hurricane) season, the annual carnival ending with the Fourth of July is a time to party with abandon and side-step misgivings about the future. On the Fourth, Mary, John and I piled into our pick-up truck and eased down our mountain via a steep series of switch backs to go to Cruz Bay to join the party.

The end-of Carnival July 4th parade was a nearly five hour affair filled with marchers and prancers in African tribal costumes and modern psychedelic colored interpretations thereof. Dancing, drinking and music filled the streets. Throughout the town, Mardi Gras style floats and paraders drifted through narrow streets. Island women – white and black and often dressed in skimpy fluorescent costumes – dazzled the eye in the midday sun.

Most impressive were the Jumbies walking and dancing on 6 foot stilts. Eerily costumed to look like a cross between menacing scarecrows and Plains Indian ghost dancers, the Jumbies displayed remarkable agility and coordination. The entertainers helped breathe life into the African/West Indian notion that these islands are alive with the spirits of the departed (Mocko Jumbies) who can live in certain trees and haunt the decaying, overgrown remains of plantation great houses. Some still believe Jumbies can possess humans when called to them by drums during fire-lit dances.

My favorite performers, though, were the Zulu warriors, authentically clothed and armed with the classic assegai thrusting spears and cow hide shields. The Zulus of southern Africa were famed for their disciplined warrior army, battle strategies, endurance and use of the steel assegai. The assegai, a long, broad bladed, short stemmed stabbing weapon, is also called the ixwa a word mimicking the sound when it is pulled from a victim's torso.

As these Virgin Island Zulus danced, uttering harsh incantations and thrusting their assegais outward toward the crowd, it was easy to imagine the fear and horror of those young British soldiers who faced tens of thousands of real Zulus who on January 22, 1879 overran their camp at Isandlwana Mountain in Natal, Africa. The Isandlwana battle was the largest defeat of a European (or American) army by an aboriginal military force. Zulus killed thirteen hundred British soldiers and local colonial allies on that hill. It was a feat of arms that made Custer's last stand on the bluff above the Little Big Horn River in Montana (where 268 U.S. soldiers were lost three years earlier in

1876) seem trifling.

In short, the Zulu home team successfully defeated invading British aliens. Today, the tribe maintains a high degree of independence and cohesion within the nation of South Africa.

Fortunately for Europeans in the audience, the Zulus in Cruz Bay moved along peacefully, followed by trained teams of youngsters jumping rope to reggae and calypso rhythms. Next came large tractor-trailer rigs sporting two floors of steel drum bands. As these monstrous diesel-powered machines squeezed through narrow streets, they often had to stop, back-up and make seemingly impossible turns to avoid scraping buildings or knocking down the Governor's wooden reviewing stand.

The best music of the day came last. Ms. Tischell Knight, in all her full-bodied grandeur, belted out Big Gyals Rule backed by who knows how many steel drums and percussive instruments. Everyone (except yours truly) danced in the streets, including the Governor's party who had descended from their seats. Mary also danced with abandon.

At days' end, the Governor hosted a reception and fireworks display over Cruz Bay harbor. We watched from the walls of the Danish colonial battery and mansion that serves as the Governor's office when he is on-island. The rainbow colors of fireworks reflecting on placid water and palm fronds are hard to beat.

When it was time to go home, I was sober enough to carefully navigate our truck through narrow, twisting streets, packed curb-to-curb and building-to-building with revelers. We inched our way through colorful, intoxicated crowds in the sultry music-filled night, stopping from time-to-time to move aside police barricades and shepherd inebriants out of the way.

Once home, sounds of music, occasional explosions and zip bangs of rockets echoed up into our mountains. The party would continue all night. Nevertheless we fell asleep exhausted.

Molly, the family dog – a husky that Mary calls "Nanook of the South" – forced me up and out for a pre-sunrise walk. We went to the top of the mountain on which we live. The wind stiffened as we walked rough paths through the overgrown ruins of a Danish plantation, one of the earliest on St. John. In the dawning light, shards of 18th century Delft china were visible, scattered around the foundation of the great house, a testament to a genteel life for some. Somewhere in the bush were Danish graves, often telling tales tale of premature deaths from yellow fever, malaria, dengue fever or other diseases that killed as many as 50 percent of European colonists in these latitudes. Below the great house ruins, a dirt road now cuts through the site of the slave village.

We came to a clearing offering a view of the full eastern sea horizon. Clouds colored purple, red and shades in between heralded the soon to rise sun. Then, the yellow shimmering ball silently rose from the sea in its daily show. Only the audiences for the spectacle have changed over the centuries: the first Indians, who canoed island-to-island from the mainland only to be supplanted and enslaved by the Spanish. Next came Northern Europeans with their African slaves, and now the descendants of all the above including us newer emigrants. Are new space-faring explorer/settlers soon to arrive?

On our walk back home, we passed a corner where children dressed in their finest clothes waited for an early morning church bus to take them to Sunday school. I had forgotten it was Sunday.

A little boy ran up to us, "Mister, Mister, is dat a wolf?"

"No, she's a husky – you know, a sled dog like the Eskimos have. She loves children."

"Loves to eat 'em, I say," he replied, smiled and walked back to the others, ignoring my encouragement to pet the dog.

After an uneventful day of chores, Mary and John

settled in with a movie. I went to my home office and fired up the computer, first checking Caribbean weather for possible tropical depressions coming across from the Sahara. Then, I explored the service history of the *U.S.S. John F. Kennedy*, the carrier on which Sergeant Baskins had served. It had first brought him to the Virgin Islands, I was certain.

After exhausting conventional sources of information – the official Navy and *Kennedy* sites that yielded nothing – I wandered into the nether world of Internet UFO research. There was the information I needed: credible eye-witness accounts of two incidents in the Caribbean in the 1970s and 80s. Neither appears in official service records, of course. But, both, I discovered, are documented indelibly in the memories of witnesses whose stories had, in-turn, been picked-up and reported by numerous, unofficial third parties.

Tree frogs and geckoes sang their nightly songs and insects beat upon my screen window, oblivious to the phenomenal story unfolding on my computer screen. The scent of a Bay Rum tree drifted in on a gentle breeze as I read about the summer of 1971, the year tattooed under the saucer on Sergeant Baskins' chest. The *U.S.S. John F. Kennedy* had been in the Caribbean and had just completed exercises near Cuba when an extraordinary event occurred. Then crew member Jim Kopf described what happened:[1]

"I was assigned to the communications department of the Kennedy and had been in this section about a year. . . [We had completed] a two week operational readiness exercise (ORE) in the Caribbean. . . I was on duty in the communications center. My task was to monitor eight teletypes printing the Fleet Broadcasts. . . .

"It was in the evening, about 20:30 (8:30 PM) and the ship had just completed an eighteen hour 'Flight Ops'. I had just taken a message off one of the broadcasts and turned around to file it on a clip board. When I turned back to the teletypes the primaries were typing garbage. I looked down to the alternates which were doing the same. I walked a few feet to the intercom between us and the Facilities Control. I called them and informed them of the broadcasts being out. A voice replied that all communications were out. I then turned and looked in the direction of the [Naval Communications Operating Network] and saw that the operator was having a problem. I then heard the Task Group [ship-to-ship] operator tell the watch officer that his circuit was out also.

"In the far corner of the compartment were the pneumatic tubes going to the Signal Bridge (where the flashing light and signal flag messages are sent/receive). There is an intercom there to communicate with the Signal Bridge and over this intercom we heard someone yelling 'There is something hovering over the ship!' A moment later we heard another voice yelling. 'IT'S GOD! IT'S THE END OF THE WORLD!'

"We all looked at each other; there were six of us in the Comm Center, and someone said, 'Let's go have a look!' . . . We went out the door, through Facilities Control and out that door, down the passageway (corridor) about 55 feet to the hatch that goes out to the catwalk on the edge of the flight deck . . . As we looked up, we saw a large, glowing sphere. Well it seemed large; however, there was no point of reference. That is to say, if the sphere were low, say 100 feet above the ship, then it would have been about two to three hundred feet in diameter. If it were, say 500 feet about the ship, then it would have been larger. It made no sound that I could hear. The light coming from it wasn't too bright, about half of what the sun would be. It sort of pulsated a little and was yellow to orange.

"We didn't get to look at it for more than about 20 seconds because General Quarters (battle stations) was sounding and the Communication Officer was in the passageway telling us to get back into the Comm Center. We returned and stayed there (that was our battle station). We didn't have much to do because all the communication was still out. After about 20 minutes, the teletypes started printing correctly again. We stayed at General Quarters for about another hour, then secured. I didn't see or hear of any messages going out about the incident.

"Over the next few hours, I talked to a good friend who was in CIC (combat information center) who was a radar operator. He told me that all the radar screens were just glowing during the time of the incident. I also talked to a guy I knew that worked on the Navigational Bridge. He told me that none of the compasses were working and that the medics had to sedate a boatswain's mate that was a lookout on the signal bridge. I figured this was the one yelling it was God.

"It was ironic that of the 5,000 men on the carrier, only a handful actually saw this phenomenon. This was due to the fact that Flight Ops had just completed a short time before this all started and all the flight deck personnel were below resting. It should be noted that there are very few places where you can go to be out in the open air aboard a carrier. From what I could learn, virtually all electronic components stopped functioning during the 20 minutes or so that what ever it was hovered over the ship. The two Ready CAPs (Combat Air Patrol), which were two F-4 Phantoms that are always ready to be launched, would not start.

"I heard from the scuttlebutt that later three or four men in trench coats had landed [on board] and were interviewing the personnel that had seen this phenomenon. I was never interviewed, maybe because no one knew that I had seen it.

"A few days later, as we were approaching Norfolk, the Commanding and Executive Officers came on the closed circuit TV system. At the very end of his [routine] spiel, he said 'I would like to remind the crew, that certain events that take place aboard a Naval Combatant Ship, are classified and are not to be discussed with anyone without a need to know'. This was all the official word I ever received or heard of the incident.

"I completely forgot about it until years later when my wife and I went to see *Close Encounters of the Third Kind* at the movies when it first came out. In fact the friend that had been the radar operator was with his wife and went with us. As we walked across the parking lot to my car, I asked him if he remembered what we had experienced years earlier on the ship. He looked at me and said he never wanted to talk about it again. As he said it he turned a little pale. I never talked about the incident again."[1]

This story by an obviously well-trained, well-positioned seaman serving on what was then one of the U.S. Navy's most important capital ships sounded similar to Sir Keithley's account of what happened forty years later on the Willy T, a very different vessel in a very different milieu.

I thought about Sergeant Baskins and his flying saucer tattoo dated 1971. He very likely witnessed this encounter. Some Marines were usually stationed on the bridge as security when a ship's commander was present, so Baskins may well have been in a position to see and hear everything that occurred that night.

This was not the only UFO incident involving the *U.S.S. John F. Kennedy*. The following eye-witness tale by another well-situated crewman describes a second sighting aboard the carrier in the Caribbean more than a decade later.[2]

"In the summer of 1983, I worked in CIC (Combat Information Center). I was an operations specialist. We were just leaving port [the U.S. base at Guantanamo Bay, Cuba] after doing a sea and anchor detail to assess our ability to navigate a mine field in a friendly harbor. It was late; I'm guessing around 2 or 3 a.m. We had just secured from general quarters . . . We had personnel at the look-out positions . . . with binoculars and on the sound powered phones. I was on the SPA 74 radar CRT (Cathode Ray Tube) in SSSC (Surface Subsurface

Surveillance Coordination) taking fixes of the Cuban coast and keeping track of all shipping both on the water and under. We had 3 Men in SSSC including myself and one officer for a total of 4 witnesses, and 4 lookouts – 8 in total.

"Every 3 minutes I would take a new round of fixes and the plotter would work our position and the other ships in company with us, their various positions, course and speed and the like. At around 20 nautical miles south of the coast our lookout on the 010 level (superstructure) called out an air contact to the west of us; he claimed 'it was blinking 4 different colors' like a Simon Says game: blue, yellow, red, and green.' He also gave me a distance of between 10 and 15 miles.

"I was on a surface radar, so I switched the SPA 74 to 48c air search radar and found a contact approximately 18 miles to our west, and this contact was not 'squawking an IFF' (Identification Friend or Foe), which got our attention. Our officer called the D&T (Detection and Tracking) module to find out what they could. This is the air search side of CIC. We had no aircraft airborne as we had secured flight ops for the night, but we did have an alert 15 Tomcat [an F-14 Tomcat fighter jet that could be airborne in 15 minutes] on deck. Of course, the Tactical Action Officer (TAO) was notified that we had an unknown bogey in the air not squawking, and the alert 15 Tomcat was activated.

"Meanwhile, all of the look outs were going absolutely crazy over this bogey – the way it moved and changed course with [our] ship, always keeping a position relative with our ship. I'm guessing that about 10 minutes into the alert . . . the bogey just disappeared, vanished off of radar, and visual. The alert aircraft stood down and was not launched . . .

"The lookouts were still jumpy and seemed to be calling out every star they saw. The ship secured from sea and anchor detail shortly after this. This is when it really gets strange. The deck department took over the lookout positions, our guys went to the racks (beds) and as I was being relieved of duty I heard the look outs shouting about the sea being completely aglow with phosphorescence. I quickly left SSSC and headed for top side. When I got there, right where the lookouts said, was a trail of glowing water crossing the bow of the ship.

"Never have I seen the ocean lighted up like that in a trail – it was so very bright going from north to south! I had just left the radar and knew no ship had crossed our path. All I could think of was that the bogey was under the water toying with us. I have sailed every ocean and I have seen phosphorescence on every tropical water; but I tell you there has never been a sea like this one. It was a continuous glowing line very well defined and we sailed right across it.

"The next day our Lieutenant told us to forget about this; and some things can't be explained. . . The last time that I talked to the Lieutenant (5 or 6 years ago) we both remembered this event like it was yesterday."[2]

I thought again of Sergeant Baskins. Decades after witnessing one of these extraordinary and frightening encounters with the unknown, he had found himself departing from the Willy T when a very similar object raced toward him – his worse nightmare come to life? Was he paralyzed by fright? As I surmised, did he indeed fall out of the kayak into The Bight breathless or hyperventilating with only water to breathe in?

The questions surrounding the unfortunate Marine's death, however, paled next to the larger mystery of the *U.S.S. John F. Kennedy's* encounters.

Was there something about the *Kennedy* that attracted UFOs – just as Jumbie drummers attract malevolent spirits? Was it the location of the ship in the Caribbean Sea that was the key to this phenomenon? If it was the Caribbean, then other ships and island inhabitants in our blessed sea must, like those drinking on the Willy T that night, have experienced similar encounters.

With these thoughts in mind, I went back to the Web and it wasn't long before my Wi-Fi captured another remarkable story about yet another renowned U.S. aircraft carrier.

Rather than being named after a heroic World War II veteran and president, this ship was itself a valiant vet of that War. The *U.S.S. Lexington* was the second carrier in World War II to carry that name, the first having been sunk in the Battle of Coral Sea.

Tokyo Rose, the English speaking Japanese radio propagandist, called the second *Lexington* the Blue Ghost because of its Navy blue paint job and the carrier's invincibility. Commissioned in February, 1943, she was the only U.S. carrier painted blue (rather than in camouflage) and was so heavily defended by the up to 103 aircraft she carried and many anti-aircraft guns that she proved unsinkable in combat.

Nevertheless, the Blue Ghost got spooked by a UFO during the Cold War on a new, less tangible front line in the waters north of Cuba. In the early 1960s, during the Cuban Missile Crisis, the *U.S.S. Lexington* was based in Pensacola, Florida, where she alternated between training naval aviators and service as an attack carrier, as events required.

Two different UFO researchers report that, while on a routine mission in the Gulf of Mexico, crew members spotted an orange glow in the sky around midnight. The first-hand account below can be found at the Web site of UFOs Northwest, a research group whose principals describe themselves as having post-graduate degrees in such relevant subjects as engineering, mathematics, meteorology and psychology.[3]

"While serving aboard the U.S.S. Lexington CVS-16 (aircraft carrier) I was an elevator operator for aircraft. One night around 12 midnight I saw a large orange glow in the sky. I called flight deck control. They said they had it on radar and tried to get it to identify itself.

"When they got no reply, they sent up 2 F4s Vietnam War era Phantom jets. You could see their after-burners which quickly boost a jet's speed, but the F4s did not even come close to catching it. The object took off out of sight. As soon as the jets returned, it came back. This pattern repeated itself three times. After the third time, I guess they the ship officers thought it was no threat. It followed us for about a half hour I guess, then left.

"We were told the next day to say nothing about the sightings. I wish I had at least written down time/day/year, but did not. Even years after, I did not know who to report it to. Then as time elapsed more, I figured no one would believe me. . . . We were operating in the Gulf of Mexico out of Pensacola Forida. I was in the V3 division/aircraft handlers."[3]

Two historic carriers steaming in the Caribbean region had had unexplainable encounters. I logged off my PC and sat back listening to the morning birds whose songs had supplanted the chirps and trills of nighttime tree frogs and geckoes. I had been at my post all night, it seemed.

Certainly these sightings by well-trained Navy technicians, backed by radar readings, pointed to solid, powerful and intelligently maneuvering air and sea vessels of some kind. Who or what was controlling them and for what purpose?

Writing an encrypted e-mail report to Lieutenant Taft on the *U.S.S. John F. Kennedy* and *U.S.S. Lexington* sightings, I put aside such musings and reported nothing but the apparent facts.

Somewhere in my studies I had come across an optimistic theory by physicist David G. Blair about any aliens visiting earth:

"[Extraterrestrials] would be curious and have a need to explore and understand the universe. Unless ET is an exploratory animal, there would be no motivation to make contact, since the vastness of space makes many other motivations, like power and greed, meaningless."[4]

6 COLD WAR IN WARM WATER (OBSERVED FROM ON HIGH?)

"The study of history is the best medicine for a sick mind . . ."

— Titus Livius (59 BC to 17 AD), the ancient Roman historian best known as "Livy," author of The History of Rome.

"I believe that there is no country in the world including any and all the countries under colonial domination, where economic colonization, humiliation and exploitation were worse than in Cuba, in part owing to <u>my</u> country's policies during the Batista regime. . . I will even go further: to some extent it is as though Batista was the incarnation of a number of sins on the part of the United States. Now we shall have to pay for those sins." — President John F. Kennedy, October 24, 1963, in comments to journalist Jean Daniel prior to her visit to Cuba to interview Fidel Castro.

Hard to believe that two of America's most famous capital ships – the *U.S.S. John F. Kennedy* and USS Lexington – encountered unknown intelligently operated flying and undersea craft that could out maneuver anything we had. Moreover, these events occurred in the Caribbean, the place millions of Americans vacation each year. How could these incidents have remained hidden?

Of course, in Cold War times, military witnesses ordered to keep quiet for the good of the country tended to do so. Mainstream media accepted with few questions the news releases and statements of government authorities who would quickly discredit civilian experiencers who told their stories.

Without Internet there were fewer outlets for

forbidden information than in today's world of 24/7 multi-media access and reporting. It was only through online research that I had today found these incredible stories from a half-century ago.

I had always subscribed to Roman historian Livy's great thought, "History is the best medicine for a sick mind," while setting aside his admittedly true follow-up explanation:

"For in history you have a record of the infinite variety of human experience plainly set out for all to see; and in that record you can find in oneself and your country both examples and warnings; fine things to take as models, base things rotten through and through, to avoid."

To ease my bewildered "sick" brain, I took a break from the inexplicable and embarked on my cover assignment of researching the Navy's role in the Cuban Missile Crisis – something rational, well-documented and openly discussed, unlike UFO incidents.

I set aside the facts that the *U.S.S. John F.Kennedy* and *Lexington* sightings had actually occurred while both vessels were on *Cuban*-related Cold War missions. In looking at the Missile Crisis I aimed to stick to pure military historical facts. Who knew that would prove impossible?

To examine the Cuban Crisis, I first looked at Cuba itself. Just what was it like in the 1950s?

"To underworld kingpins Meyer Lansky and Charles 'Lucky' Luciano, Cuba was the greatest hope for the future of American organized crime in the post-Prohibition years. In the 1950s, the Mob—with the corrupt, repressive government of brutal Cuban dictator Fulgencio Batista in its pocket—owned Havana's biggest luxury hotels and casinos, launching an unprecedented tourism boom complete with the most lavish entertainment, top-drawer celebrities, gorgeous women, and gambling galore. But Mob dreams collided with those of Fidel Castro, Che Guevara, and others who would lead an uprising of the country's disenfranchised against Batista's hated government and its foreign partners—an epic cultural battle."[1]

Daily Cuban life was grim under Batista. Dr. Eric Williams, the Oxford educated first Prime Minister of the independent Trinidad and Tobago, formerly a British colony, wrote the world's first comprehensive history of the Caribbean. He collected these and other data on pre-revolutionary Cuba:[2]

27 percent of urban children and 61 percent of rural did not attend school;

25 percent of the labor force was chronically unemployed;

75 percent of rural homes were huts made from palm trees and 91 percent had no electricity;

More than one-third of rural people had intestinal parasites.

The sad statistics go on and on. Some say that, as bad as it was, Cuba actually had it better than most Latin American countries in those days. Cuba had been liberated from Spain in 1898 by the United States and, aside from Puerto Rico (also liberated from Spain) and the U.S. Virgin Islands (purchased from Denmark in 1917), the island nation had the closest relationship with the U.S. of any country south of the border. Cubans simply had higher expectations.

Before long my research made clear that the Mafia and the U.S. government were not the only outside parties interested in Cuba during the 1950s.

Classic flying saucer reports in that troubled country date back at least to 1950. One was a 1954 sighting above Havana witnessed by many people of all walks of life. Cuban writer and researcher Antonio Santana Perez has plenty of examples and concludes:

"Cuba appears to form part of alien curiosity, perhaps with an aim toward renewed tourist purposes, or perhaps to sample the joviality and hardiness of the archipelago's inhabitants. Several eyewitness accounts recorded throughout our country, offering specific details on swift vehicles, strange lights, irregularly-moving orbs and strangest of all, the presence of ghostly beings involved in abductions and kidnappings, have led to an appraisal of these events beyond meteorological, physical or paranormal justifications."[3]

But this digression was getting me nowhere on my factual look at the U.S. Navy, the Castro revolution and missile crisis.

Back to basics.

Until 1958 the U.S. supported Fulgencia Batista, the army sergeant who became Cuba's military dictator backed by the American Mafia and U.S. agri-businesses that ran many plantation-style farms. By March of that year, the U.S. had lost confidence in the Cuban government. Some in Washington believed the insurrectionists, including Fidel Castro, might be people they could deal with. Castro, after all, was the son of a wealthy sugar plantation owner and had studied law at the University of Havana.

In 1958, Americans stopped shipping arms to Batista. Nevertheless, later that year Castro's forces kidnapped ten American engineers working for the Moa Bay Mining Company to hold as hostages. In June, Fidel's brother Raul kidnapped 29 unarmed US sailors and Marines from a bus taking them back to the Guantanamo Bay Navy base from their liberty. The hostages later told U.S. investigators they had been questioned by Raul's girl friend and future wife, the M.I.T. educated Vilma Espin.

Although the U.S. gained release of all the hostages by threatening to resume arms shipments to Batista, it was no longer safe for American civilians to remain on the island. The *U.S.S. Franklin D. Roosevelt*, a powerful aircraft carrier, was ordered to support the evacuation of 56 U.S. citizens and three foreign nationals. On October 24, 1958 they were taken on board the *U.S.S. Kleinsmith*, a World War II era destroyer transformed into a fast transport.

By dispatching the carrier *U.S.S. Franklin D. Roosevelt*

to assist, the U.S. was sending a serious cautionary message to the insurgents. Built in 1945 at the close of World War II and virtually rebuilt and modernized in the mid-1950s, the Roosevelt carried the most modern jet fighter aircraft and weaponry. Indeed, she was the first carrier to take nuclear weapons (including the hydrogen bomb) to sea, and also boasted then state-of-the art Regulas guided missiles, precursors of today's Tomahawk cruise missiles.

The evacuation was completed.

In researching the *Roosevelt*, I was shocked to see in her operational records located on the *U.S.S. Franklin D. Roosevelt*'s historical web site these notations:[4]

581028 Stand by for Rescue of Americans from Oriente Province, Cuba.

581077 UFO sighting – Cuba

"UFO Sighting – Cuba." One crew man later came forward to publicly describe that October, 1958 event. Chester Grusinski, then an 18 year old seaman, recalled that extraordinary night off Cuba:[5]

"It was dark outside, and I was down below decks at the time. There was a bunch of men who came running up from the engine room and a couple of minutes later another bunch came running up and I followed them up to the flight deck.

"I saw a bright white ball of light. It headed straight for us, getting bigger and brighter. It was spherical, approximately 75 to 100 feet long. It turned red orange and I could feel the heat on my face. As this was going on, the man on watch was yelling into the intercom for an officer to get up on deck.

"I could see silhouettes of figures looking at us from the object. They had no features and you could tell they weren't human. Then the bottom turned cherry red and it vanished in a flash."[5]

Later, investigators came on board and crew members who talked about the incident were transferred because of alleged gambling on-board. This was simply a "cover up,"

Mr. Grusinski said.

Separately, Navy petty officer Harry Allen Jordan, a radar operator, later served on the *U.S.S. Roosevelt* during 1962 and 63. While on a Mediterranean cruise in 1962, he saw a contact on his radar screen that, because of its speed and maneuvering, defied explanation. He and others plotted the course, altitude and speed and the captain ordered two Phantom jets to take-off and give chase.

The contact disappeared as the jets neared and turned on their own radar. The planes circled and landed after about a half hour. Then, the target reappeared on ship's radar. The lookouts made no visual sighting and the blip disappeared. Later Mr. Jordan's immediate commanding officer told him "this never happened."[6]

After that cruise, when he was on a different assignment, Petty Officer Jordan ran into a Navy chief who told him about a similar incident when he was on the *Roosevelt* in the Caribbean. That time the ship also went to General Quarters.

"They saw this large UFO come up out of the water and take off. And he said that the movie *The Abyss* was based on that particular story and that was a part of the Navy records."

I wondered if Jordan was correct about *The Abyss?* It was a well-received 1989 movie by director James Cameron about a team recovering a sunken nuclear submarine who run into an affable, curious alien force two and half miles below the ocean surface.

Was former Petty Officer Jordan correct about the movie? Seems he was correct about the *Roosevelt's* UFO encounters. He later ran into Chester Grosinski, the Cuban UFO witness, who was still assigned to the *Roosevelt* when Jordan came aboard in 1961.

"I learned they had a huge UFO event. This UFO came down out of the clouds – not only lights, but they saw the saucer. And photographs were taken. Chet Grazinski (sic) saw it."

Meanwhile, back in the terrestrial world of geopolitics, at age 33, Fidel Castro entered Havana on January 8, 1959 at the head of a rag tag army he had led from mountain jungles to defeat the military dictatorship. At first, many in the U.S. were hopeful a democracy might emerge, despite Cuba's history of failed republics.

William LeoGrande, an American University professor of government and Latin American policy expert, explains the context:

"The generation of 1959, which overthrew Fulgencio Batista was part of a long tradition in Cuba of revolutionary generations, of each generation defining itself in a way by overthrowing a dictatorial regime.

"When Castro said this is going to be a real revolution, in 1959, I think he was referring to the aborted revolutions of 1898 and 1933. I think he wants to carry those revolutions through to their promise – or to what he thinks their promise was, which are in particular reforms that will address the economic and social inequalities of Cuban society."[7]

It wasn't long before the Kennedy Administration agreed to demands of the U.S. military and Cuban exile community in Florida to support an invasion of Cuba by U.S.-trained and armed ex-patriots. Castro decisively repelled the disastrous landings of exiles at the Bay of Pigs and, fearing a full-scale American invasion, sought weapons from Moscow.

In addition to sending tanks, artillery and guns, the Soviets made an offer Castro couldn't (and ultimately didn't) refuse: sending nuclear armed missiles to be aimed at the U.S. In July 1962, American intelligence was closely following the massive arms build-up on Cuba that included anti-aircraft guns and jet fighters. Far worse, in October, U.S. spy planes discovered construction of the type of fortifications designed to protect and launch strategic (rather than defensive) missiles.

On October 15, the U.S. spotted a convoy of vehicles

carrying rocket launchers built for ballistic missiles capable of delivering nuclear warheads within 2,200 miles. Virtually every significant American population and military center was vulnerable to attack. Facilities were being constructed to launch or house a total of 42 missiles. And, U.S. planes had observed a ship in a Cuban port unloading a disassembled missile.

Unknown to the U.S. at the time, the Soviets had already delivered 158 nuclear warheads to Cuba.[8]

On October 21, 1962 (coincidentally, St. Ursula's feast day), President John F. Kennedy ordered a naval "quarantine" of Cuba. All ships carrying offensive military equipment to Cuba were to be stopped at sea and sent back. The Navy sent all available Polaris submarines to sea, deployed several carriers, and all US forces worldwide were placed on high alert. In all, more than 150 ships and more than 350 combat aircraft were deployed in the Caribbean.

President Kennedy also declared that any nuclear attack on the US by Cuba would be considered an attack by the Soviet Union. Washington raised defense readiness to DEFCON 2, the highest alert short of war. That meant all U.S. intercontinental ballistic missiles were ready for instant launch and the nuclear bomb carrying aircraft of the Strategic Air Command were in the air and on alert. Here is how the Department of Defense Annual Report described the situation:

"Starting on October 20, the Strategic Air Command (SAC) began dispersing its bombers and placed all aircraft on an upgraded alert – ready to take off, fully equipped, within 15 minutes. On October 22, the B-52 heavy bombers started a massive airborne alert, involving 24-hour flights and immediate replacement for every aircraft that landed. ICBM (Intercontinental Ballistics Missile) crews assumed a comparable alert status. POLARIS submarines went to sea to pre-assigned stations. The tremendous nuclear firepower of the United States was deployed to discourage any reckless challenge.

"Our air defense forces, under the operational control of the North American Defense Command (NORAD), were equally ready for any emergency. Fighter interceptors and HAWK and NIKE-HERCULES missile battalions were moved to the southeast to supplement local air defense forces. After October 22, interceptor units were either on patrol missions or on a 5-to-15-minute alert."[9]

It is now known that the Russian military commander in Cuba was authorized to use tactical nuclear weapons to repel any U.S. invasion. Equally scary, during the Navy's enforcement of the quarantine, a U.S. destroyer dropped practice depth charges (capable of only small explosions) on a submerged Soviet submarine that had come too close to Navy vessels. In response, the sub commander seriously considered firing a nuclear tipped torpedo into the destroyer.

In this extraordinarily tense environment, any incursion of North American airspace by unknown aircraft could lead to action and, possibly, a nuclear war. Francis L. Ridge, then an investigator for the National Investigations Committee on Aerial Phenomena (NICAP), explained a very real fear:

"One of our major concerns was the possibility of accidental nuclear war caused by jittery air defense radar men mistaking UFOs for Russian missiles or jets. And when we had the Cuban Missile Crisis in October of 1962 there was never a time when we were closer to a nuclear confrontation."[10]

Rear Admiral Delmar Fahrney, NICAP's first chairman, was the father of the Naval guided missile program, including the Regulas missiles carried by the USS Roosevelt, and was aware of this danger. Indeed, he was quite knowledgeable about UFOs.

In a 1957 news conference, Admiral Fahrney was quoted by the Associated Press as saying:

"There are objects coming into our atmosphere at very

high speeds. . . . No agency in this country or Russia is able to duplicate at this time the speeds and accelerations which radar and observers indicate these flying objects are able to achieve. . . . The way they change position in formations and override each other would indicate that their motion is directed. . . .[They display] a tremendous amount of technology of which we have no knowledge."[11]

Admiral Fahrney knew personally of what he spoke. In an incident reported by the Milwaukee Sentinel newspaper, in November, 1952, the Admiral – then serving as Navy Secretary – was flying in a Navy plane between Pearl Harbor and Guam. His and another plane carrying Admiral Dan Kimball were buzzed by two UFOs.

When he landed, Secretary Fahrney demanded the Air Force investigate the episode and report to him what they already knew about UFOs. The Air Force reportedly refused to give Secretary Fahrney, a member of the Cabinet, any information. Fahrney then ordered Naval Intelligence to open its own investigation.

In fact, Navy interest dated back at least to the immediate post-Second World War years when then Navy Secretary James Forrestal reportedly pressured the Army Air Force (later renamed "Air Force") to research and analyze UFOs. That the Air Force would later refuse to give information to another Navy Secretary (Fahrney) must have been infuriating.

One can guess frustration might have led Fahrney and other naval officers to organize the National Investigations Committee on Aerial Phenomena. Possibly reflecting the views of other Navy brass, retired Admiral Hillenkoetter (and NICAP board member) told the New York Times:

"It is time for the truth to be brought out in open Congressional hearings. . . Behind the scenes, high-ranking Air Force officers are soberly concerned about the UFOs. But through official secrecy and ridicule, many citizens are led to believe the unknown flying objects are nonsense . . . To hide the facts, the Air Force has silenced its personnel."

By the time of the Cuban Missile Crisis, high ranking military officers were well aware that UFOs were real objects. They worried that UFOs could be confused with Soviet missiles, possibly leading to nuclear war. NICAP investigator Francis Ridge learned from air force ground radar operators of just such an incursion at the height of the crisis:

"Something slower than an incoming missile, but faster than our jet interceptors, was violating airspace all the way from New Jersey, Pennsylvania, New York, on into Canada and Alaska, and we U.S. Air Force were ready to use tactical nuclear weapons, if necessary, to stop it."

Nuclear air-to-air missile armed fighters gave chase and tried to lock their on-board radars on the target above New York. The object immediately rose to an altitude of more than 75,000 feet, where the fighters could not follow. It then crossed into Canadian airspace and ultimately disappeared.

Today, former investigator Ridge sums up the incident:

"Forty years ago, something real was tracked by at least seven defense radars. This occurred during one of the most dangerous times in our history, the Cuban Missile Crisis. . . .   The object was not a Russian missile; Intercontinental Ballistic Missiles move ten times faster than that. It wasn't a jet. It wasn't ours and it wasn't Russian. They knew it then, but we all know now for sure. There was no visual sighting, but the UFO was 14 miles up and moving faster than anything we had in the air."[12]

Such an event would have been brought to President Kennedy's attention. He had already reportedly asked questions about UFOs. And, that incursion could only have peaked his interest. It is not surprising, therefore, that once the Missile Crisis ended (with Soviet withdrawal from Cuba in November, 1962 of all nuclear warheads and the missiles and facilities to launch them), President Kennedy took action to make sure confusion about UFOs would not trigger a nuclear war.

In a secret memo to the director of the CIA, Kennedy ordered the Agency to review the "high threat" UFO cases and separate the "known from the unknown," according to a 2011 report in The Daily Mail, a conservative British newspaper with a circulation of about 2 million. The paper reproduced the full memo:[13]

TOP SECRET
November 12, 1963
Memorandum for
The Director [BLACKED OUT] CIA
Subject: Classification of all UFO Intelligence affecting National Security

As I had discussed with you previously, I have initiated [BLACKED OUT] and instructed James Webb to develop a program with the Soviet Union in joint space and lunar exploration. It would be very helpful if you would have the high threat cases reviewed with the purpose of identification of bona fide as opposed to classified CIA and USAF sources. It is important that we make a clear distinction [between] the knowns and unknowns in the event the Soviets try to mistake our extended cooperation as a cover for intelligence gathering of their defense and space programs.

When this data has been sorted out, I would like you to arrange a program of data sharing with NASA where Unknowns are a factor. This will help NASA mission directors in their defensive responsibilities. I would like an interim report on the data review no later than FEB 1, 1964.

Signed John F. Kennedy

John McCone was then the Director of the Central Intelligence Agency and James Webb was Administrator of NASA. Kennedy's post-Missile Crisis intention to seek cooperation with the Soviets in space exploration had already been announced to the world in his speech before the United Nations in September, 1963. The secret memo hinting at sharing UFO knowledge with the Soviets is consistent with that intent.

We'll never know how history might have been changed. President Kennedy was murdered in Dallas just ten days after signing the memo.

Decades later, however, a very different president, Ronald Reagan, hit on a similar theme in his remarkable speech before the United Nations on September 21, 1987:

"Can we and all nations not live in peace? In our obsession with antagonisms of the moment, we often forget how much unites all the members of humanity. Perhaps we need some outside, universal threat to make us recognize this common bond. I occasionally think how quickly our differences worldwide would vanish if we were facing an alien threat from outside this world."[14]

According to the now declassified U.S. Department of State record of Reagan's November 19, 1985 summit with Soviet leader Mikhael Gorbachev, the President said the following in an "impromptu dinner toast" responding to Gorbachev's toast:

"He [President Reagan] said that previous to the General Secretary's [Mikhail Gorbachev's] remarks, he had been telling Foreign Minister Shevardnadze (who was seated to the President's right) that if the people of the world were to find out that there was some alien life form that was going to attack the Earth approaching on Halley's Comet, then that knowledge would unite all the peoples of the world.

"Further, the President observed that General Secretary Gorbachev had cited a Biblical quotation, and the President, also alluding to the Bible, pointed out that Acts 16 refers to the fact that 'we are all of one blood regardless of where we live on the Earth,' and we should never forget that."[15]

Kennedy and Reagan, two presidents of different

parties and philosophies – both of whom UFO researchers claim had been briefed by national security officials on the importance of the phenomena – came to similar conclusions about the need for cooperation with the Soviets and super power unity in approaching extraterrestrial life.

Meanwhile, long after the deaths of both Cold War presidents, Cuba and the Caribbean continue to be the object of unidentified aeronauts' interest. Incidents have occurred in Matanzas, Cuba's second largest province.

Stretching from Cuba's northern, Florida facing coast to the island's southern coast, Matanzas boasts world-famous beaches. Its interior is an important agricultural region, producing sugar and henequen, an agave plant with fibrous leaves used in making rope and paper.

The province is also home to the Caribbean's largest freshwater and saline swamps, preserved in a national park along the southern coast. It's a mecca for multiple species of birds and endangered Cuban crocodiles. The infamous Bay of Pigs is also located along the province's southern shores.

The provincial capital city of Matanzas, known as the "city of bridges," is called the Venice of Cuba. On December 21, 1993, four luminous spheres sped silently above the city in early evening skies. They were observed by several people from different angles in the city, which is situated on the nation's north coast.[16]

On the province's south coast and located about two miles from the vast Matanzas marsh and swamp lands, sits the quiet farming village of Torriente, the scene of a far more complicated UFO event. The Cuban Academy of Sciences reportedly studied it and their story has been disseminated by About.com.[17]

On the morning of October 15, 1995, a 74-year old farmer (and former aircraft mechanic) headed out to work in his corn fields. During a cigarette break, he spotted a round object silently approaching, which landed in a field nearby. The object, about the size of a car, was smooth and colored with multiple shades of green, like the fields. It had a clear round top seemingly made of glass. A door opened and a humanoid creature stepped out.

The farmer was very concerned about all this because two years earlier a cousin had disappeared in this same vicinity. So, he remained hidden in the bushes.

"The being's features were not visible, as it wore a cover-all outfit, which was colored like the craft. The only deviance from the green colors was the humanoid's face mask. The being seemed to wander around the UFO like he was seeing the fields for the first time. At times, he would bend down and uproot some of the flora. This was probably done to take samples back for study. For a moment, he walked to the back of the craft, then returned to the front, and leaned against the exterior of the UFO.

"In a few moments, the being went back into the ship. The door closed behind him, leaving no trace of where it had been."

With a burst of air that shook the corn stalks and other vegetation, the craft silently took off vertically and when about 50 feet high, flew horizontally out of sight. The farmer then called the police, who later found footprints and scorched plants at the landing site. The evidence was given to the Academy of Sciences. Meanwhile, other witnesses in the region saw the same or a similar object in the sky. It remains a mystery.

As I completed my Cuban studies, it became clear I would need to write a sanitized version of the Cuban Missile Crisis for the Annapolis Institute Press, while writing an unexpurgated account for the benefit of Lt. Taft.

Ironically, I had become part of the cover-up.

7 BLACKBEARD AND LINDBERGH

"Citizens of St. Thomas. First, I want to thank all of you for the welcome you gave me yesterday on my landing [here]. I appreciate very greatly what you have done to make my trip and my visit most enjoyable. I have never made a more interesting or beautiful flight than that over the islands of the West Indies, yesterday."

— Charles Lindbergh, speaking in Charlotte Amalie, February 1, 1928, after being presented with an illuminated writing desk and a mahogany table inlaid with sandalwood at a reception at Emancipation Garden. The Navy Band and an overflowing crowd sang the hymn "O God our Help in Ages Past."[1]

"No-body but me and the Devil knows where it is, and the longest *Liver* should take all."

— Blackbeard's response when asked if his wife knew where his treasure was should he be killed.[2]

I easily completed the Cuban Missile Crisis writing assignment and for the Institute Press. Then, I turned back to Sergeant Baskins.

To gain much needed perspective on my research to-date, I turned to an island friend artist Schooner Smith. A self-described "man of art and science," he is both a well-known artist and the island expert on satellite communications and dish installation. Schooner was an old Caribbean hand – having lived in the basin for 40 years – and had seen everything from Central American civil wars to the hippy invasion of the West Indies.

We had met Schooner in his science capacity soon after Mary, John and I had first moved on-island. I was doing research while waiting to take up my college post. Mary was taking John to school each day.

We had rented a disheveled house perched atop a rocky ridge on St. John's far East End – nearly as far south and east as one can go on a road (albeit, an unpaved one) and still stand on U.S. territory in the Western Hemisphere. Among the many glitches in our rental home was lack of an advertised air conditioner and a broken satellite-fed Wi-Fi system, making Internet reception impossible. That led me to phone Schooner.

It wasn't long before noisy gear changes and billowing dust blowing up our steep, rock strewn dirt road alerted me to his approach. Through the screen door, I watched an aged Suzuki SUV, armed with ladders atop a bamboo roof wrack and a rusting Ford pick-up, turn into our overgrown drive way.

Schooner and his crew had arrived, quickly disembarked from their vehicles and bounded up to our door.

After introductions, Schooner, with dark moustache and hair, sparkling black eyes and wearing a hand-dyed, hand-painted shirt sporting Mayan hieroglyphs, quickly diagnosed the satellite problem: faulty wiring between the loosely mounted and cracked dish on the tin roof and satellite modem on the hard-worn wooden dining table at which I sat. He gently directed his associates to erect ladders on our porch overlooking Coral Bay. The porch (and house itself) appeared barely attached to the rim of a precipice that dropped a few hundred feet to the bay.

After a couple hours of talk, it was clear Schooner enjoyed conversation beyond work-a-day matters. He was a man of arts and sciences, with interests ranging from aboriginal petro glyphs to telecommunications and tropical gardening.

We have since moved to the other end of the island above Cruz Bay. In addition to his other roles, Schooner now serves as communications director for Coral Bay emergency services. In that capacity, he had taken the first call that quiet April morning about the then unidentified body of Sergeant Baskins discovered by a hiker in the rocks along Privateer Bay. He had manned the radio, helping coordinate its recovery.

Phoning Schooner to find a time to talk about the Sergeant and the strange happenings was a no-brainer. We settled on a time and, since Schooner's studio and home is located in the hills above Coral Bay, Mary, John and I took the opportunity to drive out there together and first go snorkeling in one of the Bay's many mangrove fringed coves.

Swimming with sea turtles – some quite large – who come to the shallows to serenely eat sea grass is a marvel. Since they must surface to breathe air every few moments, and then dive back down for more grazing, the shallower the water the better they can access food. If one is quiet and gentle, they are surprisingly tolerant of humans swimming along above them. One can even hear the crunching as they snap off and eat grasses. Communing with them is an other-worldly experience.

Mary especially enjoys swimming with the turtles and lost 30 pounds doing so in just a few months. She told people she was on a sea turtle diet. She dropped the joke, however, after Schooner told her that the Brits, just across the Channel, still kill and eat these endangered beauties.

After our snorkel, we cleaned up and went to

Schooner's place – a West Indian style, two- story house – all tropical hard wood verandas, screened windows (no glass) with wooden shutters and built into the side of a hill. His wife Betsy offered tea to Mary and John and they caught up on island happenings. I wandered down to Schooner's work area located under the lower deck.

His open-air workshop is partially protected from the elements by a close-in bamboo forest, some mosquito netting and canvas draped from outer deck beams. Schooner was listening to vintage blue grass music as he worked on a large table littered with swaths of cloth, jars of paints, canvases and other artful odds and ends.

A freshly-made, multi-colored banner hung from a bamboo pole: "All Who Wander Are Not Lost" was the lesson painted on the canvas amid purple and pink floral and sea creature figures. That J.R.R. Tolkien aphorism brought to mind Jesus' mantra: "Seek and ye shall find." Both sayings were relevant to the task at-hand.

"Scorpion!!!" he shouted before I could even say hello. He quickly swept paint spattered fabric off the table and pointed to a section of bare wood. There a small, brown lobster-like creature stood tall on eight pincer legs with fore claws ready to pinch and tear. Rear segmented stinger was arched high. It circled slowly eyeing us humans, daring us to touch him. Then, the creature leisurely walked to the table's edge and jumped off.

"Usually, you see them in pairs – male with his mate," Schooner matter-of-factly explained, as I looked around for this specimen's paramour.

Must be here somewhere, I thought. Meanwhile, the scorpion in view had disappeared on the brick floor into the bamboo outside the work area.

"People who've been stung say the toxin induces hallucinations," he enthusiastically explained.

Probably not a good trip, I thought.

After some small talk, I described my interest in Sergeant Baskins and his apparent link to UFO activity. I recounted my conversations with Sir Keithley and Captain Hap, omitting all the other research, the link with the Navy, etc. Schooner's comments were on target.

"If it were just Keithley's story about what he saw on the Willy T, I'd say he was in his cups that night; maybe seeing things. But, Hap Collins is a reliable sailor. He doesn't drink when skippering tourists; a level headed guy."

Looking for still more evidence, I asked Schooner a key question. "By any chance did you hear any complaints from customers about interruptions in satellite TV that night?"

"I'll check my customer service log," he obligingly said, as he pulled down a paint spattered wireless key board from a wooden shelf.

After a few minutes of looking at a PC screen encased in mahogany, he grunted and gave his verdict, "Several people did lose service for about 15 minutes early that Saturday evening. Weather was clear and there was no problem with the satellite or receivers. I checked because it seemed unusual to get customer calls on such a calm night when sun spots or tropical storms were not issues."

"Very interesting. So, no obvious explanations for service disruptions. By the way, have you ever seen such lights or unexplained objects?"

"Personally, I never saw anything like that when I used to sail these waters."

"When did you have a boat?"

"When we first arrived about 1980. We rented that old falling down clap board house right on Hansen Bay. Arthur the boat builder had re-rigged an old island sloop into a small schooner. I fell in love with her and we sailed everywhere. No mortgage, no assets. Just produced enough art to sell to the occasional tourists who made it out here in those days. Kept life simple; the bare essentials. Now, between art and satellite dishes, I'm working six days a week."

"Guess the Coral Bay community was pretty small and tight in those days. You would have heard of any odd lights or UFOs."

"Yes, it was a much smaller place back then. Most people were either on the sea or focusing on making a living on land. I never heard any UFO stories. And, if I had, I would have figured the person had smoked too much ganja or eaten mushrooms. There was a lot of that back then. That being said, there could have been unexplained lights and craft. Odd things happened and still happen here every day."

Truer words were never spoken. We all reside on an island where baby goats are known to suckle on the teats of lactating mother pigs, and scores of feral donkeys, loose cows, semi-wild goats and sheep wander through yards, onto roads and across beaches at will. Then there are the local electric outages caused by iguanas that fall asleep on high branches and fall onto utility pole transformers.

"Back in the days when you first arrived, did you spend much time sailing around the BVI?"

"Of course. Who didn't? This was all paradise back then."

"What was Norman Island like?"

"Not much different – not any moorings, of course, and the original Willy T had just been towed there and was being worked on."

"Were there people camping on the beach?"

"Yes, there were hippies and treasure hunters on Norman, and wandering souls scattered throughout these islands."

"Does the name Melissa wring any bells?"

"Now that you mention it, there was a strikingly beautiful American woman camping on one of Norman's small beaches near the caves. A brunette whose name could have been Mel or Millie or something like that. She stands out in my memory because she had actually studied archaeology. Not like the stoners. Her treasure search was methodical and she kept at it for a year or so."

"What happened to her?"

"BVI immigration finally kicked-out the people camping on Norman. She came to Coral Bay for a while, and then went back to the states – California, I believe."

Another puzzle piece found! Baskins must have made it to Norman Island and camped with Melissa. It was not surprising she made a big impression. Back then, the hell of combat had been a recent experience for the Sergeant. She was, no doubt, very different from the ladies of the night he might have been accustomed to.

Baskins' story was coming together. In trying to comprehend these extraterrestrial, cosmic events in which he was caught up, however, I was stretching my brain to its limits. Nearing the edge of rationality; approaching a border Herman Melville's Billy Budd the sailor describes best:

"Who watching a rainbow can draw the line where the violet tint ends and the orange tint begins? Distinctly we see the difference of the colors, but where exactly does the one first blendingly enter into the other? So [it is] with sanity and insanity."

Schooner had resumed work on his canvas – an impressionistic seascape bordered by aboriginal style petroglyphs of sea turtles, fish and conch. He looked up.

"Why are you so interested in this, Harris?"

Since I hated to be addressed as Thayer, I encouraged people to simply use my surname.

Now, I would need to dissemble.

"I might write a fictional story based on this incident and want to get enough facts to make the plot feasible."

"Good luck, and keep me informed about what you learn. This is interesting."

"Hey, you'll be the first to know if I uncover new information. Your opinion counts."

On the way back to Cruz Bay, we stopped at Pickles, a deli that made great sandwiches. The owner puts out buckets of water for the wild donkeys that frequently pass through. We were in luck that day. John and I got to sneak food to and pet some donkeys that had stopped by for drinks.

Later, at home, I did a sanity check by going through files and rereading accounts of the most credible witnesses. And, who had a more credibly conservative slant than the Ol' Gipper himself? There was a reason why he thought seriously about alien invasions while president.

On a Discovery Channel website called "Science: How Stuff Works," there it was. One night, then California Governor Ronald Reagan was flying in a small Cessna plane accompanied by Bill Paynter, his pilot, and two security guards. Their routine business trip was upset when they spotted an unusual object in the air as they approached Bakersfield. Pilot Paynter recalled:

"It appeared to be several hundred yards away. It was a fairly steady light until it began to accelerate. Then it appeared to elongate. Then the light took off. It went up at a 45 degree angle at a high rate of speed. Everyone on the plane was surprised . . . The UFO went from a normal cruise speed to a fantastic speed instantly. If you give an airplane power, it will accelerate – but not like a hot rod, and that's what this was like."[3]

One week later, Governor Reagan was in his office speaking to the Wall Street Journal's Washington Bureau Chief, Norman Miller. The Governor told him about the encounter:

"We followed it for several minutes. It was a bright white light. We followed it to Bakersfield, and all of a sudden to our utter amazement it went straight up into the heavens."

When Miller expressed doubt, a "look of horror came over [Reagan]." Miller explained:

"It suddenly dawned on him . . . that he was talking to a reporter. Immediately afterward, he clammed up."

In other media accounts of this incident, Reagan tells

the pilot, "Hey, let's follow it!" Although Reagan never publicly spoke about it again, the story was widely reported at the time. And, Reagan's reactions sound very much in character.

Although one Governor and future President clammed up when he realized he was telling a reporter he had seen a UFO, another one (Jimmy Carter) actually officially reported his sighting to the best available authority: the National Investigations Committee on Aerial Phenomena – NICAP, the one-time bastion of disaffected Navy brass looking for answers.

According to the Washington Post, Governor Carter witnessed a UFO in October, 1969. While waiting to deliver a dinner speech to the Lions Club of Leary, Georgia, Governor Carter and several Club members watched a UFO for 10 to 12 minutes before it disappeared. Carter freely told reporters all about it:

"I don't laugh at people any more when they say they've seen UFOs, because I've seen one myself . . . A light appeared and disappeared in the sky. It got brighter and brighter . . . at one time as bright as the moon . . It seemed to move toward us from a distance, stopped and moved partially away. It returned, then departed. It came close . . . maybe 300 to 1,000 yards . . . moved away, came close and then moved away. It turned color and was bluish at first, then reddish. It was luminous, not solid. I have no idea what it was."[4]

"Another bloody multi-colored thing flying around," I muttered to myself. And, witnessed by unimpeachable (so to speak) sources. How many of these accounts must I read to fulfill the Navy contract, I asked myself. I was being paid to investigate Baskins and the *U.S.S. John F. Kennedy*, not solve the biggest mystery of our age.

Getting back to Baskins, I realized there was still work to be done. Lt. Taft said the Sergeant had arrived on St Thomas on March 26 – seven days before his rendezvous with the Willy T. What did he do on those days? And, where did he get the kayak?

An e-mail exchange with the good lieutenant revealed the Sergeant had used his credit card for six nights at the Best Western Emerald Beach resort. That was a break. The hotel was located near the college and I knew the bartender at its Polynesian style beach bar.

Baskins had made a good choice in lodging. Built on what could well be the world's best beach located across the street from an airport, the Best Western is relatively inexpensive and close to Charlotte Amalie and the old Navy base district. Neither the hotel nor the airport would be there if the Navy hadn't filled in an old malarial swamp in the early 1920's and made it a golf course. It was not a coincidence the bay there used to be called Mosquito Bay. Today, it's called Lindbergh Bay, memorializing the aviator's visit.

During his 1928 Latin America good will tour, then global super star Charles Lindbergh was met by nearly hysterical crowds each place he landed. He was flying his *Spirit of St. Louis*, the plane he had flown alone across the Atlantic.

Spirit was the first airplane ever to land in British Honduras (now the independent nation of Belize) and Lindbergh landed on St. Thomas in February, 1928 on the Navy golf course. The course was later turned into a Navy air strip and is now the airport. To many then living in the Caribbean, the silver *Spirit of St. Louis* would have been nearly as exotic as a flying saucer.

In his memoir, *Me and My Beloved Virgin*, Guy H. Benjamin, one of St. John's oldest and most revered residents (who passed away at age 98 in 2012), recalled his exciting visit to St. Thomas to see Lindbergh and the wondrous aircraft. Years later, for several hours each day, Guy would sit in his wheel chair under a small wooden framed kiosk at the edge of the road in front of his Coral Bay house, just up the road from Skinny Legs. *My Beloved Virgin* was hand painted on a sign and he would have a pile of books ready to sell and autograph to passersby. The now empty kiosk still stands.

Too bad, I thought, that Uncle Benjie (as islanders called him) passed away before I could ask him about these phenomena. But, we do have his book, and his trip to see Lindbergh illustrates the awe with which people have always viewed airships.

As a child, his family home was all the way out on the island's East End on Hansen Bay, a world away from St. Thomas, and a long walk from the Coral Bay settlement.

"I begged my grandmother with tears in my eyes to let me go see the plucky, lucky Lindbergh, the hero of the United States. I was thirteen and my mother had never permitted me to go any further than Emmaus [the Moravian Mission in Coral Bay]. [Even Emmaus] was a day's journey there and back by sailboat or row boat from my home."[5]

Young Guy, though, was given permission to go see the *Spirit of St. Louis*. Visions of "cars, electric lights, ice cream and sugar babies" filled his head as he thought about St. Thomas and the capital, Charlotte Amalie.

"The day we were to leave, I was awake at the first cock's crowing . . . and boarded my grandfather's sailboat, the *Adventure*. We leaped and jumped with the waves and the flying fish towards magical St. Thomas. The trip took us six and a half hours.

"And then St. Thomas came into view. We saw so many houses, cars and trucks, horses and donkeys, people running into each other, confusion and noise. . . . And Lindbergh, so slim and gentle as he rolled the *Spirit of St. Louis* up to a halt on the grounds of Mosquito Bay . . . We touched the *Spirit of St. Louis*, which was later roped off after so many of us had touched it."[6]

Of course, Mary, John and I had also seen the *Spirit of St. Louis* in Washington, D.C. in the Smithsonian's Museum of Air and Space, but we never got to touch it. Also in that museum are numerous rockets, a space lab and a lunar command module that brought U.S. astronauts back home from an historic extraterrestrial trip to the Moon. That museum also has spacecraft from the Soviet Union, another terrestrial civilization that once seemed as distant from American life as the Moon.

These thoughts kept me occupied as I drove beside the solar panels arrayed along the airport runway and turned into the Best Western located on Lindbergh Bay. I had guessed that Sergeant Baskins chose this hotel because he was looking to revisit old haunts from youthful liberties in St. T's decaying naval district located along the waterfront just over the hill from the hotel.

Luckily Bud, the Best Western barkeep, remembered the old, crew-cut stocky gent with the Semper Fi on his forearm who had sat at his bar for a couple of hours each night for about a week.

"He asked me a lot of questions about this or that bar or restaurant; most, I had never heard of – even asked about a brothel over in Estate Contant, just outside the Sub Base area. Who knew?"

There are still a couple of seedy bars and an old dance hall in Contant across the road from Sub Base and the French Town section along Charlotte Amalie's shoreline. Fights and worse occur there regularly after nightfall.

In the grounds of the Navy's old submarine and ship base, Quonset huts now house car repair businesses. The dry dock is a private marine repair facility with one of the best machine shops in the Caribbean. Rows of two story barracks lie mostly empty, as do several high ceilinged open machine shops where rows of heavy equipment rust in peace.

It was an old man sitting at a desk at the VFW lounge, however, who fondly remembered Putain's Bier Garten, the establishment mentioned in Baskins' notebook. With a paint flaking sign ("All who enter here are friends") over an old wooden door, the lounge was located on the first floor of Sub Base barracks near the dry dock. The aging black veteran scratched his short gray hair and smiled as he told me about the beer place.

"Yes, sir. Putain's was as fine a bar as any on the waterfront. And, all was welcome. Didn't matter what color, nationality – officer or seaman – all was equal at Putain's brass rail. Women in the old profession used to hang there, too; pretty women of all shades – clear to dark mahogany.

"But, when the base closed, Putain's closed along with it. It was run by a Dutchman. He done packed-up and went home after the sailors disappeared."

"Are you from the mainland?" I asked him.

"Yessir – Stone Mountain Village, Georgia."

"Stone Mountain," I replied, barely concealing my astonishment. "Isn't that the Mount Rushmore of the Confederacy?"

His smile turned sour. "It is."

"With Robert E. Lee, Stonewall Jackson and Jefferson Davis carved on the side of the largest granite dome in the nation? I've been there." I had spoken without thinking.

"Oh, sure you was. But, when you were there, did you see the poor little town not far from the rock? Where the majority of people is black living in or near poverty? Did ya know the Ku Klux Klan was reborn in 1915 right on the top of that devilish stone hummock? And, did ya'll know that near the end of his 'I have a Dream' speech Dr. King sang out:

'Let freedom ring from the snowcapped Rockies of Colorado!

Let freedom ring from the curvaceous slopes of California!

But not only that; let freedom ring from Stone Mountain of Georgia!'

"You see, the place is that bad that Dr. King hisself needed to tell the whole world."

Feeling guilty that I had only thought of those carved Civil War leaders in military history terms during my visit years ago, I admitted, "No, I didn't know any of that."

"Well sir, now you do. And, now you know why I stayed right here after my twenty years was up. No point going back there. None at all. Got me a fine family and fine life right here."

"I fully understand," I said. To redeem myself, I added, "On that same trip to Georgia, I also visited Martin Luther King's boyhood home and his father's church in Atlanta's Sweet Auburn neighborhood – an inspiration just to see it."

"Very glad to hear you saw all of that," he said, smiling again. "Now that's worth a body's time!"

After thanking him for the information and his Armed Forces service, I kept walking along the Charlotte Amalie waterfront. Beyond the Sub Base and French Town, one can see the stone warehouses built in the late 1600's and into the 1800s to hold trade goods – both legal and otherwise.

The island's many bays were used by vessels from all nations to replenish water supplies and provisions. As Charlotte Amalie grew from a beach village into a free port, ships and seamen came from all over Europe and the East to trade goods and find respite in taverns and houses of ill-repute.

The Virgins welcomed pirates and small landholders long before any European powers took interest in the islands. Eventually, though, the king of Denmark gave the Danish West India Company a charter to take possession of St. Thomas, St. John and the smaller other islands associated with them. The purpose was to develop sugar plantations. Early Danish governors, however, also found profit in trading with freebooters and pirates who were permitted to use Charlotte Amalie as a base in return for a share in their loot.

Although many such adventurers passed through, Blackbeard (real name Edward Teach or Thatch) was the most famous visitor and trader. Mr. Teach (or Thatch) probably had a woman on St. Thomas. Indeed, he was believed to have had 14 wives by the time he was killed in a fight with the Royal Navy off Beaufort, North Carolina.

He also loved rum. Historian Wayne Curtis describes Blackbeard's habits:

"He and his crews would make stops on islands between harrying raids for feasting and indulging in massive quantities of drink . . . Among his cocktails was a potion of gunpowder mixed with rum, which he would ignite and swill while it flamed and popped."[7]

In between parties, the pirate – who is said to have never passed out from drink – kept watch over the St. Thomas harbor. A round stone tower now called Blackbeard's Castle was built as a watchtower by the Danes in 1679 on the highest point of Charlotte Amalie's Government Hill. It commands the anchorages, bay and provides a view for miles seaward. Teach is said to have kept a look-out there for Royal Navy men-of-war and other ships of interest.

Blackbeard was comfortable, but circumspect, when in port. Consider his retort when someone got too nosy with questions about his home:

"I come from hell and I'll carry you there presently."[8]

Not a chap to belly-up to a bar with.

Not far from Blackbeard's haunts, three hundred years later I was now once again sitting comfortably among tourists and island lifers at the Best Western beach bar. Bartende Bud was in his mid-thirties and had come to St. Thomas from the Midwest five years earlier. I guessed he knew little of the colorful history of the waterfront where he now worked. But, Baskins had done a lot of talking as he drank at the beach bar and Bud is a good listener. Tips depended on it.

One day the Marine told Bud he had taken a safari taxi out to Bolongo Bay, the location of an old St. Thomas resort that had been a happening place in the 70s.

"Iggie's?" I asked, thinking of the sergeant's notes.

"The same," he answered.

Iggie's Beach Bar had a no shirt, no shoes, no problem policy. It was a place sailors could go, drink and chill with dates and enjoy a good beach – no questions asked. Iggie's is a reference to the iguanas that live all over these islands but often congregate near bars and restaurants where humans throw them scraps.

"Bolongo Bay has changed a lot since the old Marine first came off a ship here," I told Bud to keep the conversation going. "It's a lot more built-up, though Iggie's is still there and the resort has been renovated."

"Yah, I don't think your Marine found what he was looking for there, or anywhere for that matter. But, he did have fun – spent a lot of time on our beach, made friends with some women at the bar, and even went kayaking."

"Kayaking?" I blurted-out, getting excited. "Wonder where he did that?"

"He said he went over to that eco-tour place near Red Hook where they take you through the mangroves."

I knew the place – Virgin Islands Eco Tours. Better still, Mary knew the woman who owned the business. By then, Mary was assisting my research and was a good sounding board, helping to keep my focus as practical as possible.

Now, she stepped in and phoned the eco-tour owner. She learned that a few weeks earlier a retired, crew cut guy had taken the tour and, at the end, looked over the used kayaks they had on display for sale. It was the end of the season and they wanted to get rid of the older boats.

The man had paid for one in cash, but left the kayak there for a couple of days. Then, he stopped by in a rented jeep, picked it up and headed for Red Hook. He said he was catching the St. John car ferry.

I could picture the old Marine driving his jeep with kayak protruding out the canvas in the rear. He would have had to drive gingerly onto an overcrowded car barge. And, if he had caught the old *Roanoke,* he could have gone up to the sun deck, bought a couple of beers at the bar, and enjoyed the scenic ride across Pillsbury Sound to St. John.

Since we had never kayaked the mangroves near Red Hook. A few days later, Mary, John and I rented three vessels at the locals' discount. Soon we were paddling through a world of living green walled channels, sprinkled with snowy white egrets and other birds.

Eventually we came into an open bay with a boat marina to landward and more mangroves and an island to seaward. The island was called "Happy Island" by local boaters and we paddled over to take a look. Had Sergeant Baskins done the same?

First we needed to find an opening in the red mangrove trees. We navigated through their skeleton-like aerial prop roots which support the trees in the same way pilings support fishing shacks along Gulf Coast waters. But these pilings absorb the water the tree needs to live while filtering out the salt. We saw conch, mollusks and even a few red sea stars that eat the mollusks, in the shallow waters around tree roots.

Finally, we found a narrow beach, only a few yards wide, where we pulled out the kayaks. Immediately, a loud rustling sound – like the crinkling of hundreds of plastic candy wrappers – overpowered our senses. We followed a narrow sandy path through the black mangroves. Black mangroves build islands by collecting and holding the sand that washes through their red mangrove cousins living below the waterline. The black tree also absorbs saltwater, then secretes the salt from its leaves.

But, we weren't focusing on botanical wonders. Rather, the loud crinkling, crackling sound was intriguing and a little unsettling. A short way along the path we came to a small, open sandy area quite literally crawling with thousands of creatures moving like a carpet across the ground. They climbed up, over and on top of one another, building towers of struggling bodies that toppled over under their own weight. They crawled and pushed inexorably, pulling their shells with crusty red pincer feet, toward their objective.

They were soldier crabs – large hermit crabs on steroids and armed with sharp claws – competing with and fighting each other as they moved as fast as they could toward an aging, thin and weathered woman. She was throwing out bits of cat food to them. Watching from the sidelines were scores of much larger land crabs – some standing on hind legs as tall as eight to twelve inches, fore claws at the ready, waiting for their chance at food. We avoided them all.

The crab-feeding woman was one of a hundred or so hearty souls living on their boats in the coves, channels and marinas along the landward side of the large, winding mangrove lagoon. They call their community Lagoonieville. The uninhabited Happy Island (officially known as Cas Cay on marine charts) is Lagoonieville's semi-private beach and playground, reachable only by shallow dinghy, kayak or other flat-bottomed vessel that can navigate in water as shallow as one-to-three feet. The woman, we learned, lives alone on her boat with cats and comes out every day to feed the crabs – the way urbanites feed squirrels and pigeons in parks.

Happy Island stands at the end of a long thin barrier reef spanning the "False Entrance" from the sea to what is St. Thomas' largest mangrove lagoon. On the seaward side of Happy Isle, tall orange and red rock formations and cliffs emerge like small Martian mountains from sand and reef. The rocks, rock falls and reef form a barrier against the open sea, which breaks in gasps and spasms upon the natural sea wall.

The three of us kept walking along the island path beyond the crab feast and toward the seaward side. We quickly left the mangrove forest, traversing a mixture of desert-like rocks, sand, cacti, thorns and washed-up broken, dead coral. We grew hotter with each step into the interior.

Suddenly we saw high rocks – some blood red, others pink and copper – and felt a cool breeze as we caught sight of the sea. In the sun the rocks at water's edge seemed unearthly as their colors shimmered with heat waves. Among the boulders are blow holes where jets of incoming sea water race through cave-like channels and spout up as geyser blasts before collapsing into crystal pools of salt water held in multi-colored rock basins big enough to sit in. The three of us happily laid down in the blow hole pools after our hot walk. We delighted in the spa-like burst of water splashing over us and draining out to the sea.

Returning to the island's lagoon side, we saw that the thousands of exposed mangrove tree roots plunging into the shallow water provide a habitat for many life forms – both above and under the waterline. Under the trees' canopy, several species of crabs were the highest life forms on the ground. Above them, however, a variety of aquatic birds perched, watching for their chance to nab an unwary crab or plunge and skewer a fish in the shallows. Higher overhead, fork-tailed frigate birds soared in descending circles ready to pounce on fish. And, of course, pelicans dive bombed the shallows regularly.

Many people who come to the islands have no idea this alternate world lies a short distance off-shore. Only eco-tourists and marina dwellers go there. That makes it a happy island, indeed, for those who live in the lagoon.

Self-sufficient on their boats, these mahogany-skinned former mainlanders live a "non-terrestrial" life among the mangroves in Lagoonieville, depending solely upon their vessels' life-support systems.

8 IN THE TRENCHES WITH UNINVITED GUESTS

"Fifty percent of UFO encounters are connected with oceans. Fifteen more with lakes. So, UFOs tend to stick to the water."

— Vladimir Azhazha, former Soviet naval officer and Russian UFO investigator.[1]

With Sergeant Baskins' pre-Norman Island days clarified, I now had enough facts and reasoned suppositions to send Lt. Taft a fuller report. It focused mostly on Baskins and the UFO incidents he likely witnessed aboard the *U.S.S. John F. Kennedy* and in The Bight. The *U.S.S. Roosevelt* and *U.S.S. Lexington* incidents were described as corroborating and relevant evidence of apparent UFO interest in our largest warships.

Taft wasn't satisfied, however. He wanted more information about the UFOs and USOs apparently frequenting these waters. The lieutenant also demanded insight and educated conjecture.

I couldn't shake the *U.S.S. Roosevelt* seaman's comment that the movie *The Abyss* was based on a real Navy encounter in the Caribbean. When I brought it up, however, Taft denied there was anything in the files on it – at least nothing he was cleared to see.

Obviously, any undersea vessels would do best in deep water, like a Caribbean trench.

The biggest was located beyond sight of land. But, despite years of maritime study and sailing, I had little practical experience with navigating the open sea beyond our immediate islands. I'd never been near a trench.

I consulted another old Caribbean hand who probably had sailed over one. PC Matt met me at Mooey's, a West Indian bar located a block from the pier in Cruz Bay, for a before-dinner drink or two or three. Matt had been a communications tech in the Merchant marine, among other past incarnations, before washing-up on St John and becoming the island's computer guru. Over our Virgin Islands Pale Ales – brewed right on St John so we'd never run out – I told him my tale and asked what he might know.

"In all your years sailing in these waters and working in the islands, have you ever had an experience like Sir Keithley's or seen unusual flying or floating objects?" I asked.

"Can't say I have," he replied. "But, its real interesting and entertaining hearing about it."

"If extraterrestrials are really visiting the Caribbean, it would be the biggest story since Columbus came ashore in the New World," I opined.

"And, look how that turned out for the natives! Almost all islanders dead from European diseases or enslavement within a few years."

He had a point. The 1492 discovery didn't work out well for locals. Still, UFOs had been apparently visiting earth for decades and no one has been dispossessed or mass murdered yet.

I continued. "UFOs have been sighted since at least the 1940s and probably way before that," I replied, "So far, humans remain in charge of Earth for better or worse, considering the number of wars, crime, mayhem and pollution in the world."

"Good point. And, if they are visiting anywhere, why shouldn't they visit here? Everybody else does. What better place on Earth could you find?" Matt jabbed the neck of his beer bottle in the air, emphasizing his point.

"Very true! You know, this mystery has grabbed hold of me and won't let go," I said. "It's exciting. I wake up at night in bed thinking about it."

"A little insomnia, huh? Don't worry about it. You shouldn't lose any sleep over that."

He then said he had to visit the head.

I replied, "Don't get wet or fall in."

"What do you mean?"

Ever the maritime historian, I retorted, "Well, to really go to the head, don't you have to cross the street to the harbor, row out to that old wooden schooner that arrived last night, climb up on her bow and hang your rump out over her beakhead. Then let loose your effluents."

"Ha! Ha! Guess I should have said gotta go to the toilet."

PC Matt had a point – about the toilet and Caribbean tourism. The U.S. Virgin Islands alone host more than 2 million visitors a year from around the world. Why shouldn't extraterrestrials be attracted to these and the many other enchanted islands in this sea. Who doesn't like beaches and the pleasing fauna and flora and rain forests? Not to mention the underwater coral reefs, exotic fish and unknown possible attractions on the deep sea floor – such as the bottom of the Puerto Rico Trench.

The Trench, about 500 miles long and 60 miles wide, is a vast and barely understood (by humans) water world. Indeed, the deepest point in the Atlantic Ocean lies along the western end of that Trench – 28,493 feet deep; that's more than 5 miles.

This giant underwater canyon, which is just 76 miles

north and east of Puerto Rico in the Atlantic, stretches and curves slightly southwest in a bow shape extending more than 200 miles south and east of the Caribbean isles. The Atlantic and Caribbean tectonic plates grind in opposite directions near the trench with downward pressure producing the lowest gravity on Earth at the bottom of the abyss.

Never fully explored, the Trench could harbor life-forms difficult to imagine. Eternal darkness, extreme depth, high water pressure and who knows what other forces would certainly spawn strange beings – aliens, you might say.

Would such an environment attract extraterrestrials? Visitors who get their kicks buzzing and teasing the largest and most powerful war machines on Earth?

Odd to think that the Trench habitat runs uncomfortably close to our home islands – just 50 or sixty miles east of St. John out beyond the BVI island of Anegada, the outermost Virgin. Moreover, a smaller underwater canyon begins west of the Puerto Rican island of Vieques and runs southeast between the Virgin Islands of St. Croix (where the trench drop is only a few hundred yards from the north shoreline) and St. Thomas, passing 12 miles south of St. John (the "South Drop") before emptying into the Anegada Trench, which, in turn, runs out into the Puerto Rico trench.

I strongly suspected that orange-red object emerging from the sea south of Hap Collins' boat that veered off to Norman Island and The Bight had emerged from the South Drop.

Had they been above ground, these canyons would look like a drainage system leading across part of the Caribbean and flowing into the Puerto Rico trench. Could the system also provide a clandestine "highway" enabling extraterrestrials to travel deep and unobserved through vast areas of the sea?

"Matt, you're a sailor and a fisherman. Ever been out

to the Puerto Rico trench?"

"Sure. That's where you go for marlin and sailfish – the deep waters."

"Seen anything unusual out there?"

"Plenty of Sargasso seaweed, some strange currents and occasional compass problems. But, that's about it. No flying saucers, if that's what you mean."

Compass problems could certainly be caused by the gravity anomalies in the Trench. Sailing across the surface, one wouldn't expect to see much of a difference, I guessed. The odd stuff was very deep below.

Indeed, new species of very exotic fish have recently been found living in Pacific Ocean trenches as deep as 4 miles, where no complex life forms were previously thought to be able to survive. That's because the water pressure that deep would be the equivalent of "1600 elephants sitting on an Austin Mini" – to quote a Small World News Service report on the trench discoveries.[2]

Scientists also believe the exotic life forms differ from trench to trench, since they are totally isolated from each other and the rest of Earth.

The Caribbean is blessed with yet another trench nearly as deep as the Puerto Rican and likely harboring even more unusual life forms. The Caribbean Trench runs across the Sea floor from the southeastern tip of Cuba and southwest toward Guatemala, passing between Jamaica and the Cayman Islands. Though narrower than the Puerto Rican canyon, the Caribbean Trench has a maximum depth of 25,216 feet – nearly five miles. It also has "black smokers," volcanic vents three miles deep. These underwater geysers (hydrothermal vents) support unique life forms that live off the harsh chemicals emitted by volcanic plasma.

Similar active hydrothermal vents are believed to exist on the floor of the frozen sea covering the planet Jupiter's moon Europa, making that sea a prime candidate for extraterrestrial life. The remains of ancient hydrothermal vents are also believed to exist on Mars.

Could life forms comfortable in underwater extraterrestrial vent communities be dropping by ours? Are aliens vacationing in Caribbean trenches?

After finishing our drinks, PC and I went our separate ways. I went home and discussed the trenches with Mary. She thought it was a promising area for more research.

I went back to the desk top and searched for reports of deep sea USO/UFO incidents. More evidence from a credible source pointed to the Caribbean and its trenches as hot beds of highly strange activity.

Russia has recently released much of its UFO research. Since the Soviet Union's Navy routinely shadowed and observed U.S. Naval vessels (as the U.S. Navy did to theirs), the views of Captain 1st rank Igor Barklay, a former Soviet intelligence officer, might shed light on our aircraft carriers' extraordinary encounters:

"Ocean UFOs often show up wherever our [Russian] or NATO's fleets concentrate . . . especially near the Bahamas, Bermuda and Puerto Rico. They are most often seen in the deepest part of the Atlantic Ocean located in the Puerto Rico trench, in the southern part of the Bermuda Triangle, and also in the Caribbean Sea."[3]

Some official confirmation. Finally. These unknown vehicles did operate in deep warm waters.

Retired Russian submarine commander Rear Admiral Yury Beketov described how UFO encounters frequently led to electronic and other equipment failures on board the Soviet Union's most advanced subs. At other times, their vessels' sonar, radar and other instruments succeeded in tracking the mysterious objects underwater:

"On several occasions the instruments gave readings of material objects moving at incredible speed. Calculations showed speeds of about 230 knots per hour, of 400 kph [248 miles per hour!]. Speeding so fast is a challenge even on the surface. But water resistance is much higher [underwater]. It was like the objects defied the laws of physics. There's only one explanation: the creatures who built them far surpass us in development."

When did these incredible encounters with naval vessels first begin? To find answers, I looked back at the first recorded European naval activity in the Caribbean Sea.

Historians of Columbus' first voyage say he and some of his officers did see strange lights the night before they discovered the New World (or, at least, an island in The Bahamas.) Experts say these lights were too far from land to have been native fires – the only human light source available to the Taino Indians Columbus encountered the next day.

"The Life and Voyages of Christopher Columbus," published in 1838 by famed American author Washington Irving used Spanish sources to provide one of the earliest authoritative descriptions of that voyage in the English language. Irving described what happened on the night of October 11, 1492.[4]

"As evening darkened, Columbus took his station on top of the castle or cabin on the high stern of his vessel [Santa Maria], where he maintained an intense and unremitting watch. Suddenly, about ten o'clock, he thought he beheld a glimmering light at a distance. Fearing that his eager hopes might deceive him, he called one of his officers, named Pedro Gutierrez, and demanded whether he saw a light in that direction; the latter replied in the affirmative. Columbus, yet doubtful, called Rodrigo Sanchez of Segovia, and made the same inquiry. By the time the latter had ascended the [castle], the light had disappeared.

"They saw it once or twice afterwards in sudden and passing gleams, as if it were a torch in the bark [sailboat] of a fisherman, rising and sinking with the waves; or in the hands of some person on shore, borne up and down as he walked from house to house. So transient and uncertain were these gleams, that few attached any importance to them; Columbus, however, considered them as certain signs of land and that the land was inhabited.

"Four hours later, a look-out on the Pinta shot a gun to signal that he had seen signs of land about two leagues [six miles] distant.

"[At dawn,] they saw a *level* and beautiful island [Columbus named it San Salvador] covered with trees like a continual orchard."

That they made landfall on a flat island is significant. It has no hills or mountains high enough for a fire to have been visible to Columbus and his crew the night before. The highest points in all of the Bahamas are two hills, 60 feet and 100 feet high respectively, and they are not located on the island Columbus named San Salvador.

America's most eminent naval historian, Rear Admiral Samuel Eliot Morison (1887- 1976), explained why the lights Columbus and his men saw were not the work of natives:

"It cannot have been a fire or other light on San Salvador or any other island; for as the real landfall four hours later [and the speed of the ships according to Columbus' log proves, the fleet at 10 pm [October 11] was at least 35 miles offshore . . . One writer advanced the theory that the light was made by Indians torching for fish – why not lighting a cigar? – but Indians do not go fishing in 3000 fathoms of water 35 miles offshore at night in a gale wind [which was blowing then, according to the log]."[5]

Columbus himself wrote that the lights were "a sign from God" that land was near.

The Pinta lookout did see land at 2 am on October 12, 1492, and the three ships "hoved to," meaning they headed into the wind, lowered some sails, but kept enough aloft to keep the boat facing the wind and stopped. Doing so would keep them from sailing onto a beach in the dark. At dawn, they saw a very green, heavily forested, flat land with naked people on the beach.

Columbus promptly brought soldiers and banners on shore and claimed the land for Spain. He explained what happened next:

"No sooner had we concluded the formalities of taking possession of the island than the people came [closer to us on] the beach, all naked as their mothers bore them, and the women also. They are very well-built people with handsome bodies and very fine faces . . . Their eyes are large and very pretty. . . these are tall people and their legs, with no exception, are quite straight, and none has a paunch . . . I cannot get over how docile these people are."[6]

One can only guess what the Tainos were thinking as they watched these men from another world, their incomprehensible "possession" ceremony, and the large ships. After all, they navigated in cut-out log canoes. It is quite possible they viewed these strange men and imposing vessels as visitors and crafts from another world. Columbus thought as much, stating in his log:

"By the signs they made, I think they are asking if we came from Heaven. One Taino man, who climbed into one of our boats and others, shouted in loud voices to everyone on the beach, saying 'come see the men from Heaven; bring them food and drink.' "[7]

Regardless of what New World natives thought of these "discoverers" (and what Columbus thought about the strange lights the night before), many sailors coming in the years after 1492 have also seen strange lights and objects in the sea and air throughout the Caribbean and South Atlantic.

Speaking of aliens selecting lovely vacation spots, researcher Richard Hall describes a cat and mouse style game of hide and seek near Rio de Janeiro on May 19, 1986. That night, the Brazilian military air defense system was inundated with UFO reports, including visual and radar sightings. Air traffic controllers at a nearby airport actually saw "bright red and orange lights not at all like stars or planes."

Meanwhile, the Brazilian air force sent up three F-5E and three Mirage fighter jets, which made visual and radar contacts with various lighted objects before the UFOs all disappeared in sharp turns and vertical climbs "beyond the capability of [human] aircraft." Interestingly, a top Brazilian air force commander, Brig. Gen. Octavio Moreira Lima actually held a news conference at which the radar operators and air traffic controllers answered questions from the media.[8]

One air traffic controller said, "In my 14 years of experience as a radar operator, I never saw anything like this."

I had now been in my office for several hours, researching and absorbing all this hydrological and historical data. The information would need to be sorted out and culled into a suitable report for the circumspect, sober minds of Naval officers. Mary came in and forced me to go to bed, insomnia or not.

The next day was a Saturday and we decided to go out to Coral Bay for a sail. We did not discuss the UFO research or Sergeant Baskins death in front of John because it was too difficult (nearly impossible) to explain in a "nothing but the facts" fashion. John sees the world in black and white, concrete terms. He doesn't understand ambiguity and is incapable of lying. A life in politics is not in his future.

When I saw Sir Keithley and his pal Nigel walking toward us on the dock, I rushed ahead of Mary and John to intercept them first.

We had just returned from a sail to St. John's Hurricane Hole and Haulover Bay where we swam and picnicked, and were unloading our gear from the dinghy. Carrying my sea bag over one shoulder and oars over the other, I bid his Lordship "Good Day."

Lord Claymore replied, "How are you, mate? You know Nigel, I think. He's just back from St. Georges,

Grenada."

"Hey, Nigel. How goes it?"

"Goes good. Good weather, good sail up; all good."

Like his fellow countryman, in self-imposed exile Nigel favored tropical British military surplus clothing, now fraying and faded with cuts and vents where needed as air intakes. With a graying beard, wire-framed spectacles and dingy soft white hat trailing a neck flap, he looked like a Foreign Legionnaire who'd been marooned in a desert.

An old Grenada buddy of Sir Keithley, Nigel now divided his time between St John, Grenada and Venezuelan islands. The Isla de Margarita was his favorite and he was rumored to have a wife (or girl friend) and children down there.

Sir Keithley, whom I usually addressed in fun as Lord Claymore, returned the favor by referring to me by rank.

"Professor," he said confidentially, leaning closer, "Nigel and I had a bit of a chat about my Norman Island adventure and 'e 'as a story you will find captivating."

By then, Mary and John had caught up and, after making the introductions, I whispered to Mary: "The game is a'foot." I used Sherlock Holmes' saying as a private signal that John would not understand indicating I needed to speak privately with these gentlemen about the topic.

Always quick on the uptake, Mary said to John, "Dad needs to ask these men some questions about boats. Let's go feed the donkeys."

John never missed an opportunity to feed and pet wild donkeys; so off they went.

I turned to Keith and Nigel.

"Gentlemen, why don't we retire to the Coral Bay Yacht club for refreshments? The first round is on me."

Skinny's was crowded, but we found a small table at the railing overlooking the mangroves. After we gave the waitress our orders, Sir Keithley began.

"Nigel here was already on Grenada back in the late

'70s when Agatha and I arrived. After she chose a different path, it was Nigel who took charge and educated me on the ways of Caribbean living."

Nigel piped in, "Remember those hippy lasses! We won't be seeing their kind a'gin, I wager."

Keith grunted agreement, as he wistfully looked over at a table of twenty-something ladies clad in bikinis and very revealing cover-ups.

"Aye, right you are. At our age, they don't even see us. Just part of the quaint woodwork, we are."

Nigel agreed. We all ordered another round, his Lordship sticking with his Pusser's rum. Nigel continued his story.

"When Keith arrived, I was one of a small force of Royal Navy Marine Commandoes stationed there to advise the newly independent government of Grenada on defense matters – not that it was difficult duty, by any stretch of the imagination.

"My unit arrived right after independence in 1974. Spent most of our time on the beach or in the pubs.

"See, the main exports of Grenada are nutmeg and mace, the fibers that cover the nut. Nutmeg and tourism are the only industries. There's not much there needin' protectin' and the Grenada Defence Force was a fairly ragged bunch – armed with World War II British surplus junk and, frankly, ill-disciplined. We trained them as best we could and mostly played soccer and cricket with 'em. We was all on island-time, you might say."

Sir Keithley broke in.

"When I told Nigel about the Norman Island sighting, it rang bells. Tell 'em all the details. 'e's a professor and wants it in-depth."

Nigel nodded, took a sip of his beer, and continued.

"Well, I reckon t'was sometime in 1975 or '76. One night, I was an honorary security guard for Prime Minister Sir Eric Gairy. It was early evening and I was standing guard with a Grenadian soldier in front of his house – the old British governor's residence.

"And, 'ere comes four or five islanders – bare feet, straw hats – wantin' to see Sir Eric. 'And, where do we think we're goin'?' says I. They were all excited and jabbering and gesticulating in patois, they were.

"My Grenadian mate, the other guard, tells me they seen a strange, monstrous human and super strong metal wreckage washed ashore near their village on the Atlantic side of the island. They had spent several hours sailing to St George's from the other side because they wanted to tell Sir Eric. He was their hero, see – the father of the new nation, an' all.

"Fine with me, I says, and knocked on the door. Sir Eric appeared and heard them out. Next thing I know, he orders the Grenadian guard to round-up some vehicles and more men, and off we went in a nearly rusted-out Land Rover and 20-year-old British Leyland flat bed lorry.

"After three hours of driving in the dark on dodgy, unpaved roads through the mountains, we arrived at the beach. It was illuminated by bonfires built by fishermen from the village. In the flickering firelight, women, children, men were all circled around something a few feet above the water line.

"Sir Eric quickly took charge and the crowd parted as we walked over. And there, lying as though asleep was the biggest, blondest Scandinavian bloke I'd ever seen. But, you see, he was at least 7 or 8 feet tall, had six fingers on each hand and his long blonde hair was braided – probably reaching his pants belt, if 'e 'ad one. But, he didn't. See, 'e was clothed in a skin tight one piece blue suit that even covered 'is feet.

"Goes without saying, none of us ever seen the like. But old Sir Eric kept his cool, stepped over to the body, a' looken at it from 'ead to covered toe. He then grabbed the strange fabric and pulled on it to see it better. He pulled until it was stretched about two feet from the body. We all leaned in for a closer look. See, although stretched to the limit, the weave of the cloth didn't separate a bit. And then, when Sir Eric let go, the getup snaps back in place, emitting a low hummin' sound as it did so. And, wrapped itself back in place around the body's waist without so much as a wrinkle. Amazed we were, I can tell you.

"'My God, did you see that!' a village woman said. The rest of us stood silent.

"Well, Sir Eric broke the spell and ordered four of the soldiers to load the body on the lorry. Following what I took to be the village head man, Sir Eric and the rest of us walked along the beach a bit until we came to another bon fire. And, scattered around it we saw strange silver metal girders and aircraft skin-like squares and rectangles torn apart – like airplane wreckage or somethin'.

"We all picked up small pieces and played with 'em. Turned out if we bent them, they'd pop back into their original shape – even the thinnest pieces would. Later I heard that the metal could not be cut with an acetylene torch or any other tool.

"Sir Eric 'ad us collect all we could find, and lug it back to the lorry. Light as a feather, the metal was.

"While we were doin' that, Sir Eric tells the head man to send out a couple fishing boats to look for more wreckage and bodies."

Nigel then leaned in, elbows on the table and looked me in the eye.

"Them fishermen were never 'eard from again and their boats completely disappeared. Very, very strange, mate."

A cool breeze raised the hair on my arms – or something did. A donkey brayed in the distance and a mild whiff of sulpher floated in from the muddy mangrove swamp.

"What happened next?"

"Well, after we loaded everything we could find, off we went back to town. When we finally arrived, my watch was over. So, I went back to the old hotel that served as the Marines' barracks.

"I never saw any of wreckage again. But, I 'eard all the metal shreds and pieces and like were locked-up in one of them old stone warehouses on the 'arbour, and the body, it was taken up the hill to St George's Medical School. Put in their deep freeze, I suppose.

"Old Sir Eric, 'e was convinced the body was from outer space and the wreckage was from a space ship. The *Grenadian Voice* newspaper wrote all about it. Sir Eric later said he had also seen strange lights in the sky over the 'arbour that could na' be explained. I never saw 'em, but most nights, I was in the pub when not on duty.[9]

"But, Sir Eric, 'e was a man of his conviction, see. He told 'is story to all who'd listen – even traveled to New York to the United Nations and raised a big fuss about UFOs. Why was nobody studying 'em? Why it's all secret and such?

He even had Grenada issue postage stamps with flying saucers on 'em. Likely the only ones of their kind. Wish I 'ad one or two now. Probably worth some money."

Sir Keithley grunted, motioned for the waitress and ordered another Pusser. Another breeze clattered through the mangroves and blew away a few mosquitoes that had zeroed-in on our table. More donkey braying in the distance.

I was digesting Nigel's incredible tale, when Keith leaned over to pick-up the story.

"It was maybe a year or so after all that UFO craze that I arrived on-island. After Agatha departed, I met Nigel 'ere in The Sprout bar on the waterfront. I was looking for work, and 'e 'ad just left the Navy – 'ad just gotten a job on an island cargo ship going back and forth to Trinidad."

Nigel smiled and punched Sir Keithley's arm, as he excitedly interrupted.

"Next thing Keith 'ere knew it was the next mornin'; 'e was powerful hung over and 'e was signing onto the crew of the *Trinidad Star*. We both worked on 'er a year or so, until we couldn't bloody well stand it and then moved on. Keith here worked in a boat yard that was still building sailboats the old ways. But, now its' the St. Georges Yacht Club and full of toffs. Me, I bopped around Trinidad 'n Tobago. By then, all 'er Majesty's forces were long gone – and a good thing, too."

Armed with a fresh Pusser in-hand, Keith picked up the story.

"Right you are, Niig. By blind good luck, we were both out of Grenada during the Yank invasion and all the political troubles. I had left Grenada and moved north up to Antigua; learned the diving trade. And there, I run into Nigel again; only now, he has himself an inter-island trading sloop he'd rigged as a charter – takin' tourists out for overnight sails for all the romance and such. I worked with 'im, learned the charter business and then 'eaded north again a year or so later. This time to Tortola, which I 'eard was investing in the yachting business – building marinas and improving anchorages with government help."

Nigel interrupted.

"T'wasn't long before I realized Keith was on to something. With all the Brit and Yank tourists and money pouring in, the Virgin Islands looked like the place to be. I sailed my boat up to Road Town and joined forces with old Keith again. He was working with the company busy fillin' in part of the old 'arbour and building new yachting and tourist facilities."

The British had invested heavily in turning Road Town into a yacht haven. But, they didn't stop there. They tore down some of the old waterfront and rebuilt it in authentic Caribbean style to satisfy passengers on the cruise ships that now visit regularly.

Nigel continued with their story. "I worked with Keith in Road Town for a while, but got tired of the north; wanted to get back to the rain forests and Trinidadian women. Keith and I, we kept in-touch and when I 'eard he was on St. John all set to build himself a wooden brigantine, why I came north again to lend a 'and."

Nigel ordered what must have been the third round of beers for him and me and another Pusser for his Lordship. Sir Keithley now picked-up the story.

"So, now Nigel's back and forth, betwixt north and south – a few months there and a few months up 'ere. The perfect life."

I agreed, it sounded enjoyable.

Before I could turn the conversation back to Nigel's UFO tale, however, I spotted Mary and John coming in the front door.

John was bursting with news. The St. John Emergency squad was trying to extricate a donkey that had waded into the Salt Pond and sank in the muck – all the way up to its belly. John and Mary watched as Coral Bay EMS techs lassoed him, trying to pull him out. Then, they used long two-by-fours trying to leverage him out.

Another donkey on the shore line was watching in distress, very upset. We could even hear it braying and fretting sitting at our table at Skinny's.

When Mary and John had left, six emergency responders were still trying to extricate the donkey. We later heard they had succeeded by laying thick plywood over the muck and walking close enough to heave him out by-hand, using a sling under his belly.

After the donkey story, I stood up and told the lads it was time for us to leave – it being dinner time.

Later that night, after John had gone to bed, I told Mary about Nigel's story. Amazing to think the first Prime Minister of a newly independent country – and one who was knighted by the queen – would become such a UFO activist.

Naturally, I went on line as soon as possible to learn more about Grenada and try to corroborate Nigel's story. I was surprised to learn that off the coast of Grenada lays a vast abyssal area known as the Grenada Trough, complete with the type of gravity and magnetic anomalies found in the Puerto Rico Trench.

Coincidence that both trenches had apparent UFO activity?

It didn't take long to confirm Nigel's story about the Grenada's Prime Minister's finding an alien body and space ship wreckage on the beach. Nigel was also correct about Sir Eric Gairy's address to the United Nations General Assembly. It was in 1977 and he urged the UN to establish an agency to study UFOs and any signs of extraterrestrial life.

American Projects Mercury and Gemini astronaut Gordon Cooper (immortalized as Gordo in the book and movie, *The Right Stuff*) reportedly sent a letter to Grenada's ambassador expressing his belief in extraterrestrial visitation of Earth. He supported Prime Minister Gairy's position and hoped it would lead to open study.

Gairy's enthusiasm and diplomatic skill led the UN to pass a resolution (#33/426) in November, 1978 calling for peaceful international cooperation in exploring outer space and urging Member States to work together to research UFOs and extraterrestrial life and circulate the findings.

Here's how Prime Minister Gairy explained his passion about UFO's to the Associated Press:

"We've passed the stage now of whether or not these things exist. I think it is accepted that these things do exist. I think we now want to know the nature, the origin and the intent of these saucers. Some people think they have come to do good. Some think they have come to dominate human beings."[10]

Prime Minister Gairy then cited reports that military aircraft of major powers have been put out of commission, but not destroyed, after attacking saucers.

"That confirms my thought on their positive intent. I believe they are coming here to help mankind because man is so self-destructive."

Sir Eric even met with President Carter before his 1977 UN address. It's not known whether Carter shared his own UFO experience with the Prime Minister.

The world will never know how much further progress Sir Eric might have made in his crusade for open, international UFO study because his government was overthrown in a left-wing coup in 1979. Eventually, that new Grenadian government (an ally of Cuba) provoked President Ronald Reagan to order the U.S. invasion of Grenada in 1983.

Many people, however, wondered about the need for the U.S. to assault that idyllic Caribbean spice isle. America had done so against the wishes of President Reagan's friend and close ally, British Prime Minister Margaret Thatcher.

I wondered what had happened to the alien body and alleged space ship wreckage during the tumultuous years since Gairy claimed he found them.

With these thoughts in mind, I eventually fell asleep serenaded by the hundreds of night creatures in the forest around our home.

Next morning, after the dog walk, I filled Mary in about Grenada. We discussed the hard-to-explain U.S. invasion of the island, which is about the size of Martha's Vineyard.

With 100,000 people living on an island located 2,000 miles east of Guatemala and 1,500 miles south of Cuba, it seemed an unlikely target. Not to mention that Grenada was a member in good standing of the British Commonwealth with Queen Elizabeth as its official head of state.

"Really, can you imagine the Brits – the Queen for goodness sake – permitting their tiny protectorate to brazenly threaten the United States? And, what could Grenada do to us anyway?" Mary asked, following-up with, "So, why did Reagan invade against Britain's wishes?"

I attempted an answer.

"Some cynics say Reagan wanted a quick cheap military victory for political reasons. But, now I wonder if it had something to do with his obvious interest in UFOs and his wanting to recover any artifacts still on Grenada."

"Not hard to believe it was driven by politics. Certainly not the first or last war started for that reason," she said. "I don't know about the UFO stuff."

"Who does? Of course, the stated reason for the invasion was to protect a few hundred American students at the St George's Medical School; but, the school was actually founded and run by Americans to serve American kids who couldn't get into U.S. med schools. And, the kids were never in any real danger, anyway, school officials said."

"It was all very ridiculous. You know, come to think of it, a nurse practitioner who works with that gynecologist Dr. Topper over in Red Hook went to that school. One day we sat together on the ferry. One reason she moved to St. Thomas was how much she loved Grenada."

God bless Mary's network of friends and acquaintances.

"Wonder when she attended St. George's?"

"I could call her and find out. What should I say?"

"That your history professor husband is researching the U.S. invasion and would like to interview witnesses. And, if she was there, he'd appreciate the opportunity to talk."

Well, she was there during the invasion and would be happy to talk. A few days later, I went to Red Hook, walked from the ferry to the nearby building, fronted by wrought iron verandahs, and climbed the stair case to the second story. Dr. Topper's office was a few doors down the open-air porch. A nice breeze rustled the palm fronds.

Nurse Olivia Swank was an attractive woman of a certain age – probably in her early 50's to have been at St. George's in 1983, I calculated, when she answered my door knock.

"Good morning, Ms. Swank. Thanks for seeing me."

"Think nothing of it; and, please call me Olivia," she replied in a peachy soft Southern accent. "How can I help?"

"As Mary, my wife, said on the phone, I'm with the college and am writing a history of the U.S. invasion of Grenada, code-named 'Operation Urgent Fury'. I understand you were a student there at the time."

"Well, I never ever heard that ugly day called operation anything. I never knew what it was all about. Still don't, really. But, I was there."

"Do you have time to talk about what happened?"

"I sure do. Dr. Topper is off-island and I was just sitting here reading," she said.

I noticed *Celeb* magazine next to the phone and empty PC screen on the mahogany desk guarding what must be the physician's office door. A couch, potted palm, and comfortable chair were arranged in the corner opposite her desk and she motioned for me to sit down. I took the chair, she the couch. She sat down, crossed her legs, as I admired the view of the yacht harbor and ferry terminal out the picture window.

She began to talk without any prompting.

"Well now, it really was exciting, but also scary. Not much happens on an island like that. But, you know that since you live on St. Yawn. Ha!"

"Yes, it is a slow pace. All that serenity can be challenging. But, getting back to Grenada . . ."

"Well, we were all concentrating on our studies – they were haaard – and were not aware of *any* problems beyond the usual political squabbling among the natives. But, it didn't affect us on our campus. Sooo, we were very surprised when one day in October of 1983 – my second year there – Dean Crittenden, a very fine man, called us all for a special assembly in the auditorium. Lionel – that was the Dean's first name – explained that there was some trouble in Washington and that the U.S. Army was threatening to attack the island. Speaking frankly, I found it hard to believe anyone would want to hurt those people. They had so many problems just getting through their daily lives – all that poverty and everything."

"What else did the Dean say?"

"Lionel was real nice – a handsome man in his early forties from Louisiana. I do believe he'd worked for other colleges in the South. Well, I can't recall everything he said. But, he did ask if anyone wanted to leave the school. I, for one, saw no reason to go. I mean, return to my parents in Charlotte just in time for winter? Heck, my studies kept me very busy and, then, of course, we had beaches and plenty of rum punch – cheaper than Coca Cola! And, Lionel was personally tutoring me in bio-chemistry. We were making such progress."

She smiled and looked misty-eyed toward the ceiling.

"Buuut, Lionel said it was important for us to think about Washington's threats and whether we wanted to leave. He even asked us to vote on it so they'd know how many people wished to go. Well, it was all sooo silly. And, we did vote. I don't remember the numbers, but I do recollect that 90 percent or more voted to stay at school. But, over the next couple days, a few students did leave. It was soo sad."

"I'm sure it was sad. A small school like that. You must have all known each other very well. But, had you noticed any trouble off-campus – in St. George's, itself?"

"Oh well, the natives were always squabbling. But nobody bothered us. They were arguing amongst themselves, but seemed darn happy we were there and spending our money, to be perfectly frank. They wanted American students and more tourists."

"I don't doubt it."

"Sooo, things continued normally for a few days. It was very quiet on the hill of our peninsula. Sometimes we'd hear the Earth movers and heavy equipment used by that big British construction company that was rebuilding the island airport so tourists could fly in from Europe.

"But, that was it. Nothing out of the ordinary. We were making plans for a Halloween party. I was going to dress-up like Elvira, Mistress of the Night – you know, the old horror movie hostess on TV.

"Buuut, a couple days before Halloween, I was awakened about sunrise by the sounds of firecrackers going off in a long string. First, I thought it must be carnival time – but that is always in the Spring. Then, I heard even louder explosions – boom, boom, boom, boom!

"I couldn't get back to sleep, but didn't want to get up. But then, I heard the roar of jet engines and thwumping sounds of helicopters.

"Well, it wasn't long before our dorm warden came to the door and told me to get dressed and go to the auditorium – that we'd all be safe and shouldn't worry. I wasn't worried, who would want to hurt us? Lionel would take care of it all, anyway.

"Sooo, we all went to the auditorium where the nice island women brought in coffee and breakfast from the cafeteria. There was still gunfire and explosions in the distance, but we were all right."

As she spoke, I thought about the bomb drills my peers and I had been put through in elementary school. Crawl under your desks, hands over heads and all would be okay in a nuclear war. And, then there were the basement "Fall-out shelters."

Olivia continued, "Then, around 8 or 9, the auditorium doors burst open. In comes men in green camouflage helmets and uniforms – all hunched down and swinging their guns back and forth like we were an enemy army or something.

"A couple students screamed and someone yelled 'please don't shoot us' and someone started crying. I mean, it was scaaree.

"Then a soldier shouted in English that we must all sit down and stay still; but, not to worry because they were

Americans. Well, I was relieved at that. If there was a war or something going on, I surely wanted to be with Americans. But, I still can't figure out who the enemy was.

"Well, even sitting down, I could see out the arched, screen windows – big ones to let in the trade winds. And, I saw a group of soldiers rushing toward the laboratory – it was a building on the quad right next to the auditorium, you see. I couldn't believe it when a couple of soldiers kicked in the lab doors and rushed in like it was a fortress or something. A couple more soldiers stood outside the door with their guns ready and swinging back and forth like they were looking for something to shoot at.

"A few minutes later, we could hear the sound of a helicopter coming toward our hill and, in a roar and with a cloud of dust that blew into our windows, the thing landed right on our quad. Two men in dark suits – I mean wearing ties and all – jumped down. I mean, men in suits in 85 degree weather and in the middle of some kind of war or whatever!

"They walked right into the lab. Next, several men in white lab coats and wearing gas mask type things jumped down and followed the business men – or whoever they were – into the lab. Finally, a couple regular soldiers handed down from the copter a long aluminum box that looked like a casket.

"And, they carried the casket-like thing into the lab. And, you know, the lab is where we had the deep freeze room where they kept the cadavers that we used for dissection and lab work. I figured they wanted one for some reason."

A breeze came in through Olivia's open window, raising the scent of astringent Doctor's office floor cleaner. Or, was it the embalming fluid formalin?

"What happened next?" I asked.

"Well a few minutes later they all came out carrying the casket and loaded it and everyone back into the helicopter. It then took off in a roar and another blast of dust hit our faces – we were still kneeling, see, and our heads were just above the window sills. We were all looking out to see what was happening.

"After the helicopter took off, the soldier in charge of us said we could all get up and go to our rooms and start packing. We were to be taken home. I think it was a day later that we were all loaded into Army trucks – forced to sit on wooden benches under hot old canvas – and taken to the nice new airport runway where a blue passenger jet waited for us.

"They took us to Washington. I was sooo surprised to see all the television cameras and reporters with microphones, and all, waiting for us as we climbed down the steps onto the ground. Well, some kind of official had selected the first two students to get down and had brought them over to the cameras to be interviewed. I certainly didn't want to talk to any of them. I just wanted to get home, by that time.

"I saw my parents waiting just inside the door to the terminal. We hugged. Mom cried. And then, we all went to the parking lot and drove back to Charlotte.

I later heard that the Army sent most of the med school professors back to America or England or wherever they came from. It was a shame.

"But, I had already put in over a year of school down there. So, I took another year of classes and easily qualified as a nurse practitioner.

"Eventually, I got married and then divorced, and decided I wanted to see more of the world. I was lucky to get a job with Festiva Cruise Line and traveled all over the Caribbean and Mediterranean working in on-board clinics. It was fun for a while.

"But, it got to be a drag. I mean, yuck! How much diarrheal virus, seasickness and alcohol-related injuries can one stand to deal with? It was icky.

"I did want to live in the Caribbean again, though. Charlotte Amalie was the nicest port we visited on the cruises and, being American and all, it was easy to move here. So, I did!"

"Well, we're glad you're here. And yours is a very interesting story. It was extremely helpful to me to hear the story of an actual eye-witness to the events."

I was understating the importance of her story. The implications were enormous.

Olivia interrupted my thoughts: "Mary tells me you all have a sailboat. I'd love to go out for a sail sometime."

"That would be great. I'll ask Mary to phone you and arrange it."

As I went back to St. John on the ferry, I thought about Olivia's tale. Could the whole point of the invasion have been to get the alien body out of St. George's medical school deep freeze and raid the warehouses where the saucer artifacts may have still been stored? It sure seemed plausible.

One thing was certain. I knew Lt. Taft was familiar with "Operation Urgent Fury." It had opened with Navy Seals storming some of the best vacation beaches in the British Commonwealth. I also had a hunch his Annapolis history Profs had never taught the midshipmen that Prime Minister Gairy believed an alien being and flying saucer wreckage had washed up on said beaches.

After telling Mary about the meeting, I left it up to her as to whether we took Olivia sailing. I then gathered my thoughts and phoned Lt. Taft.

"Taft, here."

"Glad to reach you on the first ring."

"No problem. What's up?"

I took some satisfaction in describing in detail Sir Eric's discovery, his work at the United Nations, and the eye-witness account of the U.S. assault. I also shared my belief that the exceptional deep water troughs in the Caribbean and nearby Atlantic waters were related to the UFO phenomena in some way.

"Finally, Lieutenant, I think you should ask internally

about the Grenada operation and try to find out what cargo or artifacts might have been shipped back from the conflict. It is quite possible someone within Naval Intelligence caught wind of something very strange and very secret."

"Good suggestion, I'll see what I can find out. But, it sounds more like the Agency is the party to ask. Still, one of our intelligence people may have seen something on the ground in Grenada."

A few days later, I received an encrypted e-mail with the answer: no confirmation; no denial. We were not to speak of Grenada again.

9 FIRST CONTACTS OF AN INTIMATE KIND

"I captured a very beautiful Carib woman, whom the Lord Admiral gave to me, and with whom, having taken her into my cabin, she being naked according to their custom, I conceived a desire to take pleasure."

— Count Michele de Cuneo, an officer on Columbus' second voyage of discovery in 1493, describing an encounter off the Salt River on St. Croix.[1]

"[In October, 1957] Boas claimed he was joined in the room by another humanoid. This one, however, was female, very attractive, and naked . . . Boas said he was strongly attracted to the woman."

— Story of Antonio Vilas-Boas, a Brazilian farmer who later became a lawyer and gained unwanted fame as the first documented alien abductee.[2]

I pondered all the information and evidence we had accumulated. There certainly was a tropical connection. Was it the climate? The deep ocean canyons?

Meanwhile, speaking of climate, a late-July tropical depression had hovered over us for several days, pounding St. John with heavy rain and tidal surges. When it cleared, we decided to sail to a National Park bay for a well-deserved day of rest and recreation. Leaving Coral Bay, we rounded Ram's Head point, coasted along the empty mountains of the Park's eastern half and found a mooring in Salt Pond Bay.

John's seizure disorder was keeping him from snorkeling, but Mary swam off the boat to snorkel the bay. John and I rowed the dinghy to shore and waded in the shallow water of the pristine beach. The foliage of Salt Pond Bay, framed on three sides by black mangroves and sea grapes, seemed to have been weed whacked – beaten back from the sand beach by gale winds and tidal surge. It was as though a crew had used defoliants to clear the tree line. But, the fuller forest picked up again a few yards further in-land.

On the sand above the water line was a coconut with three tiny green blade-like leaves sprouting from a crack in its hard brown hide. With no other coconut palms on that beach or even along the bay, it must have floated a distance before the surf landed it there as a self-contained pod of life. By the time the sprouts exhausted the nourishing milk in the nut, shallow roots would be working down and across the sand.

As John and I walked in the water, at one end of the bay a half-dozen or so frigate birds circled low, skimmed the shallows, scooping fish in a nearly continuous circuit. Their six-foot plus pointed wings and deeply forked tails worked steadily. We could hear them swoosh and feel the wind as they flashed over our heads and shoulders on their runs.

With the largest wingspan to body weight ratio of any bird, the wind of their passing felt like a ceiling fan.

Pelicans, who are usually the hardest-driving, high-flying plungers and scoopers, simply floated on the placid surface, studying the shallow water and effortlessly sticking their accordion-like bill-mouths under the surface, scoring several fish each time. Sea gulls swarmed around, waiting their turn. Some landed and stood on pelican heads, looking for a chance to snatch the fish right out of their hosts' mouths.

In short, it was an avian feeding frenzy. John and I stood in chest deep water watching it unfold a few yards away. Suddenly, a vast school of frantic six or seven inch silver fish stormed toward us like stampeding submerged cattle – dashing around our feet, hitting our legs and stomachs and even slapping into our heads as they swam, leaping back and forth within the U-shaped bay. In a panic, they were looking for escape. There was none.

Pelicans now took to the air and "dive bombed" just an arm's length away from us. They were neither worried by the proximity of humans nor about slamming into us through some aero-navigational error. I wasn't concerned either. I'd seen pelicans unerringly plunge a hundred feet out of the sky into a rocky pool of water only a yard wide to safely snare a fish.

While swarms of fish swam around us under water, formations of flying sun-sparkled fish leaped and sailed over the water in great arches that delighted us.

Then, brown boobies, diving cormorant birds that actually sail under water, joined the frigates and pelicans. Splashes in the shallows and whirring and flapping wings fanned and sprayed us as birds flew by. Jumping, shimmering silver specs above and below water tickled our senses. Then, as quickly as it had enveloped us, the whole melee moved on down the bay.

We would never know what drove the school so close to shore. More storm clouds and rain were visible on the horizon. Or, perhaps more menacing predators than birds were patrolling the bay entrance? Barracuda? Sharks?

As for John and I, we swam, watched and lingered as long as we could stand the sun and its reflected beams on that becalmed afternoon that preceded yet another storm. Indeed, the very frigate birds coming in so close to shore was a harbinger of approaching bad weather.

It arrived soon after we had returned to Coral Bay, moored and rowed to shore. As we drove up Centerline Road toward the top of Bordeaux Mountain, sheets of rain swept over the car, blotting out the view and ran down the steep road as a rivulet.

Good old four-wheel drive. Don't leave home without it.

One benefit of a healthy rainy season is the full cisterns in island homes. They provide families with their main source of water. Fed by a well-tended system of roof gutters and pipes, our cistern was quite full, enabling us to do as much laundry and take as many showers as we liked. In fact, a week of heavy rain meant the cistern was re-filling every day.

Our power had remained on throughout the tempests. With plenty of water, a new bottle of bourbon for my wife, a case of St. John Pale Ale, Pusser's for painkillers, good books and a working Internet, we were ready for anything.

I was able to continue my quest with a greater appreciation for what the Europeans went through when – without four-wheel drive – they first settled these islands and Central and South America. It was within Brazil, South America's biggest country, that I found a remarkable story.

Much has been written about the first alleged alien abduction. It took place in Brazil in October, 1957 on a farm outside the village of Sao Francisco de Sales near the Paraguay River.

The abductee in question, Antonio Vilas-Boas, was a 23-year-old ranchero plowing his family's fields at night to avoid the heat of day. After the incident, he went on to become a successful lawyer, married, raised four children and died in 1992 at age 58. He stuck to his story for the rest of his life.

Before looking further into his remarkable tale, I searched for other events in Brazil that might provide helpful perspective and context. In the same Paraguay River basin, a UFO was sighted and reported by a highly reputable naval officer. This occurred nearly one hundred years before Vilas-Boas was born. The location was 1,000 miles up the 1,629 mile long river, near the deep water port of Asuncion.

On July 18, 1846 Brazilian Naval Frigate Captain Augusto João Manuel Leverger, later to become an admiral, was in command of two warships sailing to Asuncion, the Paraguayan capital. His mission was to "flex some muscle" to intimidate Paraguay, then in a border dispute with Brazil. Nineteen miles south of Asuncion, Captain Leverger saw the following (as reported in a contemporary Brazilian newspaper and translated by UFO researcher J. Antonio Huneeus):[3]

"I observed tonight a phenomenon never seen before. At 5 hours 57 minutes, while the sky was perfectly clear and calm, thermometer [temperature] 60°[F], a luminous globe performed with instant speed a 30 degree curve in a NNW direction. The direction made on the horizon angles of approximately 75 and 105 degrees opened by a steep west side.

"A light band 5° or 6° long and 30° to 35° wide remained, in which one could see three bodies whose brightness was much more lively than the band, and equaled if not exceeded in intensity the full moon in clear weather. They were superimposed and separated from each other. The middle one had an almost circular appearance; the bottom one seemed like an arc of a circle of 120 degrees with broken rays at the end; the form at the top was an irregular quadrangle; the larger dimension of the disks would be from 20 to 25°. Finally you could see above them a ribbon of very faint light in the form of zigzag about 3° wide and 5 or 6° long. The angular height of the big band on the horizon appeared to be of 8° (afraid of losing some circumstances of the phenomenon I did not go to get the instrument to measure these dimensions).

"Everything was lowering with no apparent velocity greater than the stars in their twilight, but the globes of light changed aspect, taking an increasingly flat elliptical shape, and in a mist began to look like small clouds. The big band leaned N [north] until becoming almost horizontal, but the zigzag always retained the same direction. After 25 min. it was all gone, and there was not the slightest sign of disturbance in the atmosphere.

"In the city of Asunción, I talked to the Minister [Ambassador] of Brazil [the marquis of São Vicente] and several other people who also witnessed this singular appearance."[3]

The Paraguay is South America's second longest navigable river, after the Amazon. The sightings of UFOs above or near such a large, deep body of water are not unusual.

Fast-forward to October 5, 1957. Within the same river basin north of Asuncion, 23 year-old Antonio Vilas-Boas and his brother were awakened in the bedroom they shared by a bright light – a silvery light illuminating their room and yard. But, they saw no object and the light slowly passed over. Coincidentally, the day before, the Soviet Union had launched Sputnik, the first satellite.

A few nights later Vilas-Boas and his brother were again plowing their fields at night. They both saw a circular cart-wheel in the sky, shining a red light so intense it hurt their eyes. Then, it disappeared in an instant, as though a light switch had been thrown.

The following night, October 15, Vilas-Boas was plowing the field alone. At about 1 a.m., he saw a distant red light in the sky. There are many narrative versions of what happened next. Wikipedia provides a good summary and I cited it in my Navy report:

"While riding his tractor he saw a 'red star' in the night sky. This 'star' approached his position, growing in size until it became recognizable as a roughly circular or egg-shaped aerial craft, with a red light at its front and a rotating cupola on top. The craft began descending to land in the field, extending three legs as it did so. At that point, Boas decided to run from it.

"He first attempted to leave on his tractor, but when its lights and engine died after traveling only a short distance, he decided to continue on foot. However, he was seized by a 1.5 m (five-foot) tall humanoid, who was wearing grey coveralls and a helmet. Its eyes were small and blue, and instead of speech it made noises like barks or yelps. Three similar beings then joined the first in subduing Boas, and they dragged him inside their craft.

"Boas said he was then stripped of his clothes and covered head-to-toe with a strange gel; then led into a large semicircular room, through a doorway that had strange red symbols written over it. In this room the beings took samples of Boas' blood from his chin. After this he was taken to a third room and left alone for around half an hour. During this time, some kind of gas was pumped in, which made Boas become violently ill.

"Shortly after this, Boas was joined in the room by another humanoid. This one, however, was female, very attractive and naked. She was the same height as the other beings he had encountered, with a small pointed chin and large, blue catlike eyes. The hair on her head was long and white."

A direct translation of Vilas-Boas' story, as reported by journalist Michele Bugliaro Goggia, tells us more:[4]

"Her big blue eyes, rather longer than round, were slanted outward, like those pencil-drawn girls made to look like Arabian princesses that look as if they were slit . . . except that they were natural; there was no makeup.

"Her nose was straight, not pointed, not turned up, nor too big. The contour of her face was different, though, because she had very high, prominent cheekbones that made her face narrowed to a peak, so that all of a sudden it ended in a pointed chin, which gave the lower part of her face a very pointed look. Her lips were very thin, nearly invisible in fact. Her ears, which I only saw later, were small and did not seem different from ordinary ears . . . and her breasts stood up high and well-separated. Her waistline was thin, her belly flat, her hips well-developed, and her thighs were large. Her feet were small, her hands long and narrow. Her fingers and nails were normal. She was much shorter than I am, her head only reached my shoulder . . . Her skin was white and she was full of freckles on her arms."

Back to Wikipedia:

"Boas was strongly attracted to the woman, and the two had sexual intercourse. During this act, Boas noted the female did not kiss him but instead nipped him on the chin.

"When it was over, the female smiled at Boas, rubbing her belly and gestured upwards. Boas took this to mean that she was going to raise their child in space. The female seemed relieved that their task was over, and Boas himself said he felt angered by the situation, because he felt as though he had been little more than a good stallion for the humanoids. He was then escorted off the ship and watched as it took off, glowing brightly. When Boas returned home, he discovered that four hours had passed."

After this bizarre night, Boas was restless, nervous, had difficulty sleeping and experienced nausea. Worse, lesions appeared on various parts of his body.

He told his story to a local journalist. Eventually Dr. Olavo Fontes of the National School of Medicine of Brazil heard it and examined Boas. According to Wikipedia, Dr. Fontes concluded Boas had been exposed to a large dose of radiation and was suffering mild radiation poisoning. Here's what the doctor found:

"Among his symptoms were pains throughout the body, nausea, headaches, loss of appetite, ceaselessly burning sensations in the eyes, cutaneous lesions at the slightest bruising . . . which went on appearing for months, looking like small reddish nodules, harder than the skin around them and protuberant, painful when touched, each with a small central orifice yielding a yellowish thin waterish discharge. The skin surrounding the wounds presented a hyper-chromatic violet-tinged area."

But Villas-Boas' troubles were not just medical. Former British military investigator, Nick Pope, says Villas-Boas was later "interrogated quite roughly by Brazilian military authorities, and yet he never wavered from the details of his story."

Nick Pope, a former official UFO investigator for the Ministry of Defence of the United Kingdom, concluded "it is inconceivable that everyone is lying" about such alien encounters.[5]

That Vilas-Boas did not change his story in the face of rough interrogation by a military not known for being gentle is significant.

Moreover, as Mr. Pope points out, Vilas-Boas' injuries are difficult to explain: How could a Brazilian farmer in the 1950s have come into contact conventionally with radioactive material?

That Vilas-Boas described strange red symbols written over a doorway inside the craft may be particularly significant. Years later, investigators of alleged abductees have obtained detailed descriptions of exotic symbols similar to hieroglyphs, petro glyphs or other symbolic writing.

Most descriptions, however, have not been published. Certainly there were none in Vilas-Boas' day. Back then, alien abduction had never been heard of.

During a 1992 Massachusetts Institute of Technology conference on abductions and UFOs, John G. Miller, M.D., said symbols such as those described by Vilas Boas give particular credibility to experiencers' stories. As in good criminal investigations, certain facts about abductions are not made public.

"I won't discuss what these symbols are because they have not been published; but they aren't something a person would make up. They are unique and unusual symbols."[6]

I was left with a credible story of a young man seized by apparent beings from another world who examined him, coerced him into having sex, and then let him go. This is the first recorded kidnapping and sexual assault by an alien.

But, it is not the first instance of beings from another world taking advantage of locals. During his first voyage, Columbus seized docile Taino Indians, brought them on board his ships to learn their language and customs; this to better achieve the expedition's primary objective: bringing back valuable spices, and gold and silver to sell in Europe (of which he personally would receive a generous share). In the end, lacking much treasure, he abducted a few Tainos and brought them back to Spain (along with small amounts of gold) to show off to the Court of Ferdinand and Isabelle.

On that first trip, Columbus ordered his men to treat the Tainos with respect, desiring a peaceful trade relationship. There is no written record of sexual intercourse between Old Worlders and New Worlders. For that, we must look to his second voyage and the discovery of the Virgin Islands.

On a beach in a river estuary on St. Croix, the archipelago's largest island, Columbus fought a small skirmish with members of the Carib tribe who were the dominant inhabitants. Unlike the relatively friendly Tainos, however, the Caribs were aggressive and war-like. Originally from the South American mainland, the Caribs had moved outward, island by island, slaughtering and enslaving any inhabitants they found. These, included the more civilized agricultural Tainos whose culture can still be discerned from pottery and other artifacts including petro glyphs carved in stone.

Columbus' men knew the Carib reputation and had even seen evidence they were cannibals. Indeed, 35 years later in 1528, Italian explorer Giovanni da Verrazano was killed and reportedly eaten by Caribs on the island of Guadeloupe during his third voyage of exploration. Four years before becoming a Carib dinner entrée, Verrazano had discovered New York harbor and today the bridge spanning its entrance memorializes him: the Verrazano Narrows Bridge.

Columbus and crew viewed the Caribs as monstrous barbarians. Here's how Guillermo Coma of Aragon, one of the handful of noblemen on the second voyage, described them:

"Caribs are a wild, unconquered race which feeds on human flesh. They wage unceasing wars against gentle and timid Indians to supply flesh . . . They ravage, despoil and terrorize the Indians ruthlessly."[7]

Columbus and his men dealt harshly with the first Caribs they saw. That meeting occurred at their Salt River landing on St Croix. Dr. Chanca, physician for Columbus' second expedition, described the opening events:

"At the dinner hour [on November 12, 1493], we arrived at an island which seemed to be worth the finding, for judging by the extent of the cultivation in it, it appeared very populous. We put in a harbor and the Admiral immediately sent on shore a well-manned barge to hold speech with the Indians in order to ascertain what race they were . . . and gain some information on our navigational course. And, some of the men who went in the barge went on shore and entered a village from whence the inhabitants had already withdrawn and hidden themselves. But, our men were able to capture five or six enslaved Taino women and some boys from whom they learned that the natives of this place were Caribbees.

"As our barge was about to return to the ships with the captures they had made, a canoe came along the coast containing several Caribs; and when they saw our fleet [which Dr. Chanca says consisted of 17 ships and almost 1,200 fighting men] they were so stupefied with amazement that for a good hour they remained motionless at a distance of nearly two cannon shots. In this position they were seen by those in the barge and also by all the fleet."[8]

At this point, the commander of the barge and landing party, Count Michele de Cuneo, a childhood friend of Columbus (both grew up near Genoa, Italy) saw the Carib's canoe. De Cuneo, whom Naval historian Samuel Eliot Morison describes as a jolly dog and good raconteur in contrast to Columbus and the rather solemn Spaniards, explains what happened next:

"The canoe had on board three or four Carib men with two Carib women and two [male Taino] Indian slaves, of whom they had recently cut the genital organ to the belly, so that they were still sore; and we having the flagship's boat ashore, when we saw that canoe coming, quickly jumped into the boat and gave chase to that canoe."[9]

No doubt, Count Cuneo had seen de-neutered male slaves before. Indeed, in his day, slavery was common in Genoa, where merchant sailors traveled to Muslim and Slavic lands in the East and brought home captives sold as servants. Castrated Taino males could serve Carib women without worry of unwanted sex. Eunuchs served the same function in the Middle East of Columbus' day.

Also, males would fatten-up more quickly without genitals, if destined for Carib dinner tables.

Dr. Chanca continues the story of Count Cuneo's canoe chase:

"Meanwhile, those in the barge moved towards the canoe, but so close in to shore, that the Indians, in their perplexity and astonishment as to what all this could mean, never saw them, until they [our men in the barge] were so near that escape was impossible; for our men pressed on them so rapidly that they could not get away, although they made considerable effort to do so.

"When the Caribbees saw that all attempt at flight was useless, they most courageously took to their bows, both men and women; I say courageously because they were only four men and two women [and two slaves, according to de Cuneo], and our men numbered twenty-five. Two of our men were wounded by the Indians, one with two arrows in his breast, and another with an arrow in his side, and if it had not happened that our men carried shields and bucklers, and that they soon got near the Indians with the barge and upset the canoe, most of them would have been killed by their arrows."

One of the wounded Spanish soldiers did have a shield, but an arrow went through it and penetrated his chest three inches. He died in a few days.

Dr. Chanca continues:

"The Indians, even while in the water were still using their bows as much as they could . . . so that it was very hard for our men to take them; and of all of the Indians there was one of them whom they were unable to secure until he had received a mortal wound with a lance, and whom thus wounded they took to the ships.

"The Caribbees we took had curly designs drawn with sticks on their faces and foreheads and had their eyes and eyebrows stained, which I imagine they do for ostentation and to give them a more frightful appearance. . ."

De Cuneo next describes his special conquest after the battle:

"While I was in the barge, I captured a very beautiful Carib woman, whom the Lord Admiral [Columbus] gave to me, and with whom, having taken her into my cabin, she being naked according to their custom, I conceived a desire to take pleasure. I wanted to put my desire into execution but she did not want it and treated me with her finger nails in such a manner that I wished I had never begun. But seeing that (to tell you the end of it), I took a rope and thrashed her well, for which she raised such unheard of screams that you would not have believed your ears. Finally, we came to an agreement in such manner that I can tell you she seemed to have been brought up in a school of harlots."

Columbus also gave captured Carib women to other officers, while the remaining Carib and Taino captives were sent to Spain.

Now part of Virgin Islands National Park, the Salt River landing and battle site is described by the Park Service as a "dynamic, tropical ecosystem home to some of the largest mangrove forests in the Virgin Islands" as well as coral reefs and an underwater canyon.[10]

Gone are the Carib/Taino cultivated fields and village. Even later European sugar plantation clearings are gone, covered with more than 100 years of tree and bush growth. Today, this river basin may be more heavily forested than at any time after Indians first arrived a thousand or more years ago.

The first contact experiences of Columbus and his men provided context, as I tried to understand alleged alien abductions. But, the Vilas-Boas story and other incredible reports suggested something beyond our own history of exploration and conquest. As former British Defence investigator Nick Pope put it:

"There are a number of sightings he uncovered that defied all rational explanation. Something very strange was going on."[11]

And, Mr. Pope candidly added:

"Several of my colleagues in the MOD [Ministry of Defence], military and in intelligence believe we have been . . . [visited by an extraterrestrial civilization]."[12]

All of this, of course, had to be reported to the Navy. I boiled down the research and presented Lt. Taft with the two stories of kidnapping and sexual assault in the very different first contact dramas played-out on St Croix in 1493 and in Brazil in 1957. I stuck to the facts, where they could be ascertained.

Within a few hours of receiving my e-mailed report, Lt.

Taft phoned:

"Dr. Harris, I read your analyses of the Villas-Boas and Carib contact experiences with great interest. Some of my superiors may be unable to accept the Brazilian encounter as a real event. But, that is to be expected. As for me, I found your citings of the official British Ministry of Defence UFO investigator . . . ah, Nick Pope . . . to be persuasive. And, I agree that the experiences of Columbus can shed light on all of this."

I appreciated Lt. Taft's open-mindedness. I encouraged him to look more closely.

"There are credible individuals and independent sources providing corroborative information out there. This all must be taken seriously. Your associates are in a better position than me to get the facts. You should contact the Brits and Brazilians to get more."

"Perhaps, but it's not that easy for me. You are outside the system and don't need to go through layers of often openly skeptical authority to get anything done – particularly contacting foreign officials. As an outside, paid academic consultant, your work is more difficult to deny internally."

"I can understand that. Academia has its own bureaucracies and constraints – especially when looking into these areas. Even Harvard's Dr. Mack was investigated by the University and had to hire an attorney to defend his position and the validity of his work with abductees."

Before hanging-up, I finally asked a question that had been nagging me.

"Incidentally, why do we need encrypted e-mails and a secure telephone line? Are you concerned about the media?"

He replied in a strained voice, "No, Doctor. We are concerned that other agencies may be monitoring the Office of Naval Intelligence's activities and we do not want interference with your work."

"What sort of interference?"

"Difficult to say. It depends upon how far you are able to get in your research. Now that Norman Island has become a new, well-documented UFO incident and you are uncovering new information on previous events, others in the U.S. Government would be very interested. They might even wish to step in and take over . . . or even suppress your investigation.

"And, that would be unfortunate and possibly unpleasant."

"Unpleasant for me?"

"Yes. And for your witnesses. But, you should all be fine if you follow our protocol. Thus far, most of what you've found is already in the public record – although somewhat buried. If the Norman Island event should go public, you and your witnesses can easily be discredited. I'm sure you know that.

"So far, we at the Office of Naval Intelligence have control over the physical evidence of the radar reports and Baskins' notebook and kayak . . .

"By the way, the kayak turned out to be clean of any radiation, although the plastic fibers in the hull did show signs of being super-heated at the molecular level. Oddly, the topside deck, did not. We conclude that while in the water, the hull was exposed to some type of heat or strong electro-magnetic force."

"How could that be? The object passed in the air over the kayak, not beneath it?"

"Another mystery for you to solve."

10 THE BILLIONAIRE AND THE ENCOUNTER

"I sponsored this report . . . to bring together the most credible evidence about UFO sightings in the form of eyewitness reports, official statements, and scientific views . . . I do believe that the evidence indicates that this subject merits serious scientific study. Toward that end, I hope that our government, other governments, and the United Nations will cooperate in making any information they may have available."

> — Laurence S. Rockefeller, February 29, 1996 in a cover letter to John H. Gibbons, Ph.D., President Clinton's science advisor, delivering a comprehensive report on UFOs that Mr. Rockefeller sponsored.[1]

"An interstellar flying object's advanced technology would to us be indistinguishable from magic. You have a feeling you are dealing with some very high technology devices of an entirely real nature which defy explanation in terms of present-day science. To say that we could anticipate the values, reasons, motivations, and so on, of any such system that has the capability of getting here from somewhere else is fallacious." — Dr. James E. McDonald, Senior Physicist and Professor, Institute of Atmospheric Physics, University of Arizona, and former Navy intelligence officer during World War II, in July, 1968 testimony before the U.S. House of Representatives' Committee on Science and Astronautics.[2]

As active members of the St John Historical Society, Mary and I had gotten to know many island transplants with a wide range of government and business experience.

Ms. Denise Nussbaum, with a Ph.D in astrophysics, was a Society member and a friend of Mary. She had served in President Clinton's administration, but was now retired and an avid scuba diver, exploring off-shore coral reefs and historic shipwrecks.

Denise was over for dinner, sitting at the teak table on our deck and enjoying the sunset. She had never revealed exactly what she did in the Clinton administration and Mary had not asked. As we sat there, I took advantage of Mary's momentary absence to change the subject from Hillary Clinton to unexplained phenomena.

She looked at me over tortoise shell glasses.

"Oh, are you a UFO nut?"

"I've never been diagnosed as nuts, although one of my hobbies is reading about UFOs."

Mary had returned with a fresh bottle of wine.

"He means he hasn't been diagnosed, yet," Mary observed.

Denise laughed and then turned toward me.

"Unofficially, I've also long been interested in the subject. Did you know that some of our predecessors on this island shared that interest in UFOs and the possibility of extraterrestrial life?"

"No, but I'd love to hear about it," I replied as Mary refilled Denise's wine glass.

"Sit back and I'll tell you what I know. Everyone is aware that Laurence Rockefeller was one of the fathers of the Virgin Islands National Park. When he first visited St. John after World War II, Rockefeller said it was the most beautiful island in the Caribbean. In the early 1950s, he helped buy up much of the island's mostly empty land that was then donated for the Park.

"Mr. Rockefeller was also a pilot and large investor in post-war commercial and defense aerospace industries. He was fascinated by UFOs. He even funded several UFO research organizations. Like many others, he became convinced the government knew more than it was telling the public. He even met with Bill Clinton's science advisor in a failed attempt to gain declassification of all UFO-related government documents.

"But, Rockefeller was not the only St. Johnian fascinated with extraterrestrial matters. Walter Sullivan, a prominent New York Times science reporter, was a regular visitor to the island in its early days as a vacation destination. He was a pioneer in asserting that extraterrestrial life is not only possible, it's probable."

As she made this point, I had to chime in to show off.

"I read Sullivan's excellent book, *We are Not Alone*, published in the mid-1960s, I believe. He said discoveries in meteorites and radio astronomy proved that space contains at least 20 amino acids required to form DNA molecules and cellular life."

"Correct," Denise said, like a teacher praising a struggling student. "Specifically, Sullivan argued that the presence of these chemicals in the meteorites could not have been the result of contamination upon their collision with Earth. And, most scientists agreed.

"Of course, since Sullivan's reporting, we have learned that other worlds within our own solar system – Mars, our own moon, Jupiter's moon Europa, and other bodies – have water, the other essential building block of life. Many planets in other solar systems have recently been discovered. At least one is believed to have water and an atmosphere."

"Getting back to Rockefeller, you said he met with Clinton's science advisor. What happened?"

"Nothing, I'm afraid. The President's science advisor, John Gibbons, met with him and, later, officially accepted a thorough study of credible UFO events that Rockefeller had financed and endorsed."

"Too bad nothing was done with it," I replied. Under the table, Mary kicked me to subtly indicate it was time to change the conversation back to politics. I tuned out.

After Mary walked Denise to her car with a flashlight, I went to my office and went on- line to verify her information and try to learn more.

It turned out that, beyond Rockefeller and Sullivan, another St. Johnian with a strong interest in science – and, some say UFOs – was J. Robert Oppenheimer, the father of the atom bomb. After his World War II service as head of the government's Manhattan Project, Oppenheimer was accused of being a communist and stripped of the security clearance required to conduct his research in nuclear physics. He bought property on St. John's Gibney Beach in 1957 and lived there in semi-exile until he died of cancer ten years later.

Much of the research sponsored by Laurence Rockefeller and the reporting by Walter Sullivan, I decided, should be included in my report to the Navy. As a hint to what they should do with such information, I would include Oppenheimer's view of the folly of excessive secrecy:

"We do not operate well when important facts are known, in secrecy and in fear, only to a few men . . . Follies can occur when even the men who know the facts can find no one to talk to about them, when facts are too secret for discussion, and thus, for thought."[3]

Speaking of the Navy report, a little more than three months had already elapsed. Beyond my periodic updates, a complete report that tied it all together (as much as possible) was due. I certainly had enough material –

factual and solid conjecture – to write the paper on Sergeant Baskins, the *U.S.S. John F. Kennedy*, and associated phenomena.

Still, I couldn't shake thoughts of those trenches located just a few miles off shore. What would the waters be like above them? Does the air feel or smell differently out there? Would there be more and different sea life visible on the surface? What about navigational instrument anomalies?

Certainly, one of my recommendations to the Navy would be further exploration of Caribbean trenches. I had learned that the tremendous tectonic plate movements that created trenches – combined with possible sediments deposited on the bottom – are responsible for "magnetic faults" and associated changes in gravity. Areas in the Puerto Rico Trench have the lowest gravity readings on earth.

Then there was the closer Virgin Islands trough, the South Drop, which feeds into the Anegada Trough and, then, into the Puerto Rico Trench, itself. Heck, we could actually sail there.

There was an idea. Why not sail there? Any unusual observations would be icing on the cake of my report.

It wasn't long before I went to Coral Bay to consult with Hap Collins and a very capable young man, Jonathan, who lived aboard his 26-foot sailboat. Jonathan had crewed on virtually every type of boat propelled by wind. Tragically, he had lost both parents while they were all bringing down a sailboat under contract from Bar Harbor, Maine to the Virgins. He and another crew man were the sole survivors of a sudden, fierce N'oreaster that caught them at sea and sank the boat.

"Boats sink," Jonathan stoically says about the accident.

With his slight build, agility, and an accurate square-rigged sailing vessel tattooed on his forearm, he is energetic, optimistic and the perfect able-bodied seaman. His deep black hair, light skin and freckles pegged him as a "black Irishman."

Skinny Legs was crowded that Friday. There were still tourists on-island and every seat under the roof was taken. Sitting in the open air at a wooden table in the sand, we were giving our lunch orders to a young lady when a commotion broke out at the bar.

"I don't want to sit in the sun!!!"

It was George, the Bay curmudgeon. He'd thrown up his hands, whining and asserting his rights as a regular. The bartender, conscious that heavier spending tourists also wanted room inside, stood up straight and replied:

"You live on a fucking sailboat in the Caribbean! And you can't stand a little sun?"

As it turned out, he couldn't and wouldn't. Being a Coral Bay Yacht Club member and certified character, he got to squeeze in between the end of the bar and the wall, muttering and swearing. Who knew? His long hair and beard might amuse visitors as a dash of local color, so long as they sat upwind of him.

With the entertainment concluded, Hap gave his advice.

"All you need to do is sail east beyond Virgin Gorda and then head northeast, keeping to the east of Anegada Island."

Anegada. Located 15 miles northeast of Virgin Gorda, the British island is the eastern most Virgin. I'd always meant to sail there, but its surrounding reefs and flatness made it less inviting than the others. Moreover, Anegada (Spanish for "drowned island") was a graveyard of ships. Between 1500 and 1899, more than 100 named ships had wrecked on her shores and reefs. Many more vessels were likely lost there anonymously in the days before radar. And, we had no radar on our boat.

Captain Hap continued, "Be sure to stay well east of Anegada and its Horseshoe Reef that bows out east and south almost to Virgin Gorda. Pass the reef on your port side and you'll reach the Anegada Trough before you know it."

We were looking at charts Hap had brought. Jonathan and I listened closely. Mary and John would not be making this trip. Just me with Jonathan as first mate. We went over multiple details and then went about provisioning the boat for at least a 24-hour trip.

From the college Physics department I borrowed a more sensitive compass than the one on-board and a portable gravitometer to measure the strength of gravity. Although it might not work too well on a moving sailboat, we might get some useful data – particularly if it was a calm day. I also had a hand held laser depth finder.

We studied the marine forecast, checking the readings online at relevant buoys along our course and found a three day window of calm, clear weather. Between our sails and in-board diesel engine, we could easily accomplish the mission.

Finally, the day came – August first. Mary and John waved us from the stone dock as Jonathan and I rowed out to the *Perseverance*. They had made plans to go to St. Thomas for a few days to shop and see a movie during this quiet time on St. John.

As we climbed on board, we noticed the *Bonne Chance* was just clearing her mooring, heading out on jib and staysails.

We departed a few minutes behind her and quickly threw up our sails, hoping to catch-up. The *Chance* had just lowered her square mainsail and was raising the lateen sail up her mizzen mast as we closed in. Lord Claymore, with captain's cap pulled down tight, looked astern from his ship's wheel and bellowed:

"Ahoy there, lads! Where are you headin'?"

I stood and yelled back, "Out for a pleasure sail to Anegada. How about you?"

"Makin' south for Antig'a and the Grenadines for the season"

Antigua and the Grenadine Islands for the hurricane

season. It had long been the practice of sailors in this latitude to head south where it was believed the storms are less severe and boats are safer.

As I digested his Lordship's reply, I noticed a spry man in cut-off shorts and a high-crowned, narrowly rimmed straw hat climbing down the rat line from the yard arm, where he had lowered the mainsail. His long gray hair, tied in a pony tail with a black ribbon, blew behind in the breeze like the tail of a pointer dog.

"Isn't that Lars Seligsson, the artist?" I asked Jonathan, who nodded. Lars, a very talented oil painter and seaman, had lived on the far East End since childhood. A known eccentric, his paintings of pre-National Park and pre-tourist Mecca Virgin Islanders provide snap shots of simpler lives paced by ambling donkeys and flapping canvas sails.

"Wonder where Sir Keith's pal Nigel is?"

Of course, Jonathan knew: "Left for down south about ten days ago."

Sir Keithley's third and remaining crew member was a thin, older woman of a certain age, tanned and wrinkled with strands of bleached blonde hair blowing from beneath a hand-woven palm frond hat. She was heartily pulling the halyard to raise the mizzen sail. I didn't know her by name, but had certainly seen her around – frequently sitting in worn beach chairs, swapping gossip with the other bay women under the trees near the dock. Maybe she was the current Lady Claymore.

"Best of luck to you, Sir Keith!" I yelled.

"Fair winds and followin' seas to you both!"

We knew Keith was sincere and appreciated his blessing.

We sailed by the *Bonne Chance* to her windward on the same tack. Being the smaller vessel and without a square mainsail, we were able to point much closer to the wind and our courses soon diverged. We watched them sail south and east toward the horizon as we continued due east past Norman and up Drake Channel to Virgin Gorda.

As we left Coral Bay behind, three dolphins appeared off the port bow and playfully swam a little ahead of us, matching our speed, rolling and slicing through the rising swells. Dolphins are a good omen for the start of a voyage, Jonathan noted. The sea mammals stayed with us until we came about on a new tack.

Four hours of fine sailing later, we had rounded Fallen Jerusalem heading east-north-east watching Virgin Gorda go by and heading toward Necker Island Passage. We then headed east again seeking deeper water to avoid Anegada's Horse Shoe Reef. The plan was to pass well east of the Horseshoe and then turn North, clearing Anegada on its Atlantic coast side.

By the time we passed the Horseshoe it was nearing sunset and we were in deeper water – 400 to 500 feet. Jonathan was up on the bowsprit, fiddling with the headsail sheet which had become tangled around the windless winch, when he sang out:

"Weather ahead! Look off the starboard bow."

Because we were healed over on a starboard tack, the mainsail, staysail and jib had obscured my view. I leaned over in the cockpit and looked under the mainsail boom to scan the horizon. Sure enough, there was a system approaching from due east. It was multi-hued – black in the center closest to the water and then fading into gray with billowy white towers skyward. A squall with thunderheads. Great.

Ominously, the cloud pile was intermittently illuminated from within – lightening.

"Hell, this morning the radar didn't show a thing for hundreds of miles," I called to Jonathan, as he climbed back into the cockpit. We conferred on the best moves and decided to lower the staysail, reef the main and keep the head sail up to ensure optimum maneuverability. I also turned on the engine in case we needed to hove-to and maintain forward momentum to better ship waves and handle wind gusts.

No question, we were on a collision course with the storm, which seemed too wide to go around and was approaching too rapidly to outrun. We readied ourselves as best we could.

With an air temperature of 85 degrees, we decided against foul weather gear. This looked like a fast moving baby that would quickly pass over us and move on, and we didn't want to be encumbered.

Just how violent would it be?

While we still had time, I gave Jonathan the tiller and went below to check the instruments. The digital numbers on the gravitometer, which I'd lashed alongside the nav desk with the instrument's legs firmly planted level on the cabin deck, were rapidly rising and falling, making no sense – even allowing for the angle of our hull and the sea swells. But, the depth finder showed only 500 feet. Not in the Trough, yet. So, why the gravity fluctuations?

Back in the cockpit, the compass was spinning insanely. Strange magnetic forces as well as gravity anomalies?

Very weird and scary. We waited.

As the clouds grew closer Jonathan and I tensely put on our life jackets. And waited. My hand gripped the tiller hard. My knuckles turned white. My other hand was on the main sheet, ready to uncleat it, if we needed to hove to. Jonathan sat silently with jib sheet in-hand ready to instantly uncleat it.

We stared at the approaching clouds, awaiting our fate. I looked back at our trusty, thirty year-old heavy fiberglass dinghy – virtually unsinkable – trailing on her line several yards behind us. Our lifeboat.

Oddly, we felt neither gusts of wind nor the light rain droplets that usually precede such storms. Yet, the clouds grew ever closer. Then, the maelstrom towered over us just off the bow. Still no gusts or rain.

As if in slow motion, the bow sprit entered the darkest lower clouds and disappeared. Foot-by-foot the cloud line approached from the bow toward us in the stern cockpit. Then we too were immersed in a dark, very damp fog-like cloud – but no rain. The wind had actually died.

"What the fuck," I exclaimed as the engine sputtered and fell silent just when we needed it the most.

Jonathan was no longer listening. He sat as though paralyzed with his hands still gripping the jib sheet.

Fear was rapidly building within me as I called his name with no response.

"Jesus fuckin' Christ!" I yelled desperately.

Before I descended into incapacitating panic, a soft, firm voice said:

"We will not harm you. Your friend is completely safe. Your boat is completely safe."

The boat had actually stopped dead in the water. Empty of wind, the sails hung limply.

"You are safe. Keep calm," said the voice as a narrow blue light beam hit my head. It felt as though I was being patted on the head by a parent. Instantly, I did feel calm – as calm as if I'd taken a couple of valiums. Suddenly the cloud passed over our boat and we were in a clear patch of calm sea.

Clouds and fog circled entirely around the boat a few yards beyond the placid waters immediately surrounding us – as though we were in the eye of a small hurricane. A warm, soothing sun-like light bathed us.

Looking up I saw a round, smooth, shining silver hull a few feet above our mast. It must have been about 50 feet in diameter because it extended well beyond both ends of our 32 foot boat. The "sun light" emanating from it shimmered the way heat rises from sand or a black top road on a hot summer day.

Then, a circular door opened in the hull's seamless skin. A wider blue light switched on without a sound, totally illuminating me and wiping away any residual fear. Something beckoned me to rise.

"You are safe. We will not hurt you. You will not fall."

I felt fine – "high" you might say – as I was lifted effortlessly from the cockpit and drawn up along the beam of light toward the warmth of the silver-gray hull. Looking down at our deck, Jonathan sat statuesque in the cockpit, still holding the now slack jib sheet.

"Your friend will be fine. Your boat will be fine. Do not worry."

After all the research I'd done on the experiences of abductees, I didn't worry as I floated up the beam to the circular door. I held out my hand and touched the skin of the vessel; it was smooth, silvery, metallic and warm. I thought of the young St. Johnian Guy Benjamin touching the *Spirit of St. Louis*, another wondrous air ship, the like of which he had never seen.

I was slowly tugged into a dark and noticeably more humid space. Gradually a pale green light illuminated the gray circular room in which I found myself standing. The door closed silently behind me, merging seamlessly back into the wall, as a pleasant smelling mist – aromatic like lilac flowers – filled my space.

Suddenly another seamless circular door opened opposite me. I walked through it, noticing that my legs required more strength to take each step – as though I were being pulled down.

The next circular space was vast and filled with a variety of plants and trees growing from big trays in an even warmer, more humid atmosphere. Some of the flora I recognized – orchids, bougainvillea, hibiscus, lime and mango trees, bananas, and bread fruit. Others I couldn't identify. Coconut and date palms soared up into a mist that must have concealed a ceiling somewhere. Moisture glistened and dropped from leaves as in a rain forest.

This room, which felt like a hot house, was filled by a diffuse green-violet light illuminating everything. I couldn't determine where it came from, but it reminded me of light from grow lamps.

Gurgling water sounds caught my attention. Instinct

led me to step toward where I thought the water was. Hidden behind broad banana leaves and other foliage was what appeared to be a stand of Norfolk pines. Through their limbs and green needles, I saw an arrangement of natural rocks, piled into an authentic looking cliff, standing nine or ten feet tall. A small waterfall cascaded down a series of rock ledges adorned with mosses and ferns, falling into a river stone-lined pool – perhaps twelve feet in diameter.

Walking around the pines I found a path to the pool and saw four short-legged stone benches facing the water. They were arranged to follow the contours of the semi-circular pool.

The Capitol Botanical Garden came to mind, with its rain forest growing and faux stream flowing under glass panes held aloft by 19th century steel beams. Very soothing.

"Yes, it is. We believe your equatorial flora and *ours* soothe the Universal Spirit flowing within and through us all, carrying us toward eternity – just as water flows down a mountain stream and runs to a sea.

"This is our sanctuary."

I turned and there was a short person about five feet tall with clear, white skin, large slanted blue eyes and long blonde, nearly white, hair. He was clad in a tight silver suit that ended in what appeared to be black lace-less running shoes. He had a small, straight nose, high cheek bones and a normally proportioned, smiling mouth. I realized he was reading my thoughts.

"Welcome, welcome. You are correct. We are in communication with your thoughts, and yours with ours," a soft androgynous voice said. But, his mouth didn't move. Still smiling, I noticed he had thick rounded lips similar to those crafted by plastic surgeons to serve the vanity of their clients.

"We communicate with Earth dwellers through what you call telepathy. We also communicate complex concepts and ideation within our own community in the same fashion. You are hearing our true voice, however."

I couldn't help looking at his forehead – proportionally higher and slightly more bulbous than ours. Bigger brain than us?

"Yes, our brains are configured somewhat differently than yours. As we evolved as mind-to-mind communicators, we developed a new organ in our frontal lobe.

"A crude analogy would be your radar or sonar. We transmit our thoughts and receive the thoughts of others. They are, after all, simply composed of energy – sub-atomic particles.

"We believe some of your scientists are only now discovering what we have known for thousands of years. Thoughts travel outside our corporeal bodies and, if sufficiently focused, can change aspects of our physical environment. The power of what you call 'prayer,' meditation or 'yoga' is very real. The more you focus your thoughts and the more people who join in thought, the more powerful the change effected in the physical world."

Mind over matter. If our thoughts are energy – which makes perfect sense since the brain generates electricity chemically and uses it to send messages throughout the body – then that energy can affect matter. Indeed, energy is matter, as Einstein said.

Projected matter can affect other matter. Experiments have proven telepathy exists. Subatomic particles – of which thoughts are comprised – are "entangled" with other separate particles, even when separated by vast distances of space. Einstein called such quantum entanglement "spooky".

"Good, professor. Keep thinking along those lines."

He turned and pointed to the waterfall. Suddenly, a few ribbons of water along the edge changed course and splashed out of the pool. Then he looked away and it shifted back on course.

Marvelous! Sending and receiving concentrated thoughts – energy – as a way to interact with the world. A large, bulbous forehead. Thick, rounded lips. "Sonar" energies. All familiar, but why?

Then it hit me: dolphins.

"Very good professor. Although we are bi-pedal beings living on dry ground, our organ is similar to that in your dolphins. Our home atmosphere, and here in our ship, is breathable by you. However, we have more water molecules in our 'air'- more humidity, if you will - and so our thought energy travels through our mists in the same way a dolphin's 'sonar' pierces the oceans."

Where are you from?

"A planet 55 light-years away. It is somewhat closer to our star than Earth is to yours. Our mass is also larger than Earth with slightly stronger gravity. That is why we are shorter than many humans. Our world is also warmer than yours.

"Like your Earth, however, it is composed of terrestrial rain forests, cooler mountains, desert lands and oceans. Our poles are the coldest regions. They ice over for a portion of each of our planet's solar orbits. Our 'year,' however is shorter, since we are closer to our star.

"As I said, gravity on our planet is stronger than yours and you will find that the gravity on our ship matches that of our home. That is why you find walking more strenuous. Now, come. Meet the others."

He motioned with a hand with six unusually long fingers – very similar to ours, but with extra joints and no thumb.

"No need for opposable thumbs when you have six long, four jointed fingers. Like yours, our ancestors also were forest peoples who climbed and lived among trees."

Another seamless door opened. As we stepped through the portal, the floral fragrance faded, replaced by a very faint odor of burnt electrical wires. Some astronauts have described this as the smell of space and some attribute it to particles within the vast interstellar dust clouds.

"Good, professor. Your olfactory organ is picking up a scent that we are accustomed to and no longer notice. Space does have an odor."

"What is it?" I asked aloud, forgetting he could read my thoughts.

"Your 'burnt wire' analogy is a good one and instructive. Some of the particles you call solar radiation penetrate all matter. Harmless dosages of ions and other electrically charged particles in the plasma ejected by stars like your sun even penetrate our hulls. They do smell like your primitive conductivity 'wires'."

Why hadn't I studied physics?

"Even if you had, the current limitations of the evolving human brain cannot comprehend what even your most brilliant physicists perceive as real. You can see and understand solar storms. Your scientists can also see that 'quantum entanglement' – the entanglement of minds and matter in space-time is real. But, they cannot understand what it is and what it implies.

"Similarly, your ancient Greek scientists could see the stars and constellations. They named them, navigated by them and even mapped them. But, they could not fully understand what they were observing."

At the limits of my own understanding, I looked carefully around the new room we had entered. On the curving wall opposite where we stood were what appeared to be several large geometric shapes – rectangles, squares, triangles and circles – etched into its skin. Facing the walls were cushioned chairs similar to our chaise lounges, but smaller and deeper and with soft arm rests.

"The chairs mold to our bodies, making long hours of travel and work more comfortable. Our instruments are thought controlled. Observe."

As he "spoke," a large rectangle of what must be a star map appeared in the wall. Another opened, revealing an apparent real-time view of our sea horizon with setting sun above gentle swells.

My thoughts were interrupted by a series of clicks and whistles coming from behind a wall partition. It slowly opened to reveal three other beings. Although they appeared similar in physique with the same style clothing, each wore a different color: pink, green and purple. Two had the unmistakable figures of females – mammary glands.

Their mouths opened wide enough to revealed normal looking curling tongues, as they made clicking sounds, and then formed thick-lipped "O's" to whistle. I guessed their thicker lips were useful in whistling.

"Our ancients spoke what you call a 'click' language. Some aborigines in your Africa still speak it. They are close descendants of your earliest ancestors and speak your first language – a click language like ours. These sounds carry long distances and blend-in with the natural noise of a forest - the bending and breaking of branches, fluttering leaves, avian calls and so forth. Thus, our ancients communicated while cloaking their presence from forest predators and prey. Like yours, our ancestors, too, were hunters and gatherers."[4]

The whistles and clicks ended as the others approached me. Clicks were replaced by multiple "voices" that jumbled into an unintelligible sound mash in my brain.

"Over time, we learned that thought transference was an even better, more secure, if you will, means of communication when in the presence of other species. Today, our clicks express raw emotions – joy at seeing you, in this case. We are sorry to say to you that your brain is unable to differentiate and understand the thoughts of all four of us, if expressed at the same time. Over millions of years we have developed the ability to do so.

"Regrettably, therefore, I will remain your sole communicant. Please do sit down and be comfortable while we converse."

I sat on the lounge chair, which immediately curled around my back and sides reacting to my subconscious thoughts until I was literally as comfortable as possible.

Meanwhile, the others had formed a line facing me and unfurled what could have been a red silk banner. On it were gold symbols that looked like a mixture of Sanskrit and hieroglyphs – picture-like words or letters combined with slashes and curlicues.

"It is a message welcoming you to our humble home. This vessel *is* our home and has been for 50 of your years. Our ship and this crew came to your solar system in your year 1962. But, we have a much larger mother ship in your system with which we couple from time-to-time, enabling us to commingle with other brothers and sisters, handle maintenance matters and for other purposes."

"If you have been sailing across our skies for 50 years, how old are you? What is your life span?"

"Our physical lives usually extend about 150 of your years. The average age of this vessel's team is 75 of your years.

"Our people have been coming to and living in your solar system since your year 1945 – the first time a nuclear explosion occurred on Earth. Our instruments captured that event in the North American desert. Knowing you are war-like, we were alarmed."

"Now, I am become death, the destroyer of worlds," Robert Oppenheimer had said, quoting Hindu scripture, as he watched his unprecedented atomic explosion from a bunker in the "Jornado Del Meurto" (Journey of the Dead) swath of desert near Soccoro, New Mexico.

"Quite so. And we and others from other worlds came to your planet to study your eco-systems and life forms, watching closely your nuclear weapons and power generation complexes.

"We watched as your tribe dropped nuclear weapons on two cities in the archipelago of Japan. Later, the Russian tribe developed nuclear weapons, causing a competition with your people to build the most destructive weapon.

"We watched as Russians delivered nuclear warheads to Cuba's immature leader. We observed with interest your tribe's reaction to that event.

"Indeed, we believe you have uncovered evidence of our close monitoring of nuclear weapon-bearing naval vessels and airplanes during your Cuba crisis. Had your leaders failed to halt the slide toward nuclear war, we would have done so by initiating mechanical difficulties in your respective launching systems. Fortunately, that was not required.

"It was also fortunate that, years later, a vessel similar to this one was instantly on-site at the Russian's Chernobyl nuclear power center when an explosion and fire threatened a total meltdown, rendering a considerable portion of your planet uninhabitable. With calming particle beams, we were able to drop the emitting radiation from the catastrophic 3,000 milliroentgens per hour when *we* arrived to the more manageable 800 per hour that your human responders found when they finally arrived. Your Ukraine and much of northern Europe was thereby saved from a catastrophe that would have claimed the physical lives of several generations of humans and other organisms. Vast lands and waters would have been uninhabitable for hundreds of your years."[5]

I was aware UFOs are frequently seen near nuclear missile bases and power plants; but had not heard of a Chernobyl connection. On April 26, 1986, the Chernobyl Nuclear Power Plant, in the then Soviet republic of Ukraine exploded and caught fire, spewing highly radioactive particles across much of the western USSR and northern Europe. More than 300,000 people were evacuated and resettled elsewhere within the Soviet Union. Thus far, tens of thousands of people have reportedly died from radiation related cancers.

If his story was true, it seems the death toll and long-term environmental damage could have been much higher.

But, what about the more recent Fukushima Daiichi nuclear plant disaster in Japan? And, the near meltdown at The Three Mile Island nuke plant near Harrisburg, Pennsylvania?

"Good questions, professor. Our brethren monitored both emergencies. We concluded the Fukushima meltdown, though most unfortunate, would be contained before affecting many people beyond the immediate surrounding region. Your own partial meltdown at the Three Mile Island reactor was corrected by humans before significant radioactive particles were vented into the air. The Chernobyl incident was *very* different. Tens of Millions of lives and a large portion of Earth were in imminent danger. That is why we stepped in."

How could your ship reduce the radiation? Or, for that matter, how do your vessels travel in and out of space and cross distances measured in light years?

"All good questions. We have several working 'rays' or 'beams' composed of a variety of focused particles that affect most of your mechanical devices, metals and the human brain.

"Some of the particles in our beams are unfamiliar to your scientists. For instance, we brought you up from your boat using what your Hollywood people might call a 'tractor beam.' To understand how such beams can accomplish many tasks, consider your own laser beams. They simply focus and amplify streams of photons – packets of light. Yet, these photons can accurately cut through the most delicate *and* strongest of your materials. Similarly, we apply a multitude of particles to do many types of work.

"As for our means of long-distance propulsion, we harness the power of gravity – or, rather anti-gravity. Using a form of fission requiring a very heavy metal Earth does not possess, we generate enough power to target and push the graviton particles that make up gravity, which, as some of your scientists believe, is a component of the space-time continuum. In short, we are able to generate a focused, localized anti-gravitational force of such intensity that we can bend space-time, making long distance travel fast and efficient."

"How does that work?"

"To understand, you must first realize that space-time is a real, physical entity – a fabric if you will. Consider what happens when you put a heavy ball on a tight bed sheet and then push the sheet down on one end. The ball rolls rapidly to the depression. Similarly, our anti-gravity amplifiers generate and focus targeted beams that create depressions in the fabric of space-time. We then quite rapidly travel down along the declinations to our destinations."

Sounded plausible, I thought, still wishing I'd studied physics.

"We know you are not a scientist. That is why we simplify our explanations. Anti-gravity travel is only needed for long-distance flights. For local movement, we use a simple electro-magnetic propulsion system your scientists could understand."

The electro-magnetism factor would explain the changing colors of the "fire balls" as they travel in our atmosphere. It could also explain why our electronics and machines cut off when their vessels are close. Moreover, people who have said they've been taken inside ships report time anomalies – space-time oddities, I guessed.

"All true. Aside from our anti-gravity amplifiers, we also use the energy of gravitons to create the gravity within our ships. This does create small local distortions in space-time. The time problem is why our visit must be cut somewhat short. We do not want you to suffer a significant difference between the elapsing of your personal time and that of your family and comrades. So, you should quickly ask questions and I will attempt to answer them."

"Why me?"

"We chose you as a communicant for the same reason your Navy friend chose you. You have an open, intelligent mind. You are a good investigator. You are also a good teacher and somewhat unbiased for a human."

"If you know of my Navy contact, then you must know of my investigation of the death of Marine Sergeant Baskins."

"We do. We must tell you that ours was the very vessel that your Marine and Navy men on your aircraft carrier saw near Cuba in 1971. We heard the thoughts of all the men who saw us. Several impressed us with their courage, level-headedness and unbiased curiosity. Subsequently, we have been in contact with several of them in ways neither you nor they can understand.

"By exploiting your Marine's cherished memories of a woman with whom he enjoyed remarkable sex, we did call the Sergeant back to the remote Norman Island. We wished to bring him on board to speak with us that evening. We wanted to know what he now thinks about his earlier experience and 'UFOs.' More importantly, we wished to observe his reaction to meeting us face to face."

"But why him? And why did he die?"

"We choose people from all professions and classes of your society. We wish to learn their views of us, and also their hopes and aspirations for themselves and Earth. And so, when we flew to the ship you call the William Thornton, we actually hovered over the Sergeant as he was paddling his kayak away from that entertainment vessel. All the other people who could have witnessed us were safely immobilized, as is your friend now in your boat. We did not wish them to see us raise the Sergeant up to our vessel.

"But, the Sergeant was in full control of himself – just as you were when you first looked up at us from your boat. We regret to say, however, that before we could calm Sergeant Baskins with tranquilizing particles, he panicked –

'froze up' as in your expression 'deer in a headlight.' His kayak tipped over, hull-up with him under water. We tried to pull the kayak and the Sergeant up with our beam, but he was not strapped into his vessel and the upside down hull shielded him from our beam. As we pulled the kayak up and out of the water, he rose with it for only a few feet, then plunged back down head first. For a reason we do not know, he continued falling straight down under water. He may have breathed water into his lungs when the kayak first capsized.

"After his second plunge, we perceived it was too late to revive him.

"As to your question 'why he died,' we have an expression: it was his time to transcend materiality and depart his husk.

"That being said, we do feel responsible. Had we tranquilized him more rapidly, he might be alive today. We will not make that mistake again. We will quickly sedate any humans before we communicate with them."

So, the attempt to lift the upside down kayak and Sergeant Baskins beneath it explained why Naval investigators had found heat exposure on the hull rather than the deck. The time it took them to attempt Baskins' rescue explains why the airport radars showed the space ship hovered there for a few moments.

"But, what about all the people on the Willy T and on their own boats in the harbor?"

"We immediately released them from stasis and resumed our flight past the William Thornton and up into space. They are not aware that they were immobilized."

"True. I interviewed two people who had been on the Willy's deck. They simply saw you speed by."

"Yes, they suffered no ill effects and were unaware of the incident with the Sergeant. Please be assured that your friend on your sailboat will also be perfectly fine."

"But, what is your name? What are your comrades' names?" The others were still standing off to the side watching and "listening" to our thought exchange.

"You may call me Ebe and our commonweal Ebeint."

Commonweal? What do you mean?

"The closest English word for our society. We live in a community of shared consciousness and material equality. We do have private spaces – homes, if you will - but we conserve and allocate our resources for the common good. Rather than working for a medium of exchange such as your money, we contribute our labor and skills to the community and share in its assets and benefits; from each according to ability and skills to each according to need and merit.

"We are, however, led to concordance by councils of elders. I am the eldest on this vessel, for instance. So, I bear the responsibility for our small commonweal, in accordance with the council of elders on our mother ship, who, in turn, is in accord with our planetary council. "

As he "spoke," he motioned for me to get up from the most comfortable seat I had ever sat in. The seamless door opened in the far wall and, as we moved toward it, I waved good-bye to the others. Smiling, they raised their hands palms-open toward me, a gesture I guessed was akin to waving good bye.

Ebe led me through the arboretum and into the first room I had entered.

"But, I have many more questions. Just how big is this ship? And, will I see you again?"

"This ship is 100 feet in diameter and 200 feet tall – shaped like one of your toy tops. It has three decks. The first is comprised of the anti-gravity amplifiers, the electromagnetic propulsion engine and our life support systems. It is what you might term the engineering deck. You came in on our second deck, our spiritual and command centers. We consider our communion with the Universal Spirit and the operation and control of this vessel to be virtually indivisible.

"Our third deck is devoted to day-to-day living. We

have hygiene and personal energy intake areas and rest and relaxation facilities.

"The entire interior of our vessel is always stable and steady. We feel no ill affects from travel, no external gravitational forces or other discomforts, regardless of our speed, angle of ascent or descent or navigational bearing. This is done through what you would understand as a gyroscopic process, though far in advance of your own gyroscopes.

"As to whether we see you again, it is likely. However, we cannot foretell the future with complete accuracy.

"But, we will tell you this: it was no coincidence you decided to sail to the Anegada Trough before writing your report. We will tell you that we do travel under water in the trenches, using them as discreet pathways and rest stops, as you call them."

"You know about my report?"

"We know much about you and your family. We have known you for many years. It was no coincidence that as a young man your university thesis concerned 'unidentified submersible objects' and that your paper ended up in the hands of your Navy.

"You see, we take long term interest in certain Earth individuals who come to our attention. The process by which this happens is one you could not grasp.

"We do know of your wife's work on behalf of those with disabilities; and, we ask the Universal Spirit to strengthen her and continue to assist your teenage son."

"No, wait a minute. You know of our son's condition? Your medical science must be many, many years ahead of ours. Is there nothing you can do to help him?"

"The sick, those with disabilities and the poor and hungry have always been with your species. They can be helped, restored and many cured any time your society wishes to devote the resources to do so. You have free will, as do we.

"There are many worlds, but Earth is yours. We

perceive that the Universal Spirit that flows through you and all sentient beings in the universe gives dominion of each world to the highest intelligent life form on each world. How those life forms choose to use their resources is their concern.

"Treat others as you wish to be treated. That is our most important canon. That means we try not to directly interfere in the lives of sentient beings of other worlds. Would you wish us to behave as your Europeans behaved toward the local peoples and cultures they found when they came to the 'New World'?

"And, if we started curing humans who are impaired, where and when do we stop? Would you have us re-order your society to ensure all are healthy and your resources allocated to benefit all? Any attempt to do so would be interpreted by your leaders as hostile. It would lead to conflict between your species and ours — a conflict we do not seek and do not wish to initiate.

"Non-interference is, therefore, crucial. We only make exceptions when the survival of a planet or of the highest life form on a planet is in direct jeopardy. The extinction of sentient life forms anywhere in the universe diminishes the Universal Spirit, as does destruction of a sentient life-bearing planet. Such destruction diminishes us all, including Earth's life forms.

"So, we monitor your nuclear activity. We watch your accelerating environmental and climatic challenges. But, we provide help only when it is absolutely essential.

"When we act, we do so as clandestinely as possible. That is how we would wish it, if our roles were reversed.

"Understand this: in the material stage of sentient life, all must make and walk upon their own paths. Nevertheless, we are all connected through the Universal Spirit and all will be united in that Spirit at the end of our materiality.

"You, your wife and son should, therefore, continue seeking guidance and assistance through focused, direct communication with the Spirit. Seek the best medical sciences your species' resource allocation decisions make available to you.

"Now, you must leave."

I thought back to something he had said in passing near the beginning of our conversation: "others" were also coming to Earth. Who and why?

"We can confirm that other species from other worlds have visited Earth before and after your nuclear activity began – some for many, many years."

"Do you mean the so-called 'Grays' that author Whitley Strieber and many others speculate about in our popular media[6]?"

"We may say no more about the others. You should be wary, however. That is all we can tell you without unduly affecting the course of your civilization."

"So, let me understand why you are here. Should Earth or its highest life forms be destroyed or seriously damaged it would diminish the Universal Spirit, thereby harming your spiritual lives."

"Not just our spiritual lives. A planet's unnatural and premature destruction also affects the other planets in your solar system and the changes collectively affect the space-time continuum, causing ripples in nearby systems such as ours.

"Therefore, we came and remain as semi-clandestine monitors – observers who serve the Universal Spirit and the requirements of the region of the space-time continuum in which we all live."

"And the others?"

"They may have their own agenda of which we cannot speak.

"Now, we must insist upon your departure."

"What about the big blonde body and wreckage that the Prime Minister of Grenada found several years ago? It had six fingers and blonde features like you, but was much bigger."

"Ah, our cousins. You see, a few thousand of your years ago, we were just learning to leave our home planet and we discovered another habitable world only one of your light years away. It was smaller, but had natural resources we required. We sent colonists there and over time it grew to be a thriving self-sustaining community that also explores space. Because it was smaller, that planet had less gravity and our people there grew taller and thicker. Some Earthly witnesses to their visits to *your* world call them 'Nordics' because your people say they look like your Vikings.

"But, now you should go."

"Thank you for your hospitality and information. Good bye," I said aloud and grasped his hand to shake. He took it and six long fingers completely enveloped my hand. His touch was warm and soft. Warm. Females with breasts. Warm-blooded mammals like us?

"Yes. We are all made from the same 'star dust' and our respective DNA molecules are made with the same amino acids. Our DNA structures have many strands in common with yours. And, our bodies and internal organs are similar.

"Now, we say good bye and farewell to you, our friend."

The final internal door swished open and I stepped through it. Ebe remained in the other room. As his door closed, my room slowly filled with blue light. When it reached a deep, pure cobalt blue, the external door opened and the blue light coalesced into a beam. I floated down it involuntarily, past the mast of the boat and back to my seat in the cockpit. As I grabbed the tiller and looked up, the space ship's hull shimmered with a reddish light and quite suddenly shot straight up until it was just another star – a reddish one, like Mars.

"Strangest storm I've ever seen," Jonathan said tensely, still clutching the jib sheet. Suddenly, the engine resumed, catching his attention.

"Did that clunk out? We need to check that when we reach port."

The clouds had evaporated and it was a clear night. I checked my wrist watch: 6:30 pm. The boat's clock read 10:30 pm – a four hour difference. But, my actual time aboard their ship could only have been a half-hour or hour at most. A space-time anomaly, indeed.

Fortunately, Jonathan seemed perfectly normal as he released the jib sheet and checked the wind and sails.

"The wind has shifted entirely around the compass."

And, it had. The good old compass was working again. But, we were now heading downwind, rather than on the upwind tack we'd been on when the "storm" enveloped us. Somewhat confused, we unreefed and let out the mainsail and went down wind on a new course.

I looked closely at the compass and around at the distant island lights and realized we were no longer east of Virgin Gorda nor south of Anegada, as we had been when Ebe's ship overtook us.

As Jonathan came up the companion way, I pointed out that we had sailed back into Sir Francis Drake Channel during the storm. The wind had not shifted; our boat had somehow been turned entirely around and propelled several miles through challenging waters without our knowledge or control.

"Well, thank goodness the wind shift is all the storm did. It never really hit us – just kept us in a fog bank," I explained to Jonathan. "We must have lost track of time and our true position in the fog.

"Worse, we forgot to eat dinner! I think we can relax now and get some food."

I needed a drink.

Jonathan went below to get cheese, bread and salami, never mentioning the time of night or the fact that for him the evening had changed instantly from cloudy, fog-bound sunset to full darkness.

Fortunately, we had a fair wind, following sea and were

well on our way home. We were passing Tortola's Beef Island airport to starboard and the small isle of Dead Man's Chest to port.

Soon, we saw the low lights of Peter Island Resort off our port bow, just beyond the Dead Man. I made an instant decision. We radioed the Peter Island harbor master and found they had several empty moorings. Just what a doctor would order for us. I was feeling somewhat light headed and deeply fatigued.

Jonathan went to the bowsprit with our spotlight as we passed through Peter's narrow harbor entrance and found a mooring as close to the beach as our draught would allow. The water lapping on the star-lit beach was clearly audible.

"Jonathan, we're going ashore to their pool-side bar. We've earned a few beers."

"I won't say no. I've never been here before. Looks nice."

He'd spent many of his 20 plus years on St. John – just a few miles and an easy sail away, but had never been to Peter Island Resort. An artificial socio-economic barrier and resource misallocation had prevented it, Ebe might say.

Setting aside the social and political implications, we rowed to the dock and were greeted graciously by the harbor master. We paid our mooring fee.

I was glad to be on solid ground as we walked through the discreetly illuminated, finely manicured gardens and passed through a stone archway into the open air lobby. We walked past the check-in and concierge desks, saying "good evening" to everyone and continued out through another arch onto a wide stone patio.

A table set to the side offered a silver tea service, chilled water, lemons and English biscuits. We each had some water. Then, onward to the mahogany bar, located at the edge of a large infinity pool surrounded by Royal Palms. It overlooked Sir Francis Drake Channel and the distant lights of Tortola on the other side.

British tourists, elegantly attired – as appropriate for an evening in the British Virgin Islands at one of the Caribbean's best resorts – moved their bar stools to make room for us, ignoring our bedraggled appearance.

Clearly, we were steerage passengers amidst First Class. But, the Brits were jolly enough. All equal at the bar, eh chappie?

I texted Mary that all was well; that we'd be home about noon the next day.

Jonathan and I started with shots of Pusser's to commemorate Lord Claymore's departure for more southern latitudes, and then settled in with Virgin Islands mango blended beer. Jonathan turned to me.

"So we never did make it to the Trough?"

"Well, we got close enough and into deep enough water to get the anomalous instrument readings I was looking for."

Anomalous readings and then some.

"We accomplished what we set out to do," I assured him.

Instinctively, I did not tell Jonathan the full truth about our adventure. Soon, I would have to decide whether to tell the Navy and Mary.

Several beers later, we rowed back to the *Perseverance*, shakily climbed up her side and bedded down. As I looked up from my bunk at the stars through the open foredeck hatch, I thought of the "cosmic consciousness" – that world-wide interconnected network of thoughts and souls described by turn of the 20th century philosophers like Carl Jung. Ebe seemed to be saying the consciousness network is universal and forms, or is part of, a higher Spirit that pervades the universe – God, if you will.

11 THE DEBRIEFING

"And, I alone survived to tell thee."

— Herman Melville's character Ishmael, sole survivor
of the sinking of the vessel Pequod by the great white
whale Moby Dick.

"A bad day at sea is better than a good day in an office," Cap Elliot Hooper likes to say aboard his three-master, *The Silver Cloud,* back in Coral Bay. This was not a good day in an office.

I sat before the massive oak desk of Rear Admiral Willis Turner, head of the Office of Naval Intelligence. An armed marine stood legs spread inside the closed door. A camera beamed down from a corner of the ceiling.

Shivering in a brown linen suit – purchased in Charlotte Amalie for West Indian use – I was still damp from the cold rain and sleet of a November day in D.C. Ship models in glass cases and suitable seascape oil paintings adorned the wood paneled office. But, why didn't they have the heat set higher? A government budget stricture, probably.

"I'm Willis Turner. I run naval intelligence. I know who you are."

I nervously waited for the gray haired, square shouldered stone-faced Admiral to continue. He wore gray-blue camouflaged fatigues, though I doubted he'd see combat that day.

"In case you're wondering, the video cam is turned off. Just you and me."

He'd noticed my glance at the camera as I squirmed in my seat.

"This is not an inquisition, professor."

True, thumb screws and hypodermic needles were not arrayed on his vast desk. But, they were no doubt available, if required.

"Please be at ease and proceed with any opening comments."

"Yes, sir," I automatically responded. "First, as I told Lieutenant Taft and make clear in my written report, I have used pseudonyms for the civilian sources of my information on Sergeant Baskins' experiences and the Norman Island UFO.

"I did so for a good reason. These are all independent-minded people. They're instinctively suspicious of politics, police and the military. They understood we were speaking as friends or in my academic capacity. Frankly, they'd rather face a hurricane than sit in this chair. You must understand, I will not give you the names of my sources."

"I understand completely. The thoroughness of your research and obvious credibility of your reporting makes further interviews unnecessary."

To say I was surprised by his reasonable response is an understatement. I'd had visions of men in black invading St. John in unmarked vans filled with electronics supported by black helicopters.

The Admiral continued, "I simply want you to understand our position. The Navy has been shut-out of most of the U.S. government-funded investigation of these phenomena. In recent years, when courageous naval officers or seaman actually did report sightings, men from civilian security services took their statements, warned them in no uncertain terms to keep quiet and that is the last we heard of it. So, to avoid such unpleasantness – that is totally outside our chain of command and inexcusable – we have discouraged our officers from making formal statements. Internally, we do pay attention, however."

His teeth clenched and his age-spotted, sun-blotched hands, resting on his desk became fists as he continued explaining his position.

"But, make no mistake. Like you and the public, since the days of Admirals Hillenkoetter and Fahrney, we have largely been kept in the dark about what the security agencies are doing and what they know. We don't like it.

"I personally ordered Lt. Taft to retain your services so that *we* would – how should I put this – be researching the matter of Sergeant Baskins under the radar of civilian security services. And, of course, we can at any time disavow any knowledge of, or connection with, your work. You are merely an historian who wrote a story on the missile crisis for the Institute Press – an historian with an over-active imagination, at that."

A comforting thought should any civilian operatives drop by my home unannounced for a chat. That would piss off Mary, who likes advance notice. But, as a mere historian, why should anyone care what I say or do?

"That being said, my colleagues and I deeply appreciate your work."

He chuckled to himself as he continued, "It might interest you to know that when "Ebe" told you that was his name, he was making an inside joke. In top intelligence circles, EBE is an acronym for Extraterrestrial Biological Entity. He knew that. Even we in the Navy are aware they exist, but have been excluded from the necessary investigative and policy-making processes required to understand these beings and adequately and responsibly respond to their presence."

By responding to these beings, did he mean the extraterrestrials or civilian security services?

"I have one very important question for you. You are one of the very few credible humans who have met face-to-face with Ebe. Certainly, you're the first I've talked to. Do you believe what he told you about their policy of non-interference?"

"Yes, I do," I replied, "it makes perfect sense and explains why, after a half-century, he, his people and space craft remain a mysterious enigma to the vast majority of humans on Earth. I have no doubt that should they wish to intercede overtly into our affairs, they could do so and do so decisively. The fact that they have not – even during the days of the Cold War and the U.S.-Soviet preparations for earthlings' mutually-assured destruction – proves the point, in my view. I think Ebe and his Viking cousins are anonymous friends of this planet."

"Well said. Between us, I agree. Others may not. But, what about other extraterrestrial species who might be visiting? What's their agenda? How do we distinguish between friend and potential foe?

"That is why we – the Navy, the ONI - must get back in the loop on this. We must reassert our authority as the nation's senior intelligence organization," the Admiral declared sternly.

"Did you know that? That we're the oldest intelligence agency? We were established in 1882 to obtain and analyze vital scientific and geopolitical information for the benefit of the United States government.

"Then and now, the Navy's multi-disciplinary, scientific knowledge, our behavioral know-how and diplomatic training is unsurpassed on Earth. We know how to command thousands of personnel operating the most sophisticated, technologically advanced machines on Earth. And, we drive them in the air, sea and under the sea all over this planet – everywhere. That makes us eminently qualified to evaluate the data on UFOs and USOs and communicate effectively with them.

"My fear is that civilian intelligence services and their private contractor clients are exerting undue and unhealthy control over an area of inquiry of immense importance to the U.S. government and every other government on this planet."

The Admiral's astonishing statement reminded me of President Eisenhower's famous warning about the growing influence in Washington of the military industrial complex.

"That is very interesting, Sir. I have no doubt you are correct."

The Admiral leaned forward with a fierce expression.

"You're damn right, I'm correct! Why, a naval officer was standing alongside Manhattan Project Director Robert Oppenheimer and military project commander General Leslie Groves in the bunker closest to ground zero the day the first atomic bomb was tested in the New Mexico desert.

"For us to now be shut out of operations of even more importance is not only unacceptable, but dangerous to our national security. We have the knowledge and perspective to avoid mistakes – costly, tragic mistakes in this critical matter.

"This is especially true of that other ET species, the Grays, Ebe referred to. But, I can say no more on that matter.

"The point is, we cannot leave these epic developments in the hands of for-profit contractors and their pet civilian agencies! They'd sell us all out in a minute, if the price was right. They simply cannot be trusted with the future of Earth!"

The Admiral sat back in his chair and exhaled, letting out steam. I saw an opening here to raise my key question.

"Sir, it was my hope that this research project might help lead to more open inquiry into these phenomena –

perhaps, with the President in the lead."

"Yes. Those are also the long-term aspirations of our young Turks like Lt. Taft. Aspirations that I share. I will see to it that a summary of your research into Gunny Baskins' death and encounter with Ebe is included in the President's daily intelligence report – regardless of any objections from the Director of National Intelligence or other civilians.

"The Chief of Naval Operations still has some pull in this town. Don't worry about your identity or that of your sources being compromised. We will refer to you all with code names and the CNO will give the highest assurances to the President that this report is authentic. With luck the CNO and I may get a separate private meeting with him and can go over all of it."

Like Ebe, the Admiral was telling me not to worry. That was somewhat worrisome.

"Your research regarding Caribbean trenches gives ONI an opening. The fly boys and civilians don't have deep sea submersibles and support craft in their tool chests. Our Southern Command has more than enough assets to do the job – any job. We are already working to restore a Caribbean fleet for drug interdiction and other duties. This provides further 'ammo' to continue that build-up."

"Glad to hear that, sir."

"Yes . . . well, back to the business at-hand. Because of your exposure to Ebe and immersion in his vessel's environment, you will have a thorough physical and psychological examination – blood tests, cat scans, brain MRI, those sorts of things. Once the examinations are completed, you will be free to return home at our expense, of course."

He now eyed me as though gazing upon an Annapolis midshipman with too many demerits.

"However, I must remind you of your confidentiality agreement. We take that to be an oath of silence and we take oaths extremely seriously in this service.'

I thought about the Patriot Act and provisions enabling American citizens suspected of being terrorists – or enemies of the state? security risks? – to be dealt with extra-judicially. No habeas corpus, no recourse. Locked-up and put away. Or, worse.

"I understand entirely, Sir."

With a stone, cold expression he continued, "Very good, professor. Now, Lt. Taft is waiting outside this office to take you directly to Bethesda Naval Hospital. With any luck, you will be back on your island within three days."

The Admiral smiled, rose and offered his hand.

"Please accept my personal thanks and that of the Navy for your outstanding investigation. We do not forget our friends. Don't you forget your oath."

We shook hands and I was out of there. True to his word, after three days of cat scans, blood work, psych tests, urine and feces sampling, proctologic examination, lung x-rays and more, I sat in First Class on a plane taxiing out to a Dulles runway to take me back to St. Thomas and warmth.

Angrily, I thought of the hypnosis session they had put me through. I had sat on a chair in a darkened room with a shrink, with one way windows for observers and video cameras documenting it all. The tape and transcript was immediately classified so that not even I could hear or read what I had said!

Looking out the window at the drizzle and fog I thought about how I had arrived in Washington, D.C.. This was a much, much better way to travel.

Just five days earlier, after agonizing over whether to tell the Navy about my visit with Ebe, I'd e-mailed my final and complete report to Lt. Taft. Best to let responsible people know the truth, I had concluded. Also, I realized that Ebe had told me everything with fore-knowledge that I was about to write a report to the Navy.

Did he want them to know? If so, why?

Within 24 hours of receiving said report, Lt. Taft had arrived unannounced at my door on St. John with a Marine escort. We drove to the helipad at the island medical center where we boarded a Sea Stallion helicopter that flew us to the Naval Air Station at Roosevelt Roads on Puerto Rico. Upon landing, a Navy jet flew us immediately to Andrews Air Force Base in D.C., where a dark-windowed blue Ford sedan took us directly from the tarmac to ONI headquarters inside the Beltway in Suitland, Maryland.

Now, as the stewardess offered drinks and snacks to prepare First Classers for the rigors of take-off, I thought about the difficult discussion at home before Lt. Taft had arrived.

Mary was furious about my extraterrestrial adventure, reminding me of her admonition years earlier that nothing good would come of all this. She was rightly scared and reminded me we couldn't risk anything more. John's disability provided more than enough chaos in our lives.

When Lt. Taft came to our door, she thoroughly questioned him on what was to happen next. At her suggestion, I had put on my linen suit and tie.

Mary also insisted we provide my crewman Jonathan with a medical exam and found the perfect pretext. His 25th birthday was coming up. We had long wished for him to crew on our boat as needed and, knowing he had no health insurance, Mary concocted a story that as a birthday present – and condition of employment – we were giving him a complete examination and a dinner for two for him and a friend at a restaurant of his choice on St. Thomas.

She was a born politician – able to move people in the direction she wished.

As the stewardess handed me a beer, I thought about questions I should have asked the Admiral. A summary of my report being included in the daily intelligence briefing suggests the President must already have some level of knowledge of the truth about UFOs.

How much had he been told by the civilian services? How much did they and their contractor clients think this President needed to know? As little as possible, no doubt. The less a President knows, the more freely interested parties can operate with little or no accountability.

And, what next for the Puerto Rico Trench and Virgin Islands? Would Admiral Turner lead a fleet of deep-sea submersibles and support vessels into our quiet sea? Would our sea turtles, dolphins and whales be harmed by various radars, sonars and who knows what other technologies that would be unleashed as the Admiral swept trenches and troughs?

I guessed we would find out.

As the aluminum tube in which I comfortably sat hurtled down the runway and up into dark clouds – drizzle now running horizontally across the cabin windows – I thought about Ebe and his prediction we would meet again. How would *he* react to Navy involvement? Would he be pleased?

12 MEN IN SUITS

"Don't you get the idea I'm one of those God damn radicals. Don't get the idea I'm knocking the American system."

— attributed to Chicago gangster Al Capone in the 1920s

It didn't take long for things to get back to normal. Across the islands, palms in public squares were being wrapped in white Christmas lights. Steel band orchestras and church choirs were practicing the music of the season.

From makeshift wooden stalls along the roads, West Indian families were selling homemade guava berry wine and other traditional holiday delicacies. The wine was fermented from locally grown berries, with just the right amount of aged rum added to ensure good cheer.

I was finished with the Baskins assignment and thankfully preparing for a *normal* Spring semester. It was a shock, then, when Dean Michael O'Bannon called me to come immediately to his office. It was located in one of the old senior Naval officer's houses up the hill from the faculty cubicles in former enlisted men's barracks.

"Please, sit down Thayer," the Dean said, motioning to one of his upholstered chairs in front of his well-varnished hard wood desk. Displayed on the wall were the coat of arms of the University of Massachusetts – his alma mater – and various degrees. Pushing up his gold-rimmed glasses, he picked up an official looking piece of paper.

"Do you know what this is?" he asked, waving the paper back and forth above his brown hair. This was his first job as a college dean and he loved playing the part.

"No idea, Michael. What is it?

"It arrived by certified, overnight mail from a Homeland Security Department post box in Washington, D.C. It is called a National Security Letter and orders me to provide them all paper work – no matter how trivial – concerning one of our history professors – one Thayer Harris, Ph.D. It also orders me to give them full access to our e-mail system, payroll, budget, phone and tax records regarding said professor."[1]

He leaned forward and looked me in the eye.

"Now here's where it gets real interesting. I am prohibited from telling anyone – you, my wife, anyone – about this on pain of myself being prosecuted under some provision of the Patriot Act."

He leaned back in his chair and looked at the ceiling fan before continuing.

'Now, I taught American literature before I became an administrator. I'm certainly no lawyer. But, I thought the government needed a warrant to search private property and that we had free speech – even in a U.S. Territory."

He looked back at me.

"Setting all that aside, for a moment, this whole matter begs one question: what the hell have you been doing, Professor?"

To say I was surprised by this development understated my reaction. It took a few moments to respond while I weighed my vow of silence to Admiral Turner against the requirements of loyalty to employer and the code of academic freedom. Ultimately, though, the Admiral might be able to fix this.

"Well, Michael, I cannot imagine what this is all about. The only connection I've had with the government was tangential – that article I wrote for the Annapolis Institute Proceedings journal on the Cuban Missile Crisis. Maybe that pissed off someone at the Pentagon, though I can't imagine why. Nothing at all in there went beyond the public record including DOD's own reports. There was no mention of the Middle East, terrorists or holy wars . . . You've seen it. What do you think?"

"I agree, there is nothing particularly controversial in the piece. Very little new ground, actually. But, well-documented and quite readable."

"Well, there you are. And, I didn't even use any college resources in my research. This security nonsense must be some horrible mistake. What do we do?"

"Since you are not supposed to even know about this, you should do nothing. But, I am going to discuss these outrageous demands with our school counsel before proceeding in any direction. Meanwhile, I suggest you be very circumspect in e-mails and phone calls from this hour forward."

"Thanks for alerting me to all this. I will be circumspect, although I can't imagine what could be in my e-mails – no words or phrases that would catch the eye of a National Security Agency computer in all their vacuuming, filtering and scanning – or whatever the hell they do to everyone's e-mails and phone conversations."

"Well, be that as it may, please be particularly careful, and don't tell anyone about this. We certainly can't have it leaked to the media that this institution is under some kind of national security investigation. I'll let you know what our lawyer says."

Needless to say, I was distracted for the rest of the day. First, I thought of using a pay phone to call Lieutenant

Taft. But, in today's world, where can you even find a pay phone? No, I would wait until I got home and use the land line – at least that wouldn't get the college in trouble. And, phone calls and e-mails with Taft were "secure" – encrypted or something – right?

When I got home I didn't tell Mary, preferring to learn the truth first. The hours dragged on as I waited to make the call. Finally, after dinner and multiple calming drinks while watching the sunset, I got the Lieutenant on the line. After describing what happened, I waited for his response.

"Well, Dr. Harris, someone – either working for the White House National Security Adviser or, possibly, on the Joint Chiefs' staff, must have tipped-off Homeland Security about both the UFO incident and our anonymous source. We certainly did not name you, and I can assure you that Admiral Turner and everyone at ONI is trustworthy. We know. Their work and communications are monitored."

"That's all great, but what do I do now? Shit, could I be audited by the IRS?"

"That would be the least of your worries. I will discuss this immediately with the Admiral and we will figure out how to kill Homeland's investigation before it gets started. And, we will plug the leak. Meanwhile, keep cool and stick to your story about the Cuba article. You handled your dean perfectly. We will not abandon you on the field of honor, doctor. The Navy has your back."

"Sounds good. Thanks."

"No, thank you, sir. Keep me informed."

That made me feel much better. But, I still did not tell Mary.

Things went back to some semblance of normalcy for a few days. We even went sailing the next weekend – over to Soper's Hole on Tortola's West End, where we moored for the night and enjoyed Shepherd's Pie at Pusser's Pub. I admired the historic Royal Navy photos, prints and artifacts on display.

We sat near a young couple visiting from Birmingham, U.K. Recognizing us as weathered locals, after a few painkillers they asked us questions. It was their first visit to the islands.

That gave me an opening to tell them about Joost Van Dyke, the Dutch privateer (some say pirate) and slave trader, who, in the early 1600s, founded the first village on Tortola right there at Soper's Hole. It was a perfect anchorage, protected from weather and the eyes of any Spanish naval vessels.

Van Dyke's enterprises flourished too well. They eventually attracted the interest of the Spanish who, in a last effort to reassert their original claim to the islands, invaded and occupied Tortola. Joost and his cadre escaped to St. Thomas, already home to several comrades of the brotherhood of buccaneers. There were so many gentlemen adventurers in St. Thomas harbor that the Spanish dared not attack that island. And, St John was then a mountainous wilderness – a no-man's land of little commercial value.

Today, Joost's Soper's Hole settlement is called West End and Van Dyke is memorialized by the British island that bears his name. With its two beach bars – the Soggy Dollar and Foxy's – and a population of about 200, Jost van Dyke, is a popular sailors' destination. Just sail up, anchor close to the beach, and wade in to the bar. Joost would approve.

On the way to Jost van Dyke island from Soper's Hole, to the starboard one passes Thatch Island Cut, which separates Tortola from the uninhabited – though green and inviting – Great Thatch and Little Thatch islands. The Cut and islands are named after Blackbeard (who apparently used his alternate surname Thatch on Tortola).

Despite the pleasant get-away, the following Monday I was jittery and unsettled when I arrived at my office. I realized I was still in some kind of serious legal jeopardy and had not told Mary. Yet, this could have a major impact on our lives.

At about 11 a.m., Dean O'Bannon asked me to come up for another talk. The college attorney, Tom Hatcher, was seated in one of the chairs across from the dean when I walked in.

"Well, Thayer, we have some very interesting and, if I may say so, Orwellian news on the legal front. Why don't you explain, Tom?"

Tom was a thin, balding man in his forties, wearing pressed chinos and a blue sport jacket. He looked at me through thick, horn-rimmed glasses.

"Well, here's what I found. Section 505 of the Patriot Act expanded the power of U.S. security agencies to issue these so-called National Security Letters, which, without warrant, entitles the issuing agency to obtain the telephone, e-mail, financial, credit and other records pertaining to the target – in this case, you, professor. The recipient of such a Letter is prohibited from disclosing that they received the letter."

"That's amazing," I said. "How can they do that?"

"Interestingly, the amended Patriot Act does allow a Letter recipient to challenge the demands in a U.S. Court. But, in the few cases on record in which such challenges have been made, the government provided the judge with secret evidence – so secret it was withheld from the plaintiff, the Letter recipient bringing the challenge – and his or her attorney. Because the plaintiff could not answer whatever was secretly alleged in the new evidence, the judge dismissed the plaintiff's case, and the legality of the Security Letter was upheld."

"Which book is more apropos for this occasion – *1984* or *Catch-22*?"

"Both, I would say," the dean interjected.

"So, where does that leave us?"

Tom answered for the dean.

"I will assist Dean O'Bannon in drafting a suitable reply. We will explain that the college wishes to cooperate fully, but will need Homeland Security's guidance with respect to how to proceed. It will take time for them to respond and meanwhile, we do nothing. When they finally do respond, we take our time complying. This is too important to rush. In other words, we appear to be loyally following orders, but actually drag our feet and buy time."

"Thank you counselor," Dean O'Bannon said, turning from Tom to me.

"You see, Thayer, we can't have the college targeted with any extra-judicial penalties for not complying. So, we will buy the time needed to consult our Congressional delegate. Although she does not have a vote in Congress, she is a Member of the Congressional Black Caucus, which has considerable clout. They will not be amused that a college serving a mostly African-American community on U.S. soil is being harassed by the national security complex. They know all about that. And our governor knows the President."

"Sounds like a great strategy," I replied enthusiastically.

I felt much better on the ferry ride back to St. John that evening. It wasn't until I got off at the dock that I noticed two particularly clean-cut men, aged 30 something or early forties, walking down the gangway several people behind me. They were actually wearing suits – blue, cheap ones; probably, Chinese spun polyester purchased at BaseMart, but suits nevertheless. White shirts, bland ties and skin head hair styles rounded out the picture. I thought back to Nurse Swank's comment about how odd the men in suits looked jumping out of the helicopter on tropical Grenada.

Were they salesmen? Fundamentalist missionaries? Neither was likely.

I stepped inside one of the tourist trinket shops right off the pier, hid behind some sun dresses in the window and watched. Carrying small duffle bags as luggage, they walked past the shops and up the narrow street. I followed.

Unusual for men just off the ferry, they walked right

past Woody's bar with its scantily clad waitresses serving sidewalk tables. They continued onward and turned into the Tamarind Inn, a reasonably priced small hotel. Probably getting a room there with the government's modest per diem.

I'd seen enough and quickly walked to where Mary had parked the car in the shade waiting to give me a ride home from the pier. When we got home and over drinks, I filled her in on the letter, the dean's plan and my conversation with Lieutenant Taft. I mentioned the two unlikely tourists who had come over on the ferry.

Mary was not pleased by these developments, to say the least. I realized she was correct that my activities could put John and her in danger.

That night, while reading before bed, I had a feeling I'd be learning more about the ever-vigilant civilian national security apparatus.

Sure enough the next morning the two suits came to the door. Fortunately, Mary and John were already out for the day.

"Dr. Harris, we are Homeland Security agents and would appreciate speaking with you," the taller, slightly older looking of the pair said as they pulled out leather wallet-like things with dangling gold badges.

"Well, you know, this isn't the best time. I'm trying to get ready for work."

The spokesman continued with a pained look, "Sir, I am afraid this can't wait. We've come a long way to speak with you."

"Yes, I didn't think you were from around here," I replied, motioning them to chairs out on our porch. I didn't want them inside our house.

Once seated and after they declined my offer of coffee, I asked what I could do for them.

"We want to know why you were in Washington a few weeks ago."

"If you must know, I have friends and colleagues there

from my university days. But, I fail to see how that is of interest to the Homeland Security Department."

With a gotcha kind of smile, the older agent continued.

"You see, sir, you flew back from D.C. on a commercial airline. But, there is no record of your leaving St. Thomas on an airline."

Damn that airport customs and immigration check-in! Since when does an American citizen have to show a passport and go through customs to move from one part of the U.S. to another? What's next? Customs stops for people traveling between New York and Connecticut?

But, that was a debate for another day. Reality is reality. I thought quickly about how to respond.

"Well, you see, I hitched a ride on a friend's private plane. We must have forgotten to show our identity papers to the Gestapo before traveling from U.S. soil to U.S. soil."

With the same self-satisfied smile, he shot back.

"No need to be sarcastic, sir. Just give us the name of your friend."

Now, I was getting angry – not only with these nerds, but with Lieutenant Taft – "no need to worry, if you stick with the protocol."

"Look, I don't know why you are asking me any questions or why I'm answering. Why are you here on my property?"

Smiley continued, while his younger associated stared vacantly, "Sir, we have reason to believe you have been involved in activities affecting the national security of the United States. Specifically, and I quote from the Patriot Act, we think you participated in 'an event designated under section 3056(e) of Title 18 as a special event of national significance'. We have authority to take into custody without warrant any individual who may have committed a crime related to, or who may be a material witness to, such an event of national significance."

"I don't recall any terrorist acts or any other national

emergency when I was in D.C. or here on the islands. What event are you talking about, anyway?"

"We believe you know. But, I'll spell it out. We think you aided and abetted non-resident aliens in a scheme to violate the territorial waters of the United States. Conspiring with illegals to violate U.S. sovereignty may in and of itself constitute a special event of national significance."

Holy shit! Now, I was getting scared. Did these clowns know about Ebe? Then I realized they couldn't; too far down the totem pole to know much. They were sent by someone else to intimidate me while somebody analyzed the data they expected to extract from the college. Keep cool like Taft told you, I said to myself. Aloud, I said, "Do you mean to say I somehow aided Haitian boat people or other refugees trying to come ashore? That does happen here sometimes, but I've never been involved."

"No sir, these are non-resident illegals of a different kind."

Could he possibly know? Out of the question. He was simply told what to ask.

"Well, I haven't seen any illegals of any kind."

"Sir, getting back to your Gestapo slur. You must agree that it is quite possible – easy in fact – for people without lawful visas and no background checks to step on U.S. soil in these islands. What if people with criminal or terrorist intentions came ashore here or in Puerto Rico, for that matter, and then waltzed over to the airport and got on a plane to New York or Washington, D.C.? That's why we have a customs and immigration check here, Professor.

"And, anyone assisting such illegals is violating federal law."

"Well, now that you explain it, I can appreciate that. Frankly, I have always been pleased to see the Customs and Immigration and Coast Guard patrols of our islands. And, I'm as patriotic as the next guy. Did you see the American flag above our door? Our boat flies the flag, also. But, I have had nothing to do with any illegal aliens of any persuasion."

Smiley became edgy.

"Give us the name of the friend who flew you to D.C. and the date you departed."

"That's none of your business. No crime was committed. Now, if you'll excuse me, I must get ready and go to work."

Edgy leaned toward me.

"We could arrest you right now on suspicion of involvement in a significant event. You would be wise to answer our questions here and now."

"You can arrest me, if you wish. But, I have no idea what you're talking about."

Edgy shot back.

"We will be watching you. This is a small island. You can't go anywhere without our knowing it. And, we will be talking with you again."

"I'm a lot more familiar with this island's geography than you are. If it would aid homeland security, my wife could arrange a tour for you. We have friends who are National Park rangers who actually have jurisdiction over two-thirds of this island."

I was becoming incensed and a bit self-righteous.

"And, as you say, this is a small island and community. I will be contacting our Congressional Delegate and the governor about your threats. If you wish to speak with me again, call in-advance so I can have an attorney present."

"Ha! You can't afford one." Edgy had turned Smiley, again.

He was right, of course. We had spent the first Annapolis Institute check on fixing up the house and boat and had little or nothing in reserve. But, how did he know that?

"I see I struck a nerve, Professor," Smiley said. "You just watch your step, sir."

Feeling like I was back in high school dealing with a

bully, I replied immediately.

"No, you watch your step as you climb back up our walkway, get into your car and leave my property."

I watched as they climbed the stone stairs and got into their rented, red Chevy Spark – barely big enough for them to climb into. It was probably the only vehicle they could find on short notice. Jeeps are the first rentals to be snapped up. They wouldn't win many car chases on these mountain roads with that, although they'd get great gas mileage.

As soon as they were out of sight, I phoned Lieutenant Taft and told him of the visitation.

"We'll take care of this right quick," he said angrily.

Eventually, I made it to my office and stared at the 18th century wall map of the Danish West Indies, thinking about the incredible chain of events since Taft had sat in that room only a couple months ago.

Now, I was in legal jeopardy. I thought about my older son, Samuel. He was an attorney. Idealistic and inspired, Sam was working his butt off as a second year associate at a large consumer law firm in Los Angeles. Should I call him?

I answered my own question immediately. No. The distraction and potential notoriety if this national security case went public would not help his career. Consumer lawyers already had the odds and legal playing field stacked against them.

Putting those thoughts aside, I found some busy work to occupy my mind.

When I returned home that evening, I explained the meeting with the agents to Mary.

"You mean they came to our home? That's unacceptable. This must end now!"

"Lieutenant Taft is on it."

The next morning, the boys in their Spark were waiting out on the road as Mary drove me to the ferry. They followed us at a distance, but it was impossible to be subtle in that car on our nearly empty mountain roads. I heard a loud bang. They had bottomed-out on a pot hole, as they tried to navigate a steep, hair pin curve on the descent down to Cruz Bay. Smiley must be Edgy, again.

"I hope those guys didn't wreck the suspension," I commented to Mary. "Who rents those cars?"

"You mean the Spark? Must be Rafael's Rentals in Cruz Bay."

I knew she would know.

"If you see Raf, please tell him to look over that car very, very closely when they turn it in."

"Be happy to, and I'll tell him the government is paying."

Mary dropped me off at the dock as usual. It being the 7 a.m. ferry, there were few tourists, so Twiddledee and Twiddledum stood out in their suits as they bought their tickets without saying good morning to the West Indian lady in the booth. In retaliation, she feigned not to understand where they wanted to go and then took forever giving them change and their tickets. Woe be to those who do not say 'good morning' or 'good day' to Islanders in shops and other facilities.

When they finally got their tickets, the agents found seats in the far back of the terminal, as though they were not already the focus of everyone's furtive looks – mostly, dirty looks, at that.

"Who are those assholes?" PC Matt asked as I sat next to him up front.

"Don't really know," I replied. "But they sure look like salesmen or fundamentalist missionaries."

He laughed. On the ferry I lost sight of them and chatted with PC, catching up on island and family news during the ride to St. Thomas.

As we pulled into the Red Hook dock, I saw a half-dozen Virgin Island Police Department officers hanging around the gate, waiting. Instinctively, I thought: "Fuck, what now?"

But, when the gate opened, the suits were among the first off the gangway. PC and I were still on deck, waiting for everyone else to debark to avoid the crush. At the railing we watched the VIPD officers – who had by then moved in front of the gate – stop the Homeland agents and pull them to the side, out of the stream of passengers.

Outnumbered and overwhelmed, we could see Edgy and his mute side kick angrily flashing their IDs and arguing with the police. But, arrogance – no matter who you are – gets you nowhere down here. The police simply ignored whatever they were saying, as they led them – using strong arms, as necessary – into the terminal.

PC and I watched the circus disappear.

"Fascinating," I commented. "Maybe they were soliciting donations for their sect without a license."

"Or worse; soliciting donations and not sharing the take."

"Don't be cynical, PC."

As we entered the terminal, there was no sign of agents or police; but, we could see several police cars quickly leaving the parking lot as we walked to catch a dollar safari taxi along the road. The taxis, pick-up trucks with extended beds with benches and parasol tops, were open-sided. They picked-up and dropped-off passengers at regular stops and took them anywhere along their St. Thomas circuit for two dollars. I was going to work near the end of their route, while PC had gotten out in front of Independent Boatyard, where he was working on expanding their Wi-Fi service.

As the taxi drove along Charlotte Amalie's harbor, I admired the moored sailboats, as usual. But, at the far end of the bay, at the old Navy dock (turned cruise ship dock), next to Crown Bay Marina, sat a large battleship-gray ship with high sides, many antennas and satellite dishes. On its top deck she had a couple of guns and the kind of rectangular boxes that could house missiles. Marines manned a fence that had been put up to block off the pier.

Guess *M.S. Oasis of the Seas* will have to find another place to park. Naval intelligence and the Marines had arrived!

Later that day, I was called into a meeting with Dean O'Bannon and Tom Hatcher.

It seemed the National Security Letter had been withdrawn with an apology.

That night, when I called Lieutenant Taft to report the good news, he explained.

"Seemed Homeland Undersecretary Chesney had improperly ordered the Letter without cause. And, operating outside the chain of command, Chesney had secretly sent the agents to the V.I. They, in turn, had not properly announced their arrival to the Territorial Department of Homeland Security, the U.S. Attorney's Office in Charlotte Amalie, and other officials. So, they were operating illegally.

"Since they had acted without legal authority in harassing a Territorial resident, the Governor had no alternative but to have them picked up by VIPD, taken to the airport and put on a plane to the mainland. And, those losers had even caused over a thousand dollars in damage to their rental car.

"Meanwhile, in D.C., Secretary of Homeland Security Capuano had been informed by her boss that Chesney's investigation was a non-starter and was to halt immediately."

"You mean the President?"

"That's her boss. And, Secretary Capuano had no knowledge of Chesney's actions and was very annoyed, to say the least."

"That's really something."

"I am directed by Admiral Turner to offer his sincerest apology for the inconvenience and the worry the investigation must have caused. He appreciates that you did not reveal your connection to us to anyone. In fact, in coming days, the Navy will be conducting some scientific studies of the Puerto Rico and Grenada trenches. We would like to be able to call upon you for some additional consulting work, if you are willing to continue working with us."

"Sounds exciting. But, what about other civilian security agencies? How will you keep them out?"

"As cover, we've brought in scientists from the National Oceanic and Atmospheric Administration and National Geographic. We're positioning the trough explorations as a study of trench life and a hunt for rare minerals of commercial value. Most of them will actually be engaged in that work. They won't even know what we're really looking for. So, we should be okay. No worries."

I'd heard that before. I wished these guys would send Mary flowers as a token of friendship. She was not going to like my continuing to work for these folks.

After I'd hung-up from Taft, I went online and looked up this Undersecretary Chesney.

He had spent several years as a Wall Street lawyer working on behalf of the Masters of the Universe who had concocted derivatives, mortgage-backed securities and other inventions to advance Western civilization. In so-doing, he would have become accustomed to little or no accountability to regulators or the public.

After his years on the Street, Chesney had served as a managing director of Harland Corp., a Houston-based contractor with private combatants for hire, among other services sold to the oil industry and federal government. Harland had made out like bandits during the Iraq and Afghan wars. Again, an environment with little or no accountability.

But, it was Chesney's role as counsel to Yoke Corp. that caught my eye. Yoke was another government contractor – this one rumored to work on black budgeted weapons and aerospace projects that Congress had little or no authority over. Some UFO buffs claim the company helps manage flying saucer-related operations at the shadowy Area 51.

And, the company does work there. As to UFOs? It's anybody's guess.

Based on Chesney's private sector experience selling things to the government, the previous administration had appointed him to Homeland Security. And, as a show of benevolent bi-partisanship, the new President had kept Chesney on there as Undersecretary for Operations. In that role, he had ordered an unauthorized investigation of me.

Although Chesney was apparently momentarily stymied, through his old boy network he could probably call upon the services of Harland's private security agents (unkindly called mercenaries by some) who had proven their zeal during the U.S. occupation of Iraq. Moreover, the Undersecretary's former colleagues were also experts at data and signal acquisition. In short, Harland Corp. offered one-stop shopping for consumers needing for-profit gun men and spy technology.

Not good.

I thought about Admiral Turner's worries about private contractors and their pet agencies gaining control over the most important development in human history: intelligent extraterrestrial life and technologies.

After explaining all this to Mary, she thoughtfully asked what seemed like an irrelevant question.

"Are you aware that Tim and Mia are planning a year-long trip around the world? They will be sailing their yawl and taking their time."

No, I wasn't aware our closest neighbors were planning to circumnavigate the globe in their sailboat. I was envious. Maybe we should leave with them. But, what about our pets?

"No, I didn't know. When do they plan to leave?"

"In two weeks they sail to Antigua, have their boat overhauled and provisioned and then depart from there.

I'm sure I told you about this weeks ago."

"I've been preoccupied," I said defensively. But, I didn't remember hearing about it. Our friends sailing around the world is something I'd definitely have paid attention to.

"That's very exciting. What will they do with their house and pets?"

"That's the point," she said. "They had arranged for an artist friend in Maine to come down and stay in the house; but, Mia just heard that a family illness means their friend can't come, and Mia is beside herself. They already paid a deposit at the Antigua marina to be hauled out and worked on – everything's scheduled."

"Too bad, but how does that affect us?"

"They need a house sitter and it's clear to me from what you say, we need guards."

"But, we can't afford bodyguards; what do you expect me to do? Phone Harland Corp. and see if they're running any specials on personal security?"

"No. I expect you to call your Admiral Turner friend and get us protection. The guards could move in and take care of Mia's house while they're gone. It was the Navy that got you and us into this mess and it's their responsibility to take care of it."

"Brilliant idea! I'll phone Taft immediately."

And, I did. After hearing what I had learned about Chesney's private connections, Taft promised to discuss the matter ASAP with the Admiral.

Later that night we were awakened by a phone call.

"Turner here. I hope I'm not disturbing you," he said as I looked at the clock – 11:00 pm Atlantic time; 10 pm Eastern.

"No, not at all, Admiral. Although we tend to be sunset to sunrise people on the island, I was just reading."

"Well, I wanted to personally apologize for the mix-up with Homeland Security. Taft briefed me earlier this evening on your justifiable concerns about that Chesney fellow. We are going to do all we can to protect you and your family. Some of our best men will be on that job very soon.

"If those mercenaries step one foot on your island, by God they'll wish they hadn't. I promise you that. They'll all be sorry they fucked with the Navy and our friends."

"Thank you so much, Admiral. I really appreciate that and I know my wife will be pleased."

"Our pleasure. Don't worry. Those hired guns are undisciplined and dissolute. Our boys would make mincemeat out of 'em."

The note of relish in his voice was unmistakable. I could visualize him rubbing his sun-blotched hands expectantly.

"That would be great to see, sir."

"Yes, indeedy. Now, don't you worry about a thing. Taft also said you'd be willing to help on the trench explorations. We'll be in touch about that, too. Thank you and good night."

Two days later two Navy Seals – clad in civvies – checked-in to the Tamarind Inn. As far as Tim and Mia knew – and everyone else on-island – these men (surnamed Jones and Smith) had come to open a diving business. They'd be teaching tourists and taking them out on a high speed power boat they'd arrived on. It was now moored in Cruz Bay near the ferry dock.

Providentially, they knew Mary (at least that was the story) and needed a place to live for several months or more. Jones was introduced to Mia as the son of the best friend of one of Mary's aunts. Smith was his pal and business partner.

Mia was delighted two clean-cut looking young men who knew Mary were going to look after the house while they went adventuring. Meanwhile, the men stayed at the Tamarind Inn – another day, another government per diem – and kept an eye on the car and passenger ferries.

Once our new neighbors moved in, at least one of the

Seals would always be at the house, while the other hung-out at Cruz Bay. They actually did start a diving business, though not a very successful one. They only worked a couple of days a week and spent a lot of time hanging out down town watching things and nursing drinks at popular bars.

Like the Admiral, I almost hoped Chesney's mercenaries did show-up.

We didn't have long to wait.

13 HIGH NOON ON CORAL BAY

"You see, my mule doesn't like people laughing. He gets the crazy idea that you're laughing at him. Now, if you apologize – like I know you're going to – I might convince him you really didn't mean it."

— Clint Eastwood's lines when his character enters a
Wild West town in the movie *Fist Full of Dollars* and
outlaws laugh at him because he's riding a mule. The bad
guys didn't apologize to the mule and paid for their
mistake.

Although we were now neighbors, we had little overt contact with Mr. Jones and Mr. Smith. The less contact we had, the better they could do their jobs of roleplaying. One afternoon, after picking up the mail and navigating the central round about in Cruz Bay, I spotted Jones hitchhiking in front of the Dolphin Market. I stopped, as I usually do.

"Where you heading?" I asked through the open window.

"Coral Bay," he said.

"Hop in, I'm going out there to check on my boat."

Jones got in the passenger side. As usual, he was wearing multi-pocketed shorts and a short-sleeved denim work shirt. Well-toned muscles protruded from what was visible of his arms and legs. His short-cropped hair was brown, with just a hint of grey at the temples. Early forties?

He carried a heavy looking South American-style woven bag over his shoulder. I hoped it carried armaments.

"What's up?"

"We believe they're here. Two guys in their mid-thirties of average height. One, brown haired, with an oriental dragon tattooed on his right forearm; the other, a bulked-up bleach blonde wearing wrap-around sun glasses. Checked into the Westin yesterday afternoon with a couple of heavy bags – probably using a corporate credit card with the charges heavily marked up and buried in an invoice to Uncle Sam."

"Bastards! What are we going to do?"

"First, we watch them. I saw them arrive, tailed them to the Westin and then to the Virgin Island Brewers' Tap Room. They sat at a table; I sat at the bar, but could watch them in the mirror. Blondie took off his glasses long enough for me to get a good picture with my smart phone. I'd already gotten a couple good shots of Dragon Boy; emailed all of them to ONI and they'll run them through DOD contractor data bases, looking for a match.

"But, I'd recognize their species of animal, anywhere."

"That's good to know. What's next?"

"They will be looking around, getting a feel for the island; checking out secluded places along the roads for ambushes, and there's no shortage of them."

He must have seen me flinch.

"By ambush, I'm not talking about them shooting anybody. I mean kidnapping someone – namely, you. They want to be able to grab you, pump you full of drugs and interrogate the hell out of you."

"I see."

"They won't want witnesses and they won't want the complications of taking you and your wife and son."

"Good. What do we do?"

"We set up our own ambush, using you as bait. Incidentally, do you go out to Coral Bay every day to check on the boat?"

"Every couple days. Sometimes my son comes with me."

"Let's make that a daily activity without your son. And, on your way out there, don't pick up any hitchhikers you don't know or stop for any cars that appear to be broken down. We don't want to start anything on their chosen ground.

"We want to lure them to ground of our choosing. And, Coral Bay is our territory. These assholes may not even know how to swim.

"Here's what we need: daylight, but a time of day when there are not too many people on their boats or buzzing around the harbor."

"That would be about 11 a.m. Many people out there live on their boats and are at work during the day, and any tourists will already be on the beaches. And half-day charters don't come back in until noon."

"Who else would be out there?"

"Well, there are some guys who work in the boat yard behind Skinny's; but, even if they saw something they'd support Navy Seals against bad guys, any day."

"Excellent, sounds like 11 a.m. might work out okay."

So, that was the plan. Phase one was for Jones to get familiar with Coral Bay and the positions of the moored boats. That very day, I rowed him out to our boat and showed him around. He took photos of the other boats, the nearest shoreline and other features.

In the following days I started my new routine of going out to the boat every day about 11am, trusting that Jones and Smith were watching the bad guys.

Three or four days later, I picked up Jones hitchhiking again.

"Well, Blondie checked out as a mercenary who worked in Iraq for Harland. The other guy with the dragon tat may be a new hire without combat experience. They've been watching your house from the ridge above it. One day Dragon Boy followed you out to Coral Bay and watched you row out to the boat and back. I think they'll try a road abduction off Centerline Road deep in the park as you drive to or from the boat.

"If you don't fall for their tricks, they'll probably go for you as you row to or from your boat. For that, they'll need to rent a boat of their own."

"My wife knows the lady who manages the boat rental place that has an office right in the Westin. The outfit is called 'Bad Kitty' and the crew and captains of 'manned' charters are quite attractive young women. They also rent smaller boats without crew."

"Sounds good. Sounds like the place our boys would go looking for a boat. But, we don't want your wife or her friend to know anything about this. So don't mention it. I noticed there's a public road that runs along the Westin property to the beach where dinghies are kept to go out to boats moored in the bay there."

"Correct. From that narrow strip of beach you can see the Bad Kitty boats and their rental kiosk. There are mangrove trees and dinghies pulled-up on the beach to give you cover."

"Good. Now comes the hard part for you. You must continue driving out to the boat everyday. The day you see one of these idiots hitchhiking, or see a broken-down jeep by the road, you drive right by them. Then, call Lieutenant Taft's number as soon as possible from a landline. Most importantly, trust us to do the rest. We can't tell you our plan because you might unwittingly give it away the day we pounce on them."

"Ok, 'Trust in God and Dreadnought,' as Lord

Admiral Fisher said."

"What Admiral's that?"

"He's way before your time. Let's just say, he was the father of modern battleships. And, what he meant was, 'trust in God and the power of the Navy.' "

"Amen to that, brother."

"You see, the first battleships were called Dreadnoughts and his use of the word dreadnought was sort of a double entendre – 'Trust in God and dread not.' Admiral Fisher was almost as famous in British Naval history as Lord Nelson."

"That's interesting. You do like that Admiral Fisher – don't dread about this."

The next day, half-way out to Coral Bay, just past the Reef Bay Trail, I saw a blue jeep pulled over with the hood up. I slowed, but didn't stop. There was Dragon Boy leaning over the engine. Blondie stood in the road motioning me to stop, shouting:

"Hey, my cell phone's out. Can I use yours to call for help?"

I raised my hands in a no comprende type motion, drove around him and kept going, watching them in the rear view mirror. Dragon Boy was just standing up and walking toward Blondie as I went around a curve and lost sight of them. That night, I phoned the Lieutenant as instructed.

Next day, following the same routine, I arrived at Coral Bay. The wind was gusty and the bay choppy, with some white caps frothing around the moorings and bobbing boats.

It was a struggle rowing out against the wind and waves. To get out to our boat, I moved toward the protection of the lee of each moored boat and zig-zagged my way out to *Perseverance*. With difficulty, I brought the dinghy alongside and climbed up.

As usual, I opened up the companion way hatch, went below, opened the fore hatch and turned on the batteries.

I climbed up to the cockpit and turned on the engine to idle so it would recharge the batteries and keep the bilge pump working. That's when I noticed some spray breaking over a small motorboat coming out toward *Perseverance* – not from the stone dinghy dock, but, from a somewhat concealed cove a few hundred yards away. I recognized it as a *Bad Kitty* rental. But, no pretty girls were on board.

Well, I had prepared my own reception for these guys – regardless of what Jones and Smith had planned. I went down to my nav desk and pulled out a loaded flare gun. An old live-aboard sailor once told me that whenever in a foreign harbor sleep with your flare gun under the pillow. Turns out, they're good for more than natural emergencies.

As *Bad Kitty* drew closer, I saw Dragon Boy in the bow holding a boat hook and Blondie with his hand on the throttle of the outboard engine. I made my way up to the bow sprit and sat down behind the jib sail bag. They would come that way first and the bag concealed the flare gun.

A gust of wind screeched through the wire rigging and rustled the furled stay sail as the goons came closer, bobbing over the waves on a course for my boat. When they were in hailing distance, I yelled out:

"Howdy, gents. What brings you two out in this weather?"

They pretended not to hear and came closer. When just a few feet away, Blondie yelled up:

"Good day, friend. We're trying to get back to Cruz Bay. But, we need fuel. Who knew there's no fucking gas station out here."

"Regular or diesel?"

That seemed to flummox him, as a wave brought them closer. Dragon Boy reached out with the boat hook to grab one of the mooring lines under the bow sprit.

"Guess we need regular," Blondie yelled up.

"Well, sorry. All I have is diesel. You might go over to the dock and into Skinny's. Somebody over there may have regular." I stood up, visibly holding the flare gun and continued. "That's your best move. Now remove your hook from my bow line."

"Sure mister," Blondie said as his engine stopped. "Damn! The engine went out. Could we have run out of gas already?"

With that comment, Dragon Boy pulled in closer and wrapped his hand around one of the stanchions holding up the life-lines above our bulwark.

"I've got to hold on; we can't go anywhere in these waves without the engine."

"Don't you guys have any oars or a paddle? You should head to shore right over there and walk."

Blondie responded:

"I'm afraid we'll capsize. Can we just tie up and wait for it to let up?"

"I don't think so. I don't recognize you and there've been some shady characters coming around lately, robbing boats."

As I spoke, I lifted up the flare gun so they could not mistake it. I felt a warm rage welling up, blood pressure rising. I raised the flare and wanted so much to shoot one into Blondie – or maybe just *Bad Kitty's* gas tank.

"What's that for? We're just boaters in distress, needing some help."

Blondie smiled, as he said it. Then, a wave lifted them up and Dragon Boy swung the boat hook, knocking my arm. The flare gun fell out of my hand.

"You're too timid, friend," Blondie said, pulling a real hand gun with a large magazine out from beneath his seat. Dragon Boy started trying to tie their bow line to the stanchion. But, the waves were a bit much for an inexperienced hand with no sea legs.

At that moment, on the closest shoreline, donkeys started braying and yelping angrily. The steady wind carried the sounds of hoof beats and wild thrashings in the brush. It sounded like they were in the next boat. It was a common enough sound if you're used to it. Donkeys always hang out around Coral Bay and the males will fight – usually over females.

"What the fuck's that? Mules?" Dragon Boy hesitated and he and Blondie looked toward shore.

I seized the moment, grabbed the flare gun off the deck and jumped up behind the mast, where I could look down fully into their boat. I held-up the flare gun.

"Don't do anything stupid," Blondie said, motioning Dragon Boy to tie them onto the stanchion. "Put down the flare," he said as he raised his pistol. But, it wobbled in his hand as their boat bobbed in the waves.

Standing on a far larger boat with my left arm holding firmly onto the boom, I was steadier as I aimed the flare down into their boat. I was getting hotter as my blood and anger rose.

"Hey, asshole," I shouted. "Do you really really think that gas tank over by your feet is empty?"

I pointed the flare right at the tank with a steady hand.

"Calm down," Blondie said. "All we need is some help. You're the one who threatened us. Of course the tank's empty."

"Let's find out, shall we?"

Blondie looked me in the eye.

I pulled the trigger and with a flash and smoke, the flare shot down, but bounced off the tank without exploding. Blondie, white as bleached toilet paper, stared disbelieving as Dragon Boy slipped and fell backward into their boat.

But, Blondie recovered quickly – more quickly than me. All I could do was say "Shit."

"Now, things are going to go *very* hard for you," he snarled as he raised his pistol.

"This is a Tech 9 automatic; I really don't have to aim very accurately to hit a target."

As he explained he gripped the gun with both hands and seemed to be aiming for my legs. Then, with a whoosh of air and explosion of blood and flesh, Blondie's arms were jerked to one side and the gun sprayed a dozen or so bullets as both his wrists were impaled by a two-foot long, steel spear. Bullets zinged off my heavy aluminum mast and then perforated the boom and furled mainsail, but missed me. They sounded like heavy rain drops hitting a tin roof.

What none of us had seen was Mr. Jones in scuba gear, hanging half-submerged from the opposite windward side of my boat. He now treaded water and loaded another spear into his pneumatic gun.

This was too much for Dragon Boy. As blood spurted from Blondie's helpless arms, the Boy jumped overboard and started swimming toward shore.

Suddenly, from behind a schooner moored nearby, an inflatable boat raced toward *Bad Kitty* and in seconds tied up beside it. Mr. Smith jumped in with an emergency medical kit, as Mr. Jones easily intercepted Dragon Boy and held his head under water until he blacked out, making sure not to drown him. Then, he dragged him over to *Bad Kitty*.

Meanwhile, Mr. Smith had placed handcuffs on Blondie's hands and tied two tourniquets on his forearms, careful to leave them stitched together by the spear.

"You'll be fine once we get you in the ship's brig," he said, as Blondie sat dazed, turning gray in the face. Smith injected him with something from a prefilled, disposable syringe.

"You won't feel a thing until we want you to," Smith told him.

Between Jones pushing and Smith pulling, they got Dragon Boy back on board *Bad Kitty* and handcuffed and revived him. Jones pulled out a handheld radio and apparently explained the situation to somebody. Smith tended to Blondie who was now droopy-eyed and silent.

"Hey, professor!" Jones yelled up as I continued standing by the mast, trying to take everything in. "That was a brave stunt – stupid, but courageous."

"Yes, well, too bad the flare was a dud."

"No, it's a good thing it was a dud. Now, we can interrogate these two instead of fishing pieces of them out of the bay. The explosive force of a tank of gasoline is much greater than you know."

Within moments a gray, hard-hulled Navy vessel looking something like a small World War II era PT-boat was passing Johnson Reef, heading into the harbor toward us.

"Professor, don't you worry one bit about your friend here," Jones said pointing to Blondie. "That boat has a medic on board and within a half-hour we'll have him safely in sick bay on our command ship over at Charlotte Amalie.

"By the time he's ready for interrogation, we should be about through with this piece of shit," Jones said, giving Dragon Boy a hard kick to his shin and pushing him face down into the bilge. With his hands cuffed behind his back, he was going nowhere.

"Hey, there's water and blood down here," Dragon Boy whined.

The Navy boat had pulled up to *Perseverance* and crewmen, ignoring me, tied-on. They quickly lifted up Blondie and placed him in their boat's cabin and then manhandled Dragon Boy aboard and pushed him below deck. Mr. Smith got in with them. Soon, the patrol boat was speeding back out of the bay.

Meanwhile, Jones had pulled a big water proof bag from *Bad Kitty's* cubby cabin in the bow and was rummaging through it. He pulled out a rope, a hypodermic needle kit and a small test tube of clear liquid; also an assault rifle and ammunition.

"Looks to me like they intended to tie you up, drug you and then take you back to that secluded cove," Jones explained. "I bet their jeep is parked over there near the road."

"Where did the Navy boat come from?"

"Idling over on the other side of Ram's Head out of sight. The plan was for us to take the perps out to meet them near Le Duc Island. But, all's well that ends well."

"What do we do with *Bad Kitty* and their jeep?

"Tell you what. I'm going to clean up *Bad Kitty* and return her to the Westin to keep things tidy. They won't care who returns it, as long as it's safe. You're going to meet me there in your car and then drive me back here and I'll return their Jeep to its rental place. That way the venders will be happy. No one will be alarmed. No police. I'll tell both the boat and car people that my friends were too drunk to drive the back themselves."

"Pretty slick," I said.

"You don't know the half of it. Two Navy signalmen were concealed under the mangroves on shore. Using a telephoto lens and a very sensitive long-range microphone, we captured those turds coming to your boat, the whole conversation, Blondie pulling out his gun and Dragon Boy trying to board your vessel without permission. I'd call that attempted piracy and its illegal.

"We'll use the recording internally. It'll give our team leverage as the higher-ups decide how to proceed against those two and whoever sent them. Don't you worry. Blondie and his boy will tell us whatever we want to know."

"That's way cool."

"Yes. Our signalmen were right over there in the bushes near the point where the cove enters the bay – seems they disturbed some mules or donkeys trying to have sex and almost got kicked.

"In addition to a recording, they sent a live feed to our ship in St. Thomas – animal ruckus and all. The signalmen will have already pulled out and be on their way to the ferry.

As we talked, Jones checked Kitty's fuel tank. Half full.

"Well, lookee there. She does have plenty of fuel. Imagine that. Well, let's get rolling. If you'll take the inflatable in and tie-her up, I'll see you next at the beach next to the Westin."

With that, he roared off at the helm of *Bad Kitty*, weaving between the moored boats and out into the open bay where he appeared to be slamming into one wave after another. I wouldn't have wanted to go out in that weather, but he was a Navy seal, after all.

As I watched him depart, I heard another engine speeding toward me from shore. There stood Richie, red beard blowing in the wind, at the consol of a Boston whaler. In the bow holding a long barreled shot gun stood Albert. The men from Coral Bay Boat Works coming to the rescue.

Richie pulled along side and yelled up in his rolling Iowa cadences:

"What the hell is going on out here?"

Albert ran his professional eye along the furled mainsail.

"What chewed that up?"

Fortunately, the wind had carried the sounds of gun fire to the other side of the Bay.

"Good question. I was just looking at that. This main is pretty old. Time to replace it, I guess. But, hey, thanks for coming out, guys. There were a couple of shady looking types who proved to be undocumented 'guests' from the D.R. They were nosing around my boat while I was in the cabin. I saw them and radioed the Coast Guard. A Navy patrol boat happened to be passing by out near Le Duc island, heard the call and came in; ended-up taking them into custody. Guess they'll hand them over to Immigration."

Richie scratched his beard as he listened.

"One time up in the Keys, an Immigrations dude at a road block asked me my nationality. " 'Redneck', sir," I proudly told him. The officer agreed and sent me on my way."

"Great story." I laughed, tension easing. But, Albert was skeptical.

"This all sounds very unlikely; and, since when do you have an inflatable – a fancy one at that?"

He was pointing to Mr. Jones' Zodiac tied off my stern next to the dinghy.

"I borrowed it from a friend. But, the main thing is the excitement is over. No harm, no foul. But now, I have to go meet Mary and John. Thanks so much for coming out to check on things."

"No problem, buddy," Richie said with a chuckle, as he turned the wheel of the whaler and they headed back in.

Once the vehicles and vessels were all returned and secured, I got home about dinner time. Later, I told Mary the story of the day's events. Although, relieved the bad guys were captured, she was angry about the flare misfire.

"Why didn't the damn flare gun work? I just got that for you for Christmas. The one time you need it, it doesn't work. Somebody's going to pay – who made the piece of crap? You could have died!"

The next morning, though, Mary was delighted to receive flowers and a note of apology and thanks from Admiral Turner. Better still, Mr. Smith would be returning to our neighbor's house and continuing to keep an eye on us for several weeks.

I learned from Lieutenant Taft that Blondie, who would recover use of his arms, and Dragon Boy were already on their way to D.C. for further interrogation.

14 THE BEGINNING

"The truth will set you free, but, first it will piss you off."

— Gloria Steinem, American feminist, journalist and philosopher as quoted in the 1970s.[1]

Things were really quiet after the Coral Bay showdown. Our family enjoyed a great West Indian style Christmas. We sailed as weather permitted and spent time on the beach during the school holiday break. I noticed that the Navy ship had left Charlotte Amalie and couldn't help wonder where she was heading.

One morning, while Mary and I read the newspapers online, I saw an item in *The Washington Post*: "Homeland Security Secretary Capuano Accepts Undersec's Resignation." It seemed that after six years Undersecretary Chesney was leaving public service, returning to Houston to practice law.

"Practice is the key word," Mary opined as we read the story together.

"Yes, he will need a lot of practice to get the hang of

the law. I'm sure Harland Corp. will be his client. They might not be helpful to his remedial studies in lawful conduct."

Reading on, it turned out Chesney had been away from his wife and children for too long.

"Why hadn't they been in Washington with him all these years?" Mary asked rhetorically.

Chesney was too devoted to public service to be distracted by family, I was sure.

Reading still more, it turned out that Secretary Capuano was sorry to see him depart and wished him well in the future. The President would replace Chesney with retiring Rear-Admiral Bolton. Early in his career, Admiral Bolton had served in Naval Intelligence under the command of legendary Admiral Bobby Ray Inman.

Inman had also headed the National Security Agency under President Carter and, years later, spoke-out against the warrantless wire-tapping of American citizens and politicization of the CIA in the months and years following 9/11.[2]

It was great news that the President acted quickly and chose a qualified replacement who was likely a man of integrity. And, no doubt, a friend of Admiral Turner.

Separately, *The New York Times* reported the Inspector General of the Department of Homeland Security had launched an investigation into certain unspecified contracts with Harland Corp. Irregularities in procurement were suspected.

"So, Harland will be a Chesney law client – at least unless (or until) Chesney himself is subpoenaed and indicted," I mentioned to Mary.

"Sounds like the President and Secretary Capuana are on top of things," Mary replied.

After finishing the news stories, I phoned Lieutenant Taft on the secure number. He called back within a few minutes.

"Taft here"

"I see this number still works."

"We're keeping it operational so we can safely communicate as the trench exploration and other investigations proceed."

"I appreciate that. Am I correct that Admirals Turner and Bolton are friends?'

"Close friends – Annapolis classmates, in fact."

"Great news that Chesney and, apparently, Harland Corp. are both on the defensive."

"Circling the wagons and burying bodies, to be exact."

"I hope the bodies are figurative, but wouldn't be surprised if a few aren't."

"No comment on that. But, *we* plan to root out everyone who was involved in tipping-off Chesney and take care of business one way or another with Harland. The Patriot Act works both ways and the President fully supports cutting out this cancer. "

"Who knows how many more Chesneys are playing a double game in the security agencies? ONI and the President will need good luck finding those people."

"I can assure you it's not a matter of luck. We have many committed, competent and loyal men like Mr. Jones and Smith whom we can and will deploy as needed."

"Glad to hear that. You and the Admiral should know I'm available to jump back in when and if needed as the UFO investigation moves forward."

"We'll call you. And keep that flare gun handy."

The next day, Mary and John had to go to St Thomas for a doctor's appointment. I took a walk I had been planning for some time. I hiked along the old Danish road – now a rocky trail crossing a crumbling stone bridge – out to Waterlemon Bay. I jumped in the bay to cool off, and then entered the mangrove and sea grape forest, stopping to admire the picturesque ruins of several small plantation buildings being overtaken by jungle.

Local legend has it that in 1733 this was the headquarters of King Bolombo, one of the St. John slave revolt leaders. A chief of the Adampe tribe, he had once lived near the Atlantic coast of what is now the African nation of Ghana. Bolombo is said to have been captured by a chief of another Ghanaian tribe – quite possibly King June of the Akwamu – who sold him and others at a Danish slaving camp near the port of Accra.

The Akwamu were a particularly fierce coastal tribe who caught and sold other Africans to Europeans in return for guns, steel blades and tools. Many died in their attacks upon villages and forced marches to Danish, Dutch and British trading forts on Ghana's coast.

Once the sales were made, however, the horrors for the captured were just beginning. Dr. Paul Erdmann Isert, a physician at a Danish slave trading post, described the processing of new chattel:

"As the slaves were brought in by their tribal captors, they were sold on a barter basis to the factors of the forts and then housed and guarded by their new owners in sheds or warehouses, known as barracoons, until the arrival of the slave ships. . . . [The Europeans] set them aside for branding with a hot iron on the breast or the shoulder with the indentifying mark of the company or individual purchaser."[3]

Once captives were herded aboard overcrowded ships – the like of which most had never seen, accustomed as they were to hand hewn log canoes – they were at the mercy of often horrifically cruel captains and crewman. Many were ex-convicts, bankrupts and other outcasts from European society. One historian describes the sailors' "life of indolence, with little or no restraint" by civilized authority:

"On board a slave ship they might indulge nearly every human passion with utter freedom, whether it be confirmed drunkenness or unrestrained intercourse with African girls. They knew that the deadly climate was likely to claim them so they did as they pleased."[4]

By the early 1700s, victimized tribes living further from

Ghana's coast had heard rumors and stories of what happened to those stolen from their villages. They even feared those sold would be eaten by Europeans.

So, stronger tribes retaliated against African abductors such as the Akwamu for their collaboration with slavers. They took Akwamu captives and, in turn, sold *them* to Europeans including Danes. Akwamu King June – who had earlier captured and sold Adampe King Bolombo into slavery – himself ended up enslaved and on a Danish ship heading for St. John.

Both kings were shipped there around 1730. Three years later, they worked together to stage a revolt which began in the Coral Bay plantations – just over the mountain from the Waterlemon Bay ruins – and ended with their conquest and temporary control of the entire island.[5]

Although crumbling buildings and low stone walls of Bolombo's last kingdom on Waterlemon Bay can still be seen, nothing remains of the King himself. Indeed, it is doubtful anything remains of King Bolombo or King June anywhere. Upon European re-conquest of St. John, revolt leaders were executed and probably disposed of in unpleasant ways.

As punishment, the surviving recaptured slaves are said to have each had one leg cut off, unless the former owner objected. But, most of the resident owners – or the overseers for absentee-owners who had known the slaves – had been killed during the revolt. Another catch-22, and a tragic one.

I continued through the forest and took a trail up the hill to another landmark. The Guard House was a small fort built by the Danes about 100 years following the slave revolt. Manned by 16 soldiers and housing cannons, the fort overlooked the water passages between St. John and British Tortola. Slavery had been abolished throughout the British Empire in 1834 and, in the years before Denmark outlawed slavery in 1847, the Guard House and

Danish ships intercepted runaway St. Johnian slaves who would steal boats and try to reach free British soil.[6]

As I was looking around the fort's crumbling walls and admiring the view, I slowly became aware of heat penetrating through my hat. Time to take a break and drink some water. The heat continued and then the ground around my shadow turned blue. The blue light intensified and contracted around me into a cone.

Suddenly I felt elated – as though drugged. And, then I knew.

After a few seconds the light snapped off. I looked around and there stood Ebe framed by an arch in the Guard House wall.

"Good to see you, our brother," he said (with no lip movement). "We hope your wife and son are in fine health and spirits."

Nice to see you, again, I thought, as he stepped forward to shake my hand. Mary and John are fine, though a little shaken by the events of recent weeks.

"We are sorry you have all been exposed to such unpleasantness. It does, however, illustrate why we chose you and this time and place to establish our communication."

As I absorbed what he was "saying", I noticed he wore a form-fitting green skin-like, seamless suit that covered his feet and included a hood – possibly to protect him from the sun.

"You are correct. We try to avoid direct exposure to your sunlight. Because our planet has more moisture and higher, thicker forest canopies than yours, the sunlight penetrating our surface is less strong. My green suit also provides 'camouflage,' as you call it."

That's very interesting. Where have you been?

"Where we have been is irrelevant. We are satisfied with the conduct of you and your Naval friends. We are most happy you and your family were not harmed during your adventures."

Yes, that was all quite something. We had a victory, but only a small one. It is just the beginning, I hope, of a long struggle to neutralize certain groups that have been co-opting our government for far too long.

"A journey of one thousand miles begins with a single step, your ancient Chinese philosopher Lao-tzu said."

Yes. Very true. Several times since our first meeting, I thought about the implications of your stating that you knew I was to write a report to the Navy. Did you actually want the Navy to become active in UFO investigations and explore the deep sea trenches?

"You must understand, our friend, that we initiated the events that led to your investigation and report; though, your Navy colleagues have no idea that certain thoughts were inserted into certain brains to arrange hiring you and taking action."

Why would you want the Navy involved?

"You have an expression: the lesser of evils. As we have explained, we do not wish to interfere in your affairs unless absolutely necessary; unless grave danger threatens a large part of your population or planet.

"We perceived that certain Earth humans in your country have indeed co-opted a portion of government activity vital for your future.

"The humans involved are motivated solely by greed. It is quite possible that an unholy alliance – to use one of your expressions – between opportunists and elements within your government aerospace and security authorities have seized control over the study of extraterrestrial life and technology. We perceive that this collaboration may ultimately place your own citizens and most Earth humans in jeopardy.

"These controlling humans are blind to the baseness of their motives and likely outcome of their activities. 'They know not what they do,' to quote your Jesus."

No question, certain wealthy and powerful individuals would become vastly more so if they reaped most of the rewards from non-Earth technologies. What else could happen?

"We assume most humans on Earth value freedom and peaceful planetary co-existence."

I believe they do. Does this have to do with the so-called Grays?

"We cannot comment on them. We will say this, however. This has to do with dangerous humans who lack the wisdom and morals to responsibly establish relationships with extraterrestrial civilizations. Not all who come to Earth are dedicated to non-interference."

Can you help us?

"Our friend, we already have. We have stretched our policy as far as our code permits. Earth humans do have free will. But, sometimes your people's will needs a gentle push.

"It is for Earth's legitimate governments and humans of good will to take action themselves. Your government is the most powerful on Earth and we wish responsible, accountable elements within it to take charge of further investigation into extraterrestrial life and technology. If that means your Navy must be involved, so be it."

But, will the Navy 'discover' you in the deep sea trenches or elsewhere?

"No. Our brethren choose when we can be seen by human sight and technology.

"We show ourselves and interact through individuals only when absolutely necessary.

"For instance, our ship is submerged a few miles offshore and we traveled here today in what you might call a 'scout' craft that is completely shielded from sight and radar."

Fascinating. You said human freedom is at risk? How?

"Look where we are standing at this moment. Three hundred years ago, humans in Africa seeking profit and advanced technologies including firearms and steel tools sold their fellow humans into slavery. The purchaser of the humans in this case was the for-profit human enterprise called the Danish West Indian and Guinean Company.

"Now, at this very spot, we stand within fortifications built to keep the enslaved from reaching freedom."

Yes. I know all of that.

"You don't see what we see, however. When facing 'first contacts' with 'new worlds', humans on both sides of the experience behaved with little or no morality. They were driven purely by self-interest. In Africa, humans killed and captured other humans to sell them into slavery to Europeans seemingly from another world.

"In the Americas, European humans killed and enslaved less-developed humans in a quest for gold and land."

I can't argue with you. You are correct.

"No, you cannot argue. It is true.

"Now, consider what would happen if a more advanced extraterrestrial civilization had an interest in acquiring Earth's resources including human genetic material. How and with whom would they make contact? Would they openly approach the government of Earth's leading nation – 'land on the White House lawn'? Or, secretly deal with today's versions of the West India Companies?"

They'd choose a corporation – probably an aerospace company or other military contractor – that would want their technology. Those companies could also use their influence to keep a lid on the government.

"Correct. Extraterrestrials interested in plundering Earth and humanity would choose corporations who want advanced technologies for private gain and have few scruples – just as the Akwamu tribe in Ghana captured and sold fellow humans into slavery in return for firearms and steel tools."

Is that already happening?

"That is for you and your Navy colleagues to discover.

We cannot say more."

Will I see you again?

"If it serves to strengthen the Universal Spirit. Your quest and progress may achieve that end. You have made a promising start."

NOTES

Chapter 1: The Dead Man's Chest

1. Leslie Kean: "UFO's: Generals, Pilots and Government Officials on Record," Harmony Books, 2010, page 4.
2. hamptonroads.com/2010/08/caroline-kennedy-christens-jfk-aircraft-carrier
3. home.comcast.net/~ceoverfield/sea.html

Chapter 3: Treasure Island

1. "The Republic of Pirates," by Colin Woodard, Houghton Mifflin Harcourt Publishing Company, paper back edition, 2008, pages 146 to 147.
2. "The Testimony of William Blackstock [A True Story of Piracy and Buried Treasure on Norman Island]" by David W. Knight, Vol. XI, No. 2, November 2009, St John Historical Society newsletter.
3. Robert Louis Stevenson: "To Sidney Colvin. Late May 1884", in "Selected Letters of Robert Louis Stevenson, page 263, wrote: "'Treasure Island' came out of Charles Kingsley's 'At last A Christmas in the West Indies' [1871] where I got Dead Man's Chest – that was the seed. And out of the great Captain Johnsons' 'History of Notorious Pirates.'"
4. project1947.com/shg/symposium/hynek.html
5. nytimes.com/2006/03/01/opinion/01satel.html?page wanted=print

Chapter 4: St Ursula's Bones

1. "Journals and Other Documents on the Life and Voyages of Christopher Columbus," Translated and Edited by Samuel Eliot Morison, 1963, page 212.
2. news.bbc.co.uk/2/hi/uk_news/magazine/4071124.stm

3. project1947.com/shg/symposium/sagan.html
4. Testimony of Monsignor Corrado Balducci, September, 2000, published in "Disclosure," by Steven M. Greer, MD, Carden Jennings Publishing Co., 2001, page 64.
5. catholicnews.com/data/stories/cns/0506301.htm

Chapter 5: Zulus and the End of the World

1. yorktownsailor.com/yorktown/ufojfk.htm
   galactic-server.com/radio/greer/disclosure1.html
   rense.com/ufo/kennedy.htm
2. Case published online by water UFO researcher Carl Feindt
   waterufo.net/item.php?id=1155
   Witness requested confidentiality.
3. ufosnw.com/sighting_reports/older/uslexsight/uslexsight.htm
4. As paraphrased in "After Contact: The Human Response to Extraterrestrial Life," by Albert A. Harrison, Plenum Press, 1977, page 122.

Chapter 6: Cold War in Warm Water

1. See Amazon.Com book description of "Havana Nocturne: How the Mob Owned Cuba and Then Lost It to the Revolution," by T.J. English, amazon.com/Havana-Nocturne-Owned-Cuba-Revolution/dp/0061712744/ref=sr_1_1?ie=UTF8&qid=1351526166&sr=8-1&keywords=how+the+mob+owned+cuba .
2. "From Columbus to Castro: The History of the Caribbean," by Eric Williams, First Vintage Books edition, February 1984, pages 479 to 80.
3. ufodigest.com/news/0608/cuba2.html
4. ussfranklinroosevelt.com/?page_id=2264
5. waterufo.net/item.php?id=1083
6. Steven M. Greer, M.D., "Disclosure," op cit, pages

198 and 99; See also: galactic-server.com/radio/greer/disclosure1.html

7. pbs.org/wgbh/amex/castro/sfeature/sf_experts.html #a

8. Facts about launchers, missiles and warheads drawn from the article "Caribbean Showdown," published in the U.S. Naval Institute's October, 2012 issue of "Naval History' magazine.

9. history.navy.mil/faqs/faq90-2.htm

10. nicap.org/reports/6210XXcmc2.htm

11. nicap.org/jan16.htm

12. nicap.org/ncp/cmc2.htm

13. dailymail.co.uk/news/article-1378284/Secret-memo-shows-JFK-demanded-UFO-files-10-days-assassination.html

14. reagan.utexas.edu/archives/speeches/1987/092187b.htm

15. margaretthatcher.org/document/109213

16. ufodigest.com/news/0608/cuba.html

17. ufos.about.com/od/ufossept2011/a/closeencounterin cuba.htm

Chapter 7: Blackbeard and Lindbergh

1. "Lindberg Fever Hits St Thomas," The Virgin Island Daily News, July 15, 2010.

2. See: "The Lives and Adventures of Sundry Notorious Pirates," a reprint by Robert M. McBride and Company, of an anonymous work published in 1735, page 87.
gutenberg.org/files/24439/24439-h/24439-h.htm#Page_87

3. science.howstuffworks.com/space/aliens-ufos/ronald-reagan-ufo.htm

4. The Washington Post: "UFO's Over Georgia? Jimmy Logged One," April 30, 1977.

5. "Me and My Beloved Virgin," by Guy H. Benjamin, (self published, 1998), page 40.

6. Benjamin, pages 40 – 41.
7. "And a Bottle of Rum, A History of the New World in Ten Cocktails," by Wayne Curtis, Three Rivers Press paperback edition, 2007 page 52.
8. "The Pirate Primer," by George Choundas, Writers Digest Books, 2007, page 20.

Chapter 8: In the Trenches with Uninvited Guests

1. RUSSIA TODAY, 21 July, 2009, 18:56; rt.com/Top_News/2009-07-21/russian-navy-ufo-records-say-aliens-love-oceans.html
2. news24.com/SciTech/News/New-deepwater-fish-found-20101015
3. RUSSIA TODAY, 21 July, 2009, 18:56; rt.com/Top_News/2009-07-21/russian-navy-ufo-records-say-aliens-love-oceans.html
4. "The Life and Voyages of Christopher Columbus," by Washington Irving, Collins, Keese & Co., NY, 1838; Pages 36 and 37.
5. "Admiral of the Ocean Sea," by Samuel Eliot Morison, Little Brown & Company, Boston, 1942, page 225.
6. "The Log of Christopher Columbus," translated by Robert H. Fuson, International Marine Publishing, Camden, Maine, 1987, pages 76 and 78.
7. "The Log of Christopher Columbus," page 79.
8. "Uninvited Guests," by Richard Hall, Aurora Press, 1988, page 313.
9. rr0.org/data/1/9/9/7/08/24/GrenadaSirEricGairyUfoEnthusiastDeadAt75/index.html
10. Associated Press: "United Nations Hears Case for UFO's," October 15, 1978.

Chapter 9: First Contacts of an Intimate Kind

1. "Journals and Other Documents on the Life and

Voyages of Christopher Columbus," translated and edited by Samuel Eliot Morison, The Heritage Press, New York, 1963, page 212.

2. His story is told on many Sites and in many books. See: en.wikipedia.org/wiki/Antonio_Villas_Boas for a summary, and, also "UFOs and the National Security State," Vol. 1, by Richard M. Dolan, paperback edition, Hampton Roads Publishing Company, 2002, page 202.

3. openminds.tv/brazils-first-ufo-report/

4. ufopsi.com/articles/antoniovillasboas.html

5. "Open Skies, Closed Minds," by Nick Pope, Dell Publishing, paperback, 1998, page 29-33.

6. "Close Encounters of the Fourth Kind: A Reporter's Notebook on Alien Abduction, UFOs and the MIT Conference," by C.D.B. Bryan, Penguin Paperback edition, 1995, page 280.

7. "Journals and Other Documents on the Life and Voyages of Christopher Columbus," translated and edited by Samuel Eliot Morison, The Heritage Press, New York, 1963, page 237.

8. Letter of Diego Alvarez Chanca on The Second Voyage of Columbus, American Journeys collection of Wisconsin Historical Society, pages 291 and 292. content.wisconsinhistory.org/cdm/compoundobject/collection/aj/id/4408/show/4371/rec/4

9. "Journals and Other Documents on the Life and Voyages of Christopher Columbus," translated and edited by Samuel Eliot Morison, The Heritage Press, New York, 1963, page 212.

10. See Park brochure at nps.gov/sari/index.htm

11. "Open Skies, Closed Minds," by Nick Pope, op cit, page 46.

12. Leslie Kean: "UFO's: Generals, Pilots and Government Officials on Record," Harmony Books, 2010, page 178.

Chapter 10: The Billionaire and The Encounter

1. openminds.tv/wp-content/uploads/Rockefeller-Gibbons-Letter.jpg
2. project1947.com/shg/symposium/mcdonald.html
3. "American Prometheus: The Triumph and Tragedy of J. Robert Oppenheimer," by Kai Bird and Martin J. Sherwin, Alfred A. Knopf, 2005, page 464.
4. See New York Times article on click languages: nytimes.com/2003/03/18/science/in-click-languages-an-echo-of-the-tongues-of-the-ancients.html?pagewanted=all&src=pm .
5. See "UFOs and the National Security State," Vol. 2, by Robert M. Dolan, Keyhole Publishing Company, 2009, page 366 for accounts of a UFO on site emitting a red ray as the first technicians arrived on the scene.
6. See Whitley Streiber's groundbreaking non-fiction, autobiographical book "Communion," published in 1987, and his novel, "The Grays," published in 2006.

Chapter 12: Men in Suits

1. On National Security Letters, see: en.wikipedia.org/wiki/National_security_letter
2. epic.org/privacy/nsl/
3. washingtonpost.com/wp-dyn/content/article/2007/03/22/AR2007032201882.html

Chapter 14: The Begining

1. encore.org/learn/truth-will-set-you-free
2. wired.com/science/discoveries/news/2006/05/70855
3. See pages 10 and 11, Isidor Paiwonsky, "Eyewitness Account of Slavery in the Danish West Indies," Aristographics, Inc., St. Thomas, 1987.
4. Isidor Paiwonsky, page 16.

5. There are many sources and stories about the St. John slave revolt, see:
   prezi.com/at37a6buyxxp/resistance-rebellion/;
   and
   en.wikipedia.org/wiki/1733_slave_insurrection_on_St._John

6. Gerald Singer: "St. John Off the Beaten Track," Sombrero Publishing Company, St. John, USVI, Revised Edition, 2006.)

Jeffrey Roswell McCord

ABOUT THE AUTHOR

For more than 30 years, Jeffrey R. Mc-Cord has been a
free-lance journalist and public relations/public affairs
consultant in Washington D.C. and New York City. His
by-lined work has appeared in *The Wall Street Journal*,
Barron's, *USA-UK Magazine*, the South Jersey *Courier-Post* (a
Gannett news-paper) and the online publications *Truth
Out*, *Angry Bear* and *The Activist Post*. He has also published
a blog, *The Investor Advocate*, promoting greater legal
protections for U.S. consumers and investors.

Trained as an economist and historian, Mr. McCord and
his family now divide their time between Virginia and the
United States Virgin Islands.

Photo by Alice Gebura

Made in the USA
Charleston, SC
28 October 2014